THE LAST
SYNAPSID

THE LAST SYNAPSID

TIMOTHY MASON

DELACORTE PRESS

Published by Delacorte Press
an imprint of Random House Children's Books
a division of Random House, Inc.
New York

Visit us on the Web! www.randomhouse.com/kids

Educators and librarians, for a variety of teaching tools,
visit us at www.randomhouse.com/teachers

Library of Congress Cataloging-in-Publication Data
Mason, Timothy.
The last synapsid / Timothy Mason. — 1st ed.
p. cm.
Summary: On a mountain near their tiny town of Faith, Colorado, best friends
Rob and Phoebe discover a squat, drooly creature from thirty million years before
the dinosaurs, that needs their help in tracking down a violent carnivore that must
be returned to its proper place in time, or humans will never evolve.
ISBN 978-0-385-73581-0 (trade) — ISBN 978-0-385-90567-1 (library) [1. Prehistoric
animals — Fiction. 2. Time travel — Fiction. 3. Space and time — Fiction.
4. Colorado — Fiction.] I. Title.
PZ7.M42324Las 2009
[Fic] — dc22   2008035678

Book design by Marci Senders

Printed in the United States of America

10 9 8 7 6 5 4 3 2 1

First Edition

In memory of my dad,
Reverend John Martin Mason II

I owe a lot to many.

Thanks to theater agent Buddy Thomas at ICM for passing my first draft to book agent Tina Dubois Wexler. Thanks to Tina for mighty labors above and way beyond the call of duty.

Endless thanks to Stephanie Lane, my wonderful editor, for loving this story and gently but firmly compelling me to make it better.

Others helped in countless ways. From early on, Chris Raschka was supportive and encouraging. My friends at Buon Italia in Manhattan's Chelsea Market served me good Italian coffee for years while I took up one of their tables with my laptop. I had similar help from friends at Amelia's in Santa Monica and the Van Dyke News, Miami Beach. Rusty and Gloria found a terrific young artist to see the world through Rob Gates' eyes. Other friends who read early drafts were hugely helpful: Bonnie, Ken and Anne, Michael, Victor, Bill, Diane, John, Dan, Deena, Russell, and young Malachi, the first kid to read my 450-page first draft (straight through in less than a weekend).

To Chris Buzelli and Marci Senders, my gratitude for an amazing cover and design.

To my gifted young collaborator, Paul Cronan, hats off!

Thanks to my friends in the mountains of southwestern Colorado (especially whoever left an old copy of *National Geographic* where I would find it). Thanks to Leo Geter for introducing me to them, and to a whole new world.

1
FAITH

It was generally acknowledged around the tiny town of Faith, Colorado, that Phoebe Traylor had never seemed like the lying type. Her friend Rob Gates, certainly, but not Phoebe. That was before all *this* happened. By the time the whole thing was over there weren't many in town who believed a word either one of them said. Even most of those who had actually seen "the creature" before he disappeared weren't buying it. Seeing isn't necessarily believing.

Faith is a mining town that gave up mining long ago. Today it's a little straggly thing, half circled by a ring of toothy cliffs. Winter up there in the mountains, nearly nine thousand feet above sea level, gets pretty intense. Snow can start bucketing down as early as October.

By the beginning of March, thirteen-year-old Phoebe was about cross-eyed with boredom. "What if spring never comes and it's just winter forever for the rest of time until the end of the universe?" she moaned.

Phoebe and Rob were sitting in the school cafeteria, a cheesy pizza smell hanging in the air. Rob tore open the wrapper of an ice cream sandwich and said through a mouthful, "What if Faith never existed in the first place and all this is just somebody else's boring dream?"

Phoebe was fair and freckled and a bit tall for her age. She had profoundly blue eyes. Her hair was the color of sand, and she wore it in a thick braid down her back, making her look—Scandinavian or medieval or, depending on how you felt about Phoebe—hopelessly old-fashioned. Her passion was animals, horses in particular. She thought she might want to become a veterinarian and spent a lot of time hanging out with the town's deaf vet, Janet Bright, who worked up at the Mitchelsons' stables with her deaf husband, Nick.

Twelve-year-old Rob was short and skinny, with spiky dark brown hair and dark keen eyes. He wore jeans and T-shirts exclusively, and his hands and nails were almost always dirty. Rob would have denied having a passion, but he was always sketching—portraits, landscapes and sometimes rather unkind caricatures. He was fiercely left-handed.

Their friendship was a fact of life in the tiny town of Faith. Rob-and-Phoebe had almost become one word. Their closeness hadn't been an issue when they were younger; now it could cause problems.

At that moment, Chad Scudder, an eighth grader whom Rob called "Faith's own Ken doll," swaggered by their table, making kissing noises in their direction. Rob threw the uneaten portion of his ice cream sandwich at Chad and nailed him just under his chin. Mr. Brinkley, the boys' gym teacher, busted Rob instantly, and he got detention for the third time that month, which meant that his mom would have to come in for a conference. It wasn't a good winter for anyone.

Now, though, the heavy snows were almost over. Phoebe and Rob couldn't have known it then, but as the temperature rose in the first weeks of March and the big melt began, a door on the mountain opened for the impossible to waddle through.

★ ★ ★

Rob's mother, Lucy, had been on her own since Rob's father went missing six years earlier. Faith has a population of less than five hundred, but maybe two or three times a year somebody turns up gone, nobody knows where or why. The people who disappear usually just take off in the night, no forwarding address provided.

Rob had been not quite seven years old when it happened, and in his mind it had to have been an accident—his father had climbed the mountain above town and fallen into one of the narrow cracks between the rocks. Or a mountain lion got him. Or he was rescuing a wounded mountain lion, maybe, carrying her in his arms down the mountain, when the two of them slipped into a crevasse.

There *are* places in the peaks around Faith where if you take one wrong step, nobody'd ever hear you hit bottom. And there *are* mountain lions up there, although it's rare for anyone to see one. Anyway, if you ask Rob Gates what became of his dad, he'll tell you one story; if you ask him again next week, he'll tell you something altogether different.

Lucy Gates waited tables at the diner on Main and on weekends took a shift behind the counter at the Conoco. She was in no mood for another school conference about Rob's attitude.

3

"What's wrong with you?" she shrieked in front of everybody when Rob and Phoebe came into the diner that afternoon. "The phone rings, most likely it's gonna be the principal or the guidance counselor or the vice principal calling about some prank of yours or other. I'm sick of it, Robert, I am not kidding!"

Pete the sheriff sat at the counter with a cup of coffee and a slice of lemon meringue; Adelaide and Wynola Parsons, the eighty-one-year-old twins who owned the oldest house in town, were having tea; and an alien was reading the local paper. (Aliens are what the kids called anybody who didn't live in Faith.) Everybody looked up to watch Rob get chewed out by his mom.

"Well?" said Lucy. She was in her late thirties and had dark brown hair and eyes, just like Rob's. She was always broke and often angry. Not a lot of people in town knew that she played classical piano pretty well, but she did.

Rob looked at his sneakers while Phoebe tried giving Lucy an apologetic smile.

"You've got influence over him, Phoebe," said Rob's mom. "Use it, for goodness' sake!"

"Yes, Mrs. Gates," said Phoebe.

"Throwing food around the cafeteria!"

"Sorry, Mrs. Gates," said Phoebe.

Lucy slammed a tray of dishes onto a shelf behind the counter. "Robert?"

"Sorry, Mom."

Adelaide Parsons spoke up in her small, wavery voice.

"Either of you two seen Pinkie?"

Rob was hugely relieved by the change of subject. "Is Pinkie missing, Miss Parsons?" he asked with great concern.

Pinkie was Adelaide and Wynola's toy poodle, who must have been about eighty-one dog years old itself. The poodle's pale pink skin showed through its thinning white fur, and it was always coughing and spitting, as if it were clearing its throat. The two old ladies loved it like life itself.

"She's been gone since yesterday afternoon," said Wynola, tears glistening in her eyes.

Wynola and Adelaide came from an era when the silver mines of Faith were still up and running and the town was rich and rough and wild. They were daughters of one of the mountain's legendary old miners, Patrick Parsons, and great-granddaughters of Lemuel Parsons, who was among the very first prospectors to arrive in Faith during the early 1890s. When the value of silver fell so much that it became more costly to dig it out of the mountain than it was worth, the town gradually shriveled, year after year, until it was just a dim memory of itself: two frail old ladies, crying for their lost dog.

The alien closed his copy of the *Faith Sentinel*. He was slim with thin black hair slicked back, maybe forty years old, and he looked like he wanted to sell you something.

"Your local paper's got two missing pet notices," he said with a drawl. "You folks got a coyote situation here?"

Wynola Parsons gulped back a sob, and Adelaide squeezed her hand.

The alien turned to Pete at the counter. "You're the sheriff, I imagine?"

"I imagine I am," said Pete, slow and steady. Pete was in his late sixties, and his face looked like creased leather. "Who do you imagine *you* are?"

"Jenkins, up from El Paso. Just passing through."

Phoebe and Rob knew that you don't "pass through" Faith. Faith isn't on the way to anywhere. The town's at the top of a mountain, and the only road running through it just runs down the mountain again.

"You got wildcats up here?" said the alien. "Mountain lions, wolves?"

Lucy Gates said, "What do you think was in that meat loaf you just ate?"

Jenkins from El Paso smiled wryly and pulled out his wallet to settle up, and Rob and Phoebe exchanged a quick glance.

"We'll look for Pinkie, Miss Parsons," said Rob.

"Sure we will," said Phoebe a little uncertainly.

"We'll find her, don't you ladies worry," said Rob, and he shot out of the diner, followed by Phoebe.

"Homework!" shrieked Lucy to the slamming door.

2
PINKIE

Supposedly, Rob and Phoebe were looking for Pinkie. In fact, they were on their bikes; flying down Willow, the street that parallels the flume. The flume is a cement-bottomed water chute that runs from the top of town down through the center onto the flats below, the water eventually flowing across the valley floor to the Rio Grande. Faith had burned to the ground in a terrible fire in the early 1900s, and after that they built the flume, channeling the mountain streams to provide water for fighting fires.

Rob and Phoebe's bikes splattered through silt-colored grit and skidded on the icy patches. The two of them rounded the corner at Chestnut and crossed a little wooden bridge over the flume to Main, nearly wiping out on the left turn. Pastor Mosely, about to cross from the parish house to the church, stepped back onto the curb *just* in time. Looking back over their shoulders, they caught a glimpse of Jenkins from El Paso, heading into Hotel Faith with a couple of big bags.

Rob slowed and Phoebe sped up until they were tandem.

"I thought he was just passing through," said Phoebe with a nod toward Jenkins.

"Where do you want to start?" Rob asked.

"Start what?"

"Looking for Pinkie."

"That old dog isn't missing and you know it," said Phoebe. "She's asleep under Adelaide's bed or in the linen closet. Remember when they called the fire department and Pinkie walked into the front parlor as Wynola was passing out the reward posters?"

"We said we'd look."

"It'll be dark in a minute," said Phoebe. "If we're going to do it, we need to be quick."

"Let's climb Stair-Master and look from up there."

Stair-Master was their name for the nine-hundred-foot hill that rose from the bottom of Faith to the highest of the rocky teeth above. You could see pretty much every bit of Faith from up there. The kids left their bikes lying at the bottom and headed up, Rob in the lead.

They hadn't named it Stair-Master for nothing; it was very steep. Pretty soon there wasn't any talk—all you could hear was Rob and Phoebe breathing hard as they walked almost in a crouch. There had been a big melt a couple of days earlier and then a freeze. Now they crunched over a dirty end-of-winter snow crust. Soon Rob moved out ahead, and the distance between them grew. When they needed to, they communicated with the walkie-talkies they kept clipped to their belts.

If you had been watching from the town below, you'd have seen two small figures getting smaller in the long blue shadows of the afternoon's dying light, occasionally disappearing into folds in the mountain and then reappearing, higher and higher. Maybe you'd notice also the massive black wall of cloud moving across the valley floor toward the mountain, and how one figure, far ahead of the other, stopped dead still, turned, and gestured urgently to the other.

★ ★ ★

Phoebe was out of breath and thoroughly cold when she glanced up and saw Rob on the crest above her, a scared look on his face, staring at the ground beneath his feet. She stepped up her pace but Rob held up his hands: *Stop!* He put a finger to his lips.

Phoebe stopped and listened, and then, above the sound of the wind and the distant barking of dogs in the town far below, she heard it. The cry was faint at first, not quite doglike and not quite human. Phoebe had never heard anything like it. The flesh on her arms pricked up and her stomach did a little drop.

There was a silence, and then the sound again, something between a whimper and a deep-throated moan. Phoebe suddenly remembered the walkie-talkie in her hand and clicked it.

"What *is* that?" she whispered into the mouthpiece, looking up at Rob from below.

He shook his head, his face full of dread. Phoebe moved up the slope toward him.

"Don't, Phoeb." Rob's voice crackled over the walkie-talkie. "It's nasty up here."

But Phoebe kept climbing until she reached her friend, who stood stock-still, staring at the remains of the elderly white poodle that lay at his feet.

"Oh, my God."

The dirty snow had reddish stains leading up the slope. "It's awful," said Phoebe.

Rob nodded. "Poor Pink," he said.

"Poor Adelaide, poor Wynola," said Phoebe.

"Do you think coyotes did it?" said Rob doubtfully.

And, as if in answer, the cry came again, guttural and drawn out and very un-coyote-like. The two kids jumped and whirled around: the sound seemed to be coming from a fold of earth and rock between a couple of tall boulders. A sudden warm odor, like a horse's breath, wafted over them. The two kids stared at each other in the silence that followed. And then they ran.

The sun set quickly, as it does in the mountains, the darkness closing down like a shutter. Rob and Phoebe were stumbling and falling on the steep descent, skidding on the crusted ice and tearing their jeans and jackets and scraping the palms of their hands. Thick wet snowflakes started hitting their faces, and the wind began to shriek.

★ ★ ★

The snowstorm that sprang up turned out to be one of those big March blizzards that come out of nowhere and make all your plans for spring look like a sad joke. The town was blanketed overnight and very still for days after.

That night, Jane Traylor, Phoebe's mom, got Phoebe and Rob out of their wet, torn clothes and into a couple of big fluffy robes and scratchy wool socks. Rob's mom drove over and everybody had mushroom-barley soup in the Traylors' kitchen, with the wood-burning stove blazing.

Phoebe and Rob couldn't get the words out fast enough, talking over each other, shivering with the memory of what

10

they'd seen and heard on the mountain. The two moms looked pretty doubtful.

"I imagine it was coyotes," said Jane Traylor.

"It wasn't!" said Phoebe.

"You're sure it was Pinkie up there?" said Lucy Gates, looking hard at Rob and Phoebe. "You're sure she was dead?"

The two kids glanced at each other.

"Mom, she was in pieces," said Rob.

"Do we call Wynola and Adelaide?" asked Lucy, turning to Jane.

"This isn't a phone-call kind of thing, Lucy. I'll go over there in the morning and tell them in person."

Jane Traylor was what some people in town called a hippie. She made all her own clothes and was a vegetarian and meditated. She sold baked goods and medicinal herbs out of a shop on Main, and she could crack your back like a pistol shot. Jane's husband, Phoebe's dad, had left five years earlier and lived in Denver with a whole other family.

"It wasn't coyotes, Mom," said Phoebe. "I've heard coyotes all my life and that wasn't one."

"It smelled," said Rob.

"It smelled," Phoebe echoed.

Lucy Gates shot Jane Traylor a glance. "What did it smell like?" she asked.

"It wasn't bad," said Rob, "it was just strong or something."

"Like a swamp," said Phoebe.

"Or the Mitchelsons' stables, only different."

The two moms looked at each other in that infuriating way grown-ups have when they don't believe you but they're not going to make a big deal out of it.

"Just keep off the mountain, okay, guys?" said Lucy Gates. "Until spring?"

"Geez!" said Rob. "Why do I even tell you stuff if you don't listen?"

Eventually they said their goodnights. Long after Rob went to bed, Lucy sat up late with the lights off, looking out the kitchen window at the night, thinking about her absent husband and all the other things the mountain hid. Phoebe dreamt that someone she couldn't find was crying for help, and Rob dreamt about absolutely nothing, and the next morning Jane Traylor sat in Wynola and Adelaide's front parlor and held their hands while they cried and cried.

3
A VERY BAD SMELL

The Parsons sisters held a memorial service for Pinkie Saturday morning at the diner. Pastor Mosely declined to officiate and Father Conklin said he'd have to check with his diocese, so in the end Jane Traylor just said some holy words in a foreign language and Wynola gave a little talk about Pinkie belonging to the mountain now, and the ages.

Lucy Gates served everybody a slice of Adelaide's red-velvet cake, which had been Pinkie's favorite. Rob presented the sisters with a pencil sketch

"Pinkie"
by Rbt. Gates Jr.

he'd done the night before from memory, and Wynola and Adelaide hugged him and cried all over again.

By Wednesday the drifts were still too deep to make it back up the mountain. A clear, cold wind had moved in after the storm, and the two kids stood bundled up on one of the little footbridges over the flume, pondering their options.

"Let's think this through," said Phoebe. "Something got Pinkie, right? So either Pinkie went up Stair-Master or the wildcat or whatever it was came down."

"That wasn't a wildcat we heard," said Rob.

"I know, I'm just saying. Whatever it was."

"And Pinkie never went up that mountain," said Rob. "She was too old."

"So the thing came down into town and carried Pink back up."

The thought of some unknown bloodthirsty beast walking the streets of Faith at night, right outside their windows, was chilling and kind of great at the same time.

"What about the other two?" asked Phoebe suddenly.

"What other two?" said Rob, dropping a snowball from the bridge into the flume and watching it shoot out of sight.

"Don't you remember? The alien said there were two other missing-pet notices in the *Sentinel*—come on!"

Minutes later they were in the diner, going through a copy of last week's *Faith Sentinel*.

Their next stop was Jack and June Ford's, an older couple whose house backed onto the flume near the bottom of town. Jack used to be a miner but now he was an interstate trucker, off on a run between Colorado Springs and Phoenix. June answered the door.

Yes, Booties had gone missing the previous weekend, when it

had been so warm, June said. Which was strange, she said, because that cat hated to get wet and the backyard was all puddles and so it was odd that she should wander off in all that, didn't they think? Jack was going to be heartsick when he got back and heard the news, he loved that little kitty, the two of them were a regular item and him such a big man, wasn't it a shame?

The other missing pet was a stray dog that the hotel staff had adopted, feeding it from bowls set out back of the hotel, on the landing above the flume. Rob and Phoebe talked to Jimmy, who worked in the hotel kitchen and behind the front desk on the night shift. Jimmy played in a band and had green-painted fingernails and, once in a while, green hair.

"We called him Buddy," Jimmy said, and suddenly Rob and Phoebe knew exactly which dog he was talking about.

"Oh, no," said Phoebe. "I loved Buddy. He'd come by my mom's shop and we'd feed him and a couple of times my mom gave him a bath—remember, Rob?"

Rob nodded.

"Well, then your mom's got a strong stomach," said Jimmy. "Buddy was about the smelliest, scruffiest, mangiest, most beat-up old bag of fleas I ever saw. Like he'd been run over by a road grader and sprinkled with cooties."

Both kids nodded sadly and smiled.

"But he had a good spirit, you know?" continued Jimmy. "That dog always had a big smile for pretty much everybody. He spent his whole life just one step ahead of the coyotes, so I guess I'm not surprised if they got him in the end."

"You notice any coyote tracks, Jimmy? Around the back of the hotel?" asked Phoebe.

"Buddy went missing before the last snow. Town was all water, there weren't no tracks. So what's up? You kids playing investigator? Hey, you want some nice hot cocoa in the dining room?"

Something in the way he said it made Phoebe feel very young and a little dumb.

"No, thank you," she said, just as Rob was about to say yes. "We gotta go."

Rob looked at her with some annoyance as they walked away down Main. "What's up?" he said.

"I don't know. Maybe we're making a big deal out of nothing."

"Nothing? Three small animals disappear in less than two weeks?" said Rob. "That can't be a coincidence."

"Of course it can," said Phoebe.

Rob bristled. "Are you saying we didn't hear what we heard on the mountain that night?"

"I'm just wondering if maybe, you know . . ." Phoebe's voice trailed off. "It *was* kind of a crazy night."

"I saw what I saw," said Rob. "I heard what I heard."

"I know."

"You don't sound like it. You sound like one of the adults all of a sudden."

"Well, I *am* older," said Phoebe unwisely.

Rob stopped on the pavement and stared at her for a moment, and Phoebe wished she could take the words back. Then he turned and stalked off.

★ ★ ★

"Rob and I never used to fight," Phoebe complained to her mother that night, looking up from her homework at the kitchen table. Jane Traylor was working at the big loom in the living room.

"Well, you know, honey. . . . Hormones."

16

"That's your answer for everything!" said Phoebe. "And it answers nothing!"

Phoebe grabbed her textbooks from the kitchen table and stomped off into her bedroom.

"I rest my case!" Jane shouted after her.

Phoebe dumped her books on the bed and looked longingly at the glowing red light on her walkie-talkie. She and Rob usually talked to each other this way in the evenings. There was no cell phone service in Faith, and walkie-talkies were more interesting than regular telephones.

"He can call me if he wants to," she said to herself. She put down the walkie and picked up her copy of *My Ántonia,* and although it was her favorite book that month, she didn't manage to read a single paragraph.

★ ★ ★

That afternoon Rob had stalked away from Phoebe with a burning face. The few months that separated them in age had never been an issue, but in the past year Phoebe had shot up and she now stood a good three inches taller than Rob. There were people at school who called Rob "Phoebe's little friend." It was galling.

He'd been in no mood for home or homework, so without any kind of a plan Rob headed up Main, past the hotel and the diner and the bank and the police station, up the steep gravel road leading to the abandoned mines. The flume roared clear and cold on his right, and the jagged cliffs loomed overhead on either side.

Rob glanced up and there was the alien, Jenkins of El Paso, coming toward him down the gravel road in the cleft between the cliffs. He was wearing a backpack and stabbing at the

17

ground with a long metallic walking stick. He flashed his teeth in what Rob guessed was supposed to be a grin.

"You headed up the canyon, little buddy?" said Jenkins. The man paused for a moment, giving Rob an odd, questioning look, and then glanced back over his shoulder at the old mine shacks above.

"Don't you let the bogeyman getcha, y'hear?" And he crunched on down toward town.

What a creep, thought Rob, watching Jenkins disappear, suddenly aware of how far up the canyon he had climbed. The gravel and ice crunched beneath Rob's boots, the air grew colder, and Rob thought about his father.

When Rob was younger, his dad, Robert "Jake" Gates, had taken him through many of the old sheds and shacks that once belonged to the mines, and—with a miner's lantern—into old mine shafts that wound into the depths beneath the mountains, pitch-black and cold and filled with sudden drafts from far within and distant, dripping echoes. Jake Gates was the son of one of Faith's last generation of miners and had done some mining himself when he was in his teens. He could drive a steel spike into solid rock in less than ten minutes during the town's annual mining competition. Or he had done, until he disappeared.

That was the thing that was always on the other side of a door that Rob kept tightly closed in his mind. His dad had gone missing. If it hadn't been an accident, then it was deliberate, and that would mean that Jake Gates had *wanted* never to see Rob again. It was a dangerous door. It needed to stay shut.

Rob stepped into one of the falling-down mine buildings, one that his father had shown him, where blacksmiths had been kept busy twenty-four hours a day, forging and sharpening the miners' tools, and shoeing their horses. Right away he knew something was wrong.

Something stank. It was dark in the old shack, with just a few streaks of afternoon sunlight managing to penetrate the broken rooftop slats. Rob's head spun from the odor, and he felt suddenly dizzy and sick. The smell was foul and dark and seemed to contain a spirit of actual malice. Rob took a quick step backward and broke through a piece of rotting floorboard, dropping him down to just above his waist before his feet landed on the bare earth and rubble beneath the shed. An awful scraping pain shot up and down his left leg, and he braced his hands to push himself up out of the hole. That was when he saw the eyes.

They glared at him from a distance of maybe a dozen feet. Rob froze.

He couldn't see anything but two dull yellowish orbs. There was an unnatural warmth in the old smithy that didn't belong there, and Rob felt a strange spinning sensation, as though the entire room were moving through a warm, stinky wind. As his vision adjusted to the dark he saw a tangle of bone and flesh just a foot or two from him. Perhaps it was bits of Buddy, or Booties, or both.

The yellow eyes lurched forward, and there was a sound of something big dragging across the floor of the shack that made Rob think of a heavy tail. Rob pushed up frantically with both hands until his butt just cleared the jagged splintery hole. The eyes paused, unblinking and intense. Rob, frozen by fear, waited for the thing to spring.

Suddenly there was a crackling, electrical noise in the room. The crackle came again, and there in the dark shack, between him and the yellow-eyed beast, was the voice of Phoebe Traylor, faint and staticky, coming from the walkie-talkie stuck in his jeans pocket.

"Rob, come in."

For the first time, the eyes blinked.

"Rob, do you read me?"

Rob didn't dare breathe.

"Rob, come on! Answer me! Don't be so stubborn!"

The room was really spinning now, and the stink was nauseating. A hot wind whipped round Rob's head. The last thing he saw before he passed out was a glimpse of the creature's head as it turned away from him. It was the head of an insane horse or a long-faced open-mouthed lizard—he didn't know what it was, but its fangs glinted wet and sharp and long.

★ ★ ★

The sun was down when Rob Gates stumbled out of the smithy. His leg hurt like anything and he could see a long angry scrape where his jeans were torn.

When he had opened his eyes the thing was gone, the smell was gone, and he was sitting in a hole in the floor. In the dim light he could see bits of bone scattered on the floor, but it wasn't unusual to find dead critters in these abandoned shacks. Everything was utterly ordinary, while just moments before it had been anything but.

Rob found a casserole and a note on the kitchen table when he got home. Fortunately, his mom was out for the evening, playing cards with the Zimmermans. He put his torn jeans at the bottom of the trash barrel, hoping his mother wouldn't notice there was a pair missing. He zapped the casserole and ate half of it, and then he eased himself into a hot bath, wincing with the pain from his scraped-up leg and gingerly washing the grit out of the cuts. He spent a good half hour trying to sort through what had happened to him on the mountain.

He couldn't.

At school the next morning, when Phoebe asked him somewhat coldly why he hadn't answered his walkie-talkie, Rob told her the batteries were dead, and he was silently grateful when she seemed to believe him.

4
JOHNNY B. GOODE

In the days that followed, the weather grew warmer and more springlike, and the teachers of Faith celebrated by piling on the homework. The high school baseball team started spring training, and the track team huffed and grunted their way around the gritty oval, their breath trailing behind them.

Phoebe started riding again with her mom. The horses belonged to the Mitchelsons' stables, and renting them was one of the great joys of their lives. Once a week Jane would saddle up a lovely golden mare named Sally May, and Phoebe would be reunited with her dearest four-legged friend in the world, the beautiful black stallion Johnny B. Goode. She told Johnny B. Goode all her secrets as they rode together, all her hopes and fears, and he listened like no one else.

Rob and his friends Billy Springer and Aran McBell went on their first overnight camping trip of the season, pitching their tent in the meadow just above the miners' cemetery. They made a fire and roasted hot dogs and ate too many s'mores, and around midnight Billy Springer managed to crawl out of the tent just before he puked. Overall they had a great time.

Between them, Phoebe and Rob said not one word about their disagreement or missing pets or dead poodles or the thing on the mountain. Even as the snow receded invitingly from Stair-Master and a fresh pale baby-green fuzz began to take its place, they didn't talk about any of it.

Of course, there were other things to distract them.

Mr. Brinkley, the boys' gym teacher and Rob's personal nemesis, stood on the school's cinder track with a stopwatch as the sixth-grade boys ran hundred-yard wind sprints.

"Hey, Gates!" he shouted. "Whatta you got, lead in your boots?"

Sprinting, pumping his arms and legs, Rob felt as though his chest were about to burst, but he gritted his teeth and transferred his loathing for Mr. Brinkley into his legs. He actually managed to put on more speed as he crossed the finish line.

He staggered and stumbled to a stop, and put his hands on his knees and tried to breathe. He wasn't the only one in pain; Billy Springer was throwing up right there on the track, and Rob had a moment when he thought, *Well, things could be worse.* Then he looked up and there was Mr. Brinkley, standing right over him, looking at the big scrape on Rob's left leg.

"You been shaving your legs, Miss Gates?" he said. "You need to change blades once in a while." All the boys howled with laughter, and Rob did his best to grin, like, *Yeah, good one, Mr. Brinkley.*

With Phoebe later that day he vented his anger.

"I can't make a move in his dumb class without him yelling

at me or making me stay after. Doesn't he have anything better to do?"

"Try to picture Mr. Brinkley's life, Rob," said Phoebe. "He really *doesn't* have anything better to do. You should pity him."

Phoebe had her own burdens that spring. Arabella Giddens, a seventh-grader with perfect teeth, hair, figure, and clothes (Rob called her "Faith's own Barbie doll"), had become Phoebe's dedicated tormentor. Arabella was always there to make sly comments on Phoebe's homemade wardrobe or long thick braid. She made fun of the number of books Phoebe always carried with her and the scent of patchouli that Phoebe unwillingly bore, just by virtue of living in her mother's house. Arabella called Phoebe "Earth Mother," and the nickname stuck, thank you very much, Arabella.

And even though there was a new, uncomfortable distance between Phoebe and Rob, there was always Chad Scudder to call Phoebe "Mrs. Gates" or to whistle when she and Rob walked together in the hall or sat together in the auditorium. Middle school isn't the safest territory on earth.

★ ★ ★

As the days passed, for no reason they could name, both Rob and Phoebe felt a growing apprehension.

One Sunday morning a terrible odor filled the church in the middle of Pastor Mosely's sermon. Rob, sitting beside his mother, had been nearly dozing, and then suddenly he was very much awake. People glanced at each other, silent and embarrassed, and a couple of the teenagers snickered. Deacon Fitterman moved to the windows overlooking the flume and shut each one of them.

"Was it that funky barn smell from the night we found

Pinkie?" Phoebe asked after Rob had described the Sunday service with a forced laugh.

"No, actually . . . this was really nasty."

"Remember last year when the body of that mule deer floated through town on the flume? Maybe it was something like that."

"Yeah," said Rob, knowing that it wasn't—knowing for sure he had experienced that very same odor up close, in the abandoned blacksmith's shack, and wishing he could tell Phoebe about it.

The following Saturday Phoebe's mom sent Phoebe and Rob over to the Parsons sisters' to clear and rake their yard for the coming of spring. It was hard work, but when they were finished Wynola and Adelaide had fresh pecan pie for them, just barely cooled from the oven, with scoops of homemade vanilla ice cream, and the two kids were in some kind of heaven, it was so delicious. Adelaide was talking about her childhood in Faith.

"Our father used to talk about things coming out of the mountain," she said wistfully, through a mouthful of pecan pie. "Out of the shafts. Not often, just every once in a great while. Creatures."

Rob and Phoebe stopped chewing.

"They'd swim the flume," said Adelaide, beaming. "Dad loved to scare us girls with the creatures that came out of the mountain."

The two old sisters laughed. Rob and Phoebe glanced at each other.

"Claws and fangs," said Wynola, chuckling quietly. "He'd paint quite a picture."

"One of them got Abe Adams, dragged him screaming back into the mountain, Dad said." Adelaide's eyes brimmed up, and Wynola squeezed her hand.

"I miss him so," said Adelaide. "Dad, I mean. I never really knew Abe Adams, I was just a girl."

"More pie, you two?" said Wynola brightly.

After school a few days later, when they passed crazy Mickie Pine's place, they saw him sitting on a lawn chair out back near his little chicken coop, bundled up in a parka and holding a .22-caliber rifle across his lap. Mickie looked up at them, his grizzled face and bloodshot eyes looking a little more crazed than usual.

"You seen it yet?" he rasped. "The chicken-killer?" Mickie grinned like the madman he was. "Whatever it is, it comes at night. It's a sign of the end times, that's for sure. It ain't just about chickens anymore."

Rob couldn't help it: a choked laugh escaped him. Mickie Pine glared at him murderously, and Phoebe dragged Rob on down the street until they both could safely dissolve into gales of giggles. Their laughter freed them finally, and as they walked together along Willow, Rob told Phoebe about the yellow eyes in the abandoned smithy.

"I wasn't sure if I was nuts, you know?" said Rob. "Or just imagining stuff."

Phoebe nodded.

"But I'm pretty sure I wasn't. I'm pretty sure if you hadn't walkied me just then, I would've been in big trouble. Oh, and by the way, that awful smell in church was the same dang stink."

Phoebe didn't seem surprised or anything, just quiet.

"Maybe you don't believe me," said Rob, tense again.

"It's not that," said Phoebe. "I do." And then she told Rob about the voice. It seemed that Rob hadn't been the only one holding back information.

It had started two weeks earlier, at the very moment when she and Rob stood over the body of Pinkie.

"I kept hoping you'd say you heard it, too," said Phoebe. "You didn't, did you?"

"Hear what?"

"The words. That sound that seemed to come from out of the ground, that cry . . ."

"Yeah?"

"I thought there were words in it." Phoebe blurted it out in a rush. "English words, foreign words. I thought if you heard them, too, that would mean I wasn't crazy, but you didn't, so I had to wonder, you know?"

"But I was right there with you," said Rob.

"Exactly."

"So what was it saying?" said Rob.

Phoebe walked on for a moment in silence. "I think it was saying the same thing a lot of different ways," she said finally. "Trying different languages, maybe." Phoebe glanced over at Rob. "I think it was saying, 'Help me.' "

They had reached the base of Stair-Master now.

"I decided it was my imagination," said Phoebe, looking up the steep slope, "because it was all just too weird. That's why I said those things that day we went to the hotel. I'm really sorry, Rob."

"Forget it," he said, also staring up Stair-Master.

Phoebe glanced at Rob.

"Let's do it," he said, and the two of them started up the mountain's flank, the ground wet and squishy with the runoff.

"I heard it again, Rob—the voice," said Phoebe as they climbed.

"Yeah?"

"Same voice. I was in my room. It was like it came out of the floorboards, saying the same thing over and over again."

"The floorboards?" said Rob incredulously.

"I know, I know. Maybe it wasn't coming from anywhere, maybe it was just in my head."

"What was it saying? 'Help me'?" said Rob.

"No. 'Call him, call him, call him, call him, call him.' So I did."

"On the walkie? The day I was with that thing in the old shack?"

Phoebe, just ahead of him, nodded. They climbed for a while in silence.

"That doesn't make any sense," said Rob finally. "Are you saying there's two different whatevers out there? And one of them is trying to warn you about the other?"

"*None* of this makes much sense, Robert," said Phoebe.

By the time they reached the top of Stair-Master, long shadows undulated over the moist new spring grass. A couple of mule deer lifted their heads as Phoebe and Rob approached. They stood motionless and staring for an instant before they twitched their long ears and sprang off, disappearing over the mountain's crest. Phoebe and Rob stopped and sat together on a boulder and looked out over Faith.

"It ain't just about chickens anymore," said Rob, finally, and the two of them laughed until tears came.

At last Phoebe said, "I'm scared, Rob."

"Yeah?"

Phoebe's hand found Rob's.

"Hey!" said Rob, startled. "Don't!"

"Sorry," said Phoebe, pulling her hand away.

"What was that?" Rob almost shouted.

Phoebe didn't *know* what it was. "I said I'm sorry!"

"It's okay. Just, you know, *don't*," said Rob.

"It was an accident, okay? An accident!"

"Okay!"

"Geez!"

Phoebe was deeply irritated to realize that she was blushing. They sat in silence for several minutes, watching the sun sink. "I'm really scared," she said finally, "and I don't know why."

Rob thought it over, looking out at the shadows lengthening across the valley.

"Me too, I guess," he said.

That night something got into the Mitchelsons' stables and attacked the lovely mare named Sally May, and the beautiful stallion Johnny B. Goode disappeared from the face of the earth.

5
THE STRANGE DOG

Janet Bright, the veterinarian, and Nick, her husband, the young deaf couple who lived above the Mitchelsons' stables, had set up an emergency operating room on the premises and were struggling to save Sally May's life when the townspeople began to arrive. It was nearly 11:00 P.M. Usually Faith is about asleep by then, but when the sirens go and the volunteer fire truck heads out on a call, so do the citizens.

Brad Mitchelson and Deputy Keith Springer were leading the remaining horses from the stable to adjoining corrals, trying to calm them down, when Phoebe and her mom arrived.

The cop car's spinning red lights competed with the fire truck's red and orange ones. Volunteer firefighters Ben and Ernie and Pastor Mosely were putting up yellow police tape around the scene. The crowd of townspeople was growing: there was green-haired Jimmy from the hotel, and Philippa

Larson, the middle school's librarian, and Sam and Emma Decker, who ran Faith Rep, the summer-stock theater in town.

Phoebe and her mom stood nearby, their arms around each other, their faces smeared with tears.

Pete the sheriff was standing just outside the stable with Thelma Mitchelson and her fourteen-year-old daughter, Donna. Thelma's face was ashy white and she was stroking Donna's hair. Donna looked like she was in shock.

"This is how a lion kills, generally," said Pete the sheriff. "Throat first, then the gut."

"You think this is a mountain lion's work?" said Thelma Mitchelson.

"Don't know what to think. The meltwater's pretty much wiped out any tracks. You can tell something heavy come from up there behind the barn. Could be mountain lion, could be black bear. I just don't know."

Rob rolled up on his bike next to Phoebe, flannel pajama bottoms showing beneath the cuffs of his jeans. He saw that Phoebe'd been crying, so he didn't say anything, just nodded and looked away.

"But where's my other horse, Pete?" said Brad Mitchelson, joining his wife and daughter. "Where's my Johnny B. Goode? Where are the tracks? I know it's been melting, but Johnny's a big boy, and if he took off runnin', we'd see tracks!"

Sheriff Pete squinted up into the starless night sky. "I know," he said. "It's just real dang strange."

The stable door opened and Nick Bright came out. For a brief moment before he closed the door again, they all had a glimpse of a large shape lying on the stable floor, covered in blood-soaked sheets and lit by bright work lights. Janet Bright was bent over the horse, working intently, in a tangle of intravenous bags and tubes.

31

Nick was signing urgently.

"Nick's saying they were asleep," Phoebe translated, "and when they woke up . . . Oh, geez. There was a bad smell, very bad, and then the horses started screaming."

Rob nodded grimly.

"Nick got up and started down the stairs to the stables with a flashlight," Phoebe said. "The stable door was open. Sally May was lying there bleeding and sort of snapping at herself. Johnny B. Goode was gone."

"Nick," signed Phoebe, speaking at the same time, "is Sally May gonna be all right?"

Nick took a deep breath. He made the sign for "I don't know," then headed back into the stable. Phoebe moved to Donna and the two girls held each other.

"Okay," said Pete, "the stink does it for me. You ever been up close with a full-grown black bear, Brad? The males especially can stink like all heck."

The sheriff turned to his deputy. "Keith, get some of the fellas together, first light tomorrow. We're hunting bear."

A sigh of relief seemed to go through the crowd. Black bear: the thing had a name now, and a named fear is a lot easier to live with than the nameless kind.

Rob nudged Phoebe and the two of them moved away.

"That was no bear in the old blacksmith's shack," whispered Rob. "Yellow eyes and—I don't know, Phoeb, but from what I heard, a tail scraping across the floor."

"You think we should say something?"

Rob shook his head. "What are we gonna say? To who?"

"To whom," said Phoebe absently, staring off across the barn-yard.

"Phoebe," Rob hissed, "this is no time for grammar!"

"Rob—look over there. Did you ever see that dog before?"

He followed her gaze, and there, in alternating shadow and spinning red light, stood a broad-faced dog. Its body sloped oddly downward from its head to its hind parts—or maybe it was sitting, it was hard to tell. It had a short grayish or greenish coat that in that dim light seemed to shimmer, and its big dark eyes seemed to be gazing intently at Rob and Phoebe.

"I don't know," whispered Rob. "Why?"

"I'm getting goose bumps here," said Phoebe. "I'm not sure it's a dog."

"Sure it's a dog," said Rob. "Of course it is. Isn't it?"

Rob stared intently at the animal across the stable yard, and it stared right back. The hairs on Rob's arms tingled. "Are there things hanging from its mouth?" he asked.

"It's built sort of wrong, isn't it? For a dog?" whispered Phoebe.

"What's built sort of wrong?" said Jenkins of El Paso, suddenly at their side. Where had he come from?

"I wasn't talking to you," said Phoebe, startled and angry. "I don't even know you!"

"Jenkins, up from El Paso. Just tryin' to be friendly."

Phoebe tugged Rob and they moved off through the crowd together, Rob wheeling his bike beside him. But there was no dog there when they looked again.

"Where'd it go?" said Rob.

"You didn't hear anything just now, did you?" asked Phoebe hesitantly.

"What do you mean? Did *you?*"

"No," said Phoebe uncertainly, still looking for the creature. "I mean, I don't know."

"*What?*" demanded Rob.

"I thought . . . I thought I heard someone saying your name, that's all. Sort of a low, raspy voice, 'Rob, Rob, Rob.' Sort of like

33

a dog barking. Just my imagination, I guess," she added, noticing the discomfort in Rob's eyes.

They were crisscrossing the stable yard, moving among the volunteer firefighters and the onlookers.

"It wasn't very big. Could something that size take down a horse?" whispered Rob.

"I don't know," said Phoebe.

At that moment Lucy Gates appeared.

"Where have you been?" was her opener to her son. "What makes you think you can take off this hour of the night without saying a word to me?"

"The whole town's here," said Rob.

"Yeah, great. No more bike, no more mountain, no anything, no anywhere, until they find whatever did this and shoot it dead. Do I make myself clear?"

"Mom," Rob said through clenched teeth, "people are listening."

"Are *you* listening is what I want to know!"

Jane Traylor joined them, and Lucy turned to her. "This is nuts, Jane," she said. "This is scary. I've lived my whole life in Faith and I never saw anything like this." She turned back to Rob.

"Come on, let's get your bike in the back of the car and go."

"I'll just ride home," said Rob curtly.

"You're not riding anywhere tonight!" Lucy yelled.

She grabbed Rob's handlebar, but Rob jerked it away again, his eyes flashing.

"Don't! God, I hate you," he said.

Lucy took a deep breath, and then her face wrinkled into a brief sad smile. "You're not supposed to start hating me until you turn thirteen. You're ahead of schedule."

She turned and started out through the spinning red and orange lights and the gathered townspeople. Rob stood struggling with himself, and then he finally climbed onto his bike and followed her out without a backward glance.

Jane Traylor looked at her daughter. "He's a little rough on his mom, don't you think?"

Phoebe was silent. She glanced around at the stables, the corral, the stable yard. No dog, no voice in her head.

"Can we just go?" she said finally.

Jane put her arm around Phoebe's shoulders and gave a little squeeze, and the two of them headed down the hill together. Phoebe was already in bed and just on the verge of sleep when her walkie-talkie beeped. It was Rob, laying out his plan of action for the morning.

6
FIRST CONTACT

It was the first time Phoebe had ever sneaked out of her mother's house in the night, and she was feeling a little conflicted about it. She'd never had a lot of secrets from her mom. But there was no way Jane Traylor was going to give her permission for this, and according to Rob it was something they absolutely needed to do.

Rob was more used to disappearing from his home than Phoebe (chores to avoid, groundings to escape), but today felt different. What he'd said to his mother the night before rattled around in his head uncomfortably as he tiptoed out, his sneakers in one hand and a flashlight in the other. He thought about leaving a note on the kitchen table, something like "I don't hate you, Mom," but that felt awkward and he ended up not.

Phoebe was waiting for him on the bridge above the flume

near the Conoco when Rob arrived at 4:30 A.M. The two of them moved silently through the sleeping town. It had been Rob's plan to start before dawn, before the hunters set out, and it looked as though they'd succeeded in that.

As plans go, it wasn't much of one. They had encountered something unusual in three locations: on Stair-Master, in the old blacksmith's shack, and at the Mitchelsons' stables. Rob and Phoebe would travel between these sites, looking for . . . Tracks? Droppings? The thing itself? Anyway, they'd do it all before school and be in their classrooms by eight, with no one the wiser.

What they would do if they actually came face to face with the beast that had attacked the horses, neither was sure.

The two kids made their way up the steep slopes of Stair-Master to the spot where they'd found Pinkie. In the town far below them they saw the hunters setting out from the tiny police station, two by two, in the dim predawn light. They were ghostlike shapes that got into Jeeps and took off for the valley while others drove up the hill opposite, past the old miners' cemetery and into the mountains beyond. Eventually a small group of hunters huffed and puffed their way on foot up Stair-Master, and Rob and Phoebe tucked themselves under an overhanging boulder near the top. The kids held their breath, but the sleepy hunters fanned right past them, unseeing, up and over the crest of the mountain.

The kids crawled out of their hiding place.

"Now what do we do?" whispered Phoebe.

"Do you have any food?" said Rob.

Phoebe rolled her eyes heavenward. "Is this a picnic, Robert? Is that what this is?" she hissed.

"Come on, Phoeb," said Rob, with an imploring-puppy sort of face.

Phoebe looked at her friend for a moment, exasperated, then yanked a zipper on her backpack and pulled out a homemade breadstick.

"I'm serious. What exactly are we supposed to do up here?" she snapped as Rob crunched the breadstick.

"I don't know," said Rob. "Look around."

"Brilliant, Robert," said Phoebe drily. "Absolutely brilliant."

"Shut up! And stop calling me Robert!" Rob yelled angrily.

At that moment, several things happened at once. Mickie Pine stood up from behind two upright boulders at the mountain's peak and aimed his .22-caliber Winchester directly at Rob Gates.

At the same moment, something hit Rob from behind and he went facedown to the sod as a rifle blast shattered the still dawn air.

A blur on four legs leapt over him and raced toward the figure with the rifle.

Mickie Pine, weapon in hand, opened his mouth to scream but nothing came out. Instead, he turned and ran like a crazy man after the hunters.

Rob was struggling to his feet, and Phoebe gave him a hand up. The two of them stood in a daze, staring.

A short, broad-faced creature was standing at the top of the crest, looking off at the disappearing Mickie Pine. Then it turned and faced the kids.

It was the same thing they'd glimpsed outside the Mitchelsons' stables the night before. It had a blunt face, like a pit bull's, and a narrow body with broad shoulders. Its front legs were bowed and its "elbows" stuck out. Its eyes were big and dark. Its coat shimmered wetly, a glistening gray or green. From its upper jaw, two small tusks curved downward.

No. No, it wasn't a dog.

It stepped forward, and Rob and Phoebe both took a step backward. It sniffed the earth at its feet, then looked up and sniffed the air, and then its gaze settled again on the two kids. They had goose bumps, and a tingling skittered up their spines. The air began to feel warm and humid.

Suddenly the creature turned around in a full circle and lay down, just as a dog would—its head up, facing them, its front paws folded under its chest. Nothing could have surprised Rob and Phoebe more.

"What kind of a thing is it?" whispered Rob.

"I don't know," Phoebe whispered back. "But I think it just saved your life."

"I guess."

"Is that fur? Or hide?"

"I'm not sure." All this in whispers.

The beast seemed to be studying Rob and Phoebe as well, its deep black eyes moving over them slowly. It stood again, and the kids nervously stepped back.

A long silent moment passed among them. The first pink rays of dawn touched the tip of Stair-Master and leapt from peak to peak, on into the distance. A gentle spring wind tousled the kids' hair. The beast cocked its head and sniffed, and its brow furrowed just a bit.

"Phoebe," Rob whispered, "I don't think this guy attacked any horses."

"I don't know," said Phoebe. "Those tusks . . ."

The beast snorted and gave its head a little shake.

"I'm going to touch it," said Rob.

"No," breathed Phoebe. "Rob, you don't know anything about it, it's not safe—"

But Rob had already taken a step toward the animal, which responded by lifting its head and gazing at him intently.

"Okay, fella," said Rob. "I'm just gonna give your head a little pat here, just a friendly little pat."

The creature didn't move. Its big dark eyes followed Rob as he approached. Rob's left hand was actually shaking as he slowly reached down to put his fingertips on the top of the animal's glistening head. The moment he made contact, Rob was engulfed in a hot wind, strange cries shrieked in his ears, and beads of sweat sprang out on his forehead.

He pulled his hand away fast, like he'd burned it, staring with wide fearful eyes at the creature.

"What?" said Phoebe. "What is it, Rob? What just happened?"

Rob was breathing hard. He shook his head.

And then the beast opened its jaws and said, "That's where I come from."

★ ★ ★

The voice was coarse and gravelly, and as crazy as it seemed, both kids would later say it had a British accent.

"Did it just speak?" Phoebe asked.

"You heard it, too?" whispered Rob.

"I think so," said Phoebe. There was a silence. Somewhere far below, down in the town a dog barked. "Did you speak?" said Phoebe faintly. Was that a nod in reply? It was hard to tell.

"Who are you?"

The creature regarded them gravely. Its deep dark eyes rested slowly on Phoebe and then Rob. Just when they thought that it would never speak again, and probably never *had* spoken, a voice rumbled up out of it.

"You've grown," it said.

Phoebe shivered. *"What?"*

A low cough rumbled in the creature's chest, and it drew in a long raspy breath.

"In this era, in your language," said the beast at last, "people who know about such things call me a synapsid."

Phoebe and Rob stared, bewildered.

"Synapsid?" it said again, and waited. "We used to be rather the thing, once upon a time. You're descended from us, after all."

Phoebe and Rob just stared.

"You might say that I'm the *Last* Synapsid, or nearly. There's the gorgonopsid, of course. One mustn't forget the Gorgon." It gave a throaty chortle, like it was laughing quietly, but the deep eyes looked sad.

"It's a little lonely being the last of something."

The synapsid sniffed, like a dog picking up information from the air.

"Methane," he said, and his brow wrinkled. "It's all happening again."

Rob and Phoebe glanced at each other. What was happening again? What was it talking about?

"What's a Gorgon?" asked Rob in a hoarse voice.

"The Gorgon is the other synapsid—we're almost all that's left. You've seen him, Rob."

Rob shuddered to hear the creature call him by name.

"Worse—he's seen you." The synapsid regarded them gravely. "You mustn't let him eat you."

Rob was suddenly angry. "Okay, this is where I wake up, right?" he blustered. "And it was all a dream?"

But he didn't wake up. Phoebe was still standing there gaping, and the creature was still staring at him. Rob felt light-headed.

"Where?" said Phoebe faintly. "Where do you come from?"

41

"Your past," the creature said simply. It sniffed the air and its brow wrinkled again. "My world is dying. The earth erupted and the air turned bad. You mustn't let such things happen here. I need to get back to my world to try to save it. If I succeed, then you'll have a chance to save *yours.* If I fail, your world will never come to be."

"Excuse me, but my world *is,* last time I checked," said Rob.

The creature seemed to smile. "It seems to be, I'm sure, to *you,* but your world is just a possibility. You've wondered about such things yourselves, haven't you? 'What if all this is just a dream?' If we don't succeed, I'm afraid that's all you and your world will be: a glorious dream that never came to be."

Rob and Phoebe looked at each other again.

"How did you know Rob's name? How do you know English, for that matter?" said Phoebe. "How are you physically able to speak in the first place?"

"And what do you mean, we've grown?" said Rob.

"I've had plenty of time to learn the languages of humankind, Phoebe. I taught myself to speak long ago. Your larynx actually owes quite a lot to mine, if I say so myself. As to knowing your names, I was here when you found the little white dog; I heard what you called each other then. But I've known you for longer than that, even if you didn't know me. I've been looking for you for . . . Well, for longer than you can imagine."

Phoebe took a deep breath and shook herself a little. None of it was making any kind of sense. "Did you kill Pinkie?" she demanded.

"The little white dog? She'll be thought of as one of the most important little white dogs in all history. Her death brought us together, after all my searching."

Phoebe persisted. "Did you attack the horses?"

The deep black eyes looked sad again. "It was the gorgonopsid, the Gorgon. It's always been the Gorgon. We need to stop him, or there won't be any such thing as horses, or dogs, or you."

They heard men's voices from the other side of the crest.

"The hunters are coming back," said the synapsid, turning back to the cliff's edge. "We have a lot to do together, and you have much to learn. Look for me." The creature turned and crouched as though it was about to leap.

"Wait!" said Phoebe. "How do we look for you?"

"Watch, and listen," said the synapsid, and then it sprang from the edge of Stair-Master into space. Rob and Phoebe rushed to the brink and saw it land on an outcrop of rock a dozen feet below, and watched it leap like a mountain goat from crag to crag, down into the furrows of the mountains and the mines and out of sight.

Phoebe and Rob managed to hide again just before the hunters passed, Mickie Pine babbling madly about a vicious green beast with tusks.

7
THE ASSEMBLY

The two kids made it to school that morning moments before the eight o'clock bell. First they found Donna Mitchelson, to ask about the horses. The report wasn't great: Sally May was in critical condition, and there was still no trace of Johnny B. Goode.

Rob and Phoebe went from class to class in a kind of speechless daze. Mrs. Peabody, the seventh-grade English teacher, had to call on Phoebe three times before she heard her, and when she asked Phoebe how many lines there were in a sonnet, Phoebe said, "Robert Louis Stevenson, I think."

Mrs. Peabody's pumps clicked down the aisle to Phoebe's desk. She looked down at Phoebe intently, felt her forehead for a moment, then clicked back to her desk, where she scribbled on a pad for a moment, her many bracelets jangling and her elaborate earrings tinkling.

"Take this to the nurse's office, Phoebe. I think you may be coming down with something."

Phoebe took the note and walked out into the hall toward the nurse's office. Then she stopped, glanced up and down the empty corridor, and sprinted for the library.

Philippa Larson, the librarian, looked down at Phoebe from the top of a rolling wooden ladder, an armful of books tucked precariously under one arm. "Hello, Phoebe," she called. Phoebe beamed brightly and waved Mrs. Peabody's note at her as though it were a library pass, feeling like a total criminal. "Give me a little push, will you?" said the librarian.

Phoebe went to the base of the ladder and looked up hesitantly. "Just a few feet north should do," said Ms. Larson. "Go ahead, push away!"

Phoebe moved the ladder slowly along the stack, Ms. Larson teetering alarmingly. "Stop! Perfect! Thank you, dear."

Phoebe took a seat in front of one of the computers. She made her best guess at the word the creature had used on the mountain, and typed it into a search engine. She had her result within moments:

In the latter days of the Permian Era, 250 million years ago, the earth was dominated by creatures we call synapsids, the ancestors of mammals and ultimately the ancestors of us. Synapsids are sometimes called "mammal-like reptiles," because they seem to have had physical characteristics of both groups. Synapsids came in many shapes and sizes, and were very different from each other. The greatest difference lay in what they ate: some ate leaves and grasses only, and some ate only other synapsids.

Phoebe entered the word *Permian* and sifted through the many sites that came up. She was reading fast, growing more excited by the moment. She pulled her walkie-talkie from her belt and pushed the call button.

"Rob, come in," she whispered into the walkie. "Rob? This is crazy, this just can't be!"

In her excitement, of course, she'd forgotten that Rob would be in the middle of Mr. Brinkley's seventh-grade boys' physical education class. The boys were all listening to Brinkley reading from a completely embarrassing pamphlet called "Hygiene— Physical and Moral" when Phoebe's voice squeaked excitedly into the room.

"Rob, the last synapsid went extinct at the end of the Permian era!"

Rob was desperately trying to switch off his walkie, but Mr. Brinkley plucked it from his hands and held it up for the whole class to listen.

"Rob, the Permian era ended two hundred and fifty million years ago! That's way before the dinosaurs, millions and millions of years before the first dinosaur! Rob! Robert?"

The other boys were all grinning, and Rob turned a deep shade of red. Mr. Brinkley pressed the button and spoke into the walkie.

"Earth to Earth Mother, do you read me?" he said, and the boys all howled.

In the library, Phoebe nearly died.

"The what went extinct at the end of the what-what?" said Brinkley in mock horror. "Over!" There was another round of laughter from the boys in Rob's class.

"Ro-bert, perhaps you can explain what your girlfriend is talking about."

The boys started chanting. "Ro-bert, Ro-bert, Ro-bert!"

The walkie crackled and Phoebe's voice was very small. "Sorry, Mr. Brinkley."

"Switch it off, Traylor, pronto!" snarled Mr. Brinkley. He turned to Rob.

"As for you, Gates—" he began, but just then Rob was literally saved by the bell: the ringing sounded throughout the school, and the voice of Lily Sweet, the principal's secretary, came over the loudspeaker, announcing a special assembly commencing immediately in the auditorium.

Even as the kids moved in a noisy mass through the corridors a rumor began to circulate: something had been spotted on the mountain. The beast had been seen.

★ ★ ★

The kids in the assembly were quiet for once.

Principal Dunne was talking to them weightily about Recent Occurrences, and everything he said seemed to have capital letters. He talked to them about Safety and Common Sense. He told them that Hiking was Discouraged for the Time Being, and the Mines of course were Always off limits and he Hoped they wouldn't have to resort to a Curfew for those under sixteen but they would Do so if Necessary. A Literal Army of volunteers would assist the Authorities, and Principal Dunne assured them that they would Find this Menace, whatever it was, and Destroy It.

"No!" The cry jumped involuntarily from Phoebe's mouth. She was seated toward the back of the auditorium with Angela Cruz and Donna Mitchelson. Mr. Dunne didn't seem to hear her, but the kids around Phoebe did, and they turned quizzical eyes on her.

47

"What's wrong, Phoebe?" whispered Donna. Her eyes were red from crying.

"It's hard to explain," said Phoebe.

Rob was sitting in the row ahead, between Billy Springer and Aran McBell. He glanced over his shoulder at Phoebe and their eyes met.

Principal Dunne continued in his ponderous tones.

"Some of you may have heard Rumors, and I want to Emphasize: that's Just what they Are. But there has been an Unconfirmed Sighting of a Wild Animal on the mountain above town."

The auditorium buzzed with excitement, and Principal Dunne seemed to inflate a bit.

"The Source may be Unreliable," he said. "But for Now, this party's description is all we have to go on. It is Possible that the creature we're hunting is a type of Wild Boar."

A buzz went through the auditorium. Black bears were suddenly yesterday's news; wild boars were catapulted to stardom in an instant.

"Excuse me? Excuse me!"

Phoebe was on her feet, waving her hand at Principal Dunne. Rob closed his eyes and sank down in his seat. Slowly the crowd noticed Phoebe and gradually quieted down.

"I'm sorry, but . . . what if that's not what attacked the horses?" said Phoebe, trembling a bit, with the eyes of the entire school on her. "What if the hunters kill the wrong thing?"

Except for a couple of snickers here and there, there was silence in the auditorium.

Principal Dunne looked over the top of his glasses and leaned forward over the podium.

"Well, then, Miss Traylor, I for one should be glad to Partake of some Wild Boar Stew."

Which wasn't a particularly funny remark, but the audience acted like it was about the wittiest thing they'd ever heard.

"Yes, well," continued Principal Dunne. "We will be out in Force hunting this Beast, and until further Notice, no one, and I mean No One, is allowed on the Mountain."

Well, that was like waving a red flag in front of a bunch of middle-school bulls. Before the assembly was over there were probably half a dozen plans hatched to search the mountains surrounding Faith.

Billy Springer and Aran McBell nudged each other and Rob at the same time.

"After school?" whispered Aran.

"Totally," said Billy. "You with us, Rob?"

"Sorry," he said hesitantly. "Got detention." Which he didn't, but it was so often the case that Aran and Billy believed him and nodded sympathetically.

As the student body filed out of the auditorium, Donna Mitchelson came abreast of Phoebe and whispered in her ear.

"You're not saying they shouldn't hunt it, are you? Phoebe, you love these horses. You love Johnny B. Goode as much as I do."

Phoebe nodded. "I just . . . I just want everybody to be careful, you know? 'Cause it's so easy to make a mistake, and some mistakes you can't take back."

Donna stopped walking and looked hard at Phoebe. Her eyes filled with tears and she pushed on through the crowd, leaving Phoebe standing there, feeling awful.

"What were you thinking?" Rob whispered fiercely, appearing at her side.

"You know exactly what I was thinking," said Phoebe. "Thanks a lot for backing me up!"

"You're lucky I'm still talking to you," snapped Rob.

"Oh, am I?" When Phoebe got angry her freckles got darker.

"You keep this up, I'm gonna have to move to a new town," Rob hissed.

"Yeah, well, until that glorious day arrives let's just move on to the library," said Phoebe, her eyes flashing with irritation. "I've got something to show you."

8
THE FOSSIL RECORD

The library was still mostly deserted, for which Phoebe was grateful. She and Rob were hunkered over a computer terminal, and when Phoebe typed in an address, the image that appeared was unmistakably the creature they'd met that morning on the mountain.

"Wow," Rob whispered. "That's almost like it. The real one's tusks aren't quite that big, though."

"There are a lot of different varieties of synapsid. This is just some artist's guess about one of them."

"What's this one called?" said Rob. "Diictodon?"

"Yes," said Phoebe, "but you pronounce it 'di-ictodon.'"

"The real one's not as green and not that scaly. I could do better."

"That's because you've actually seen him!" said Phoebe. "Given that the fossil record is over two hundred and fifty million years old, I'd say this is a pretty good guess."

Rob tore a page from one of his notebooks, closed his eyes for a moment, and then began moving his pencil rapidly over the page. Before long, he slid the drawing across the desk to Phoebe.

"There you go—Sid."

"Who's Sid?"

"The Last Synapsid," said Rob. "Obviously."

Phoebe smiled. "I like it," she said. "Wait a minute—you think it's a he?"

"I dunno. I haven't really got that far with this whole thing. I don't have a lot of experience guessing the sex of—"

"Sid"
by Rbt. Gates Jr.

Ms. Larson appeared from the stacks, pushing a cart overloaded with books. "Back again, Phoebe?"

"Hi, Ms. Larson," said Phoebe.

"And Robert Gates, what a pleasant surprise!"

Rob took this as a dig, which it was, and merely grunted in reply.

Ms. Larson moved off, chuckling.

"Have you tried finding a picture of the other thing?" Rob whispered. "The stink bomb?"

"I'm afraid I have," whispered Phoebe, typing a new address on the computer keyboard. "There was a predator back then, a carnivore called gorgonopsid. Scientists think it gave off very strong-smelling secretions, for some reason." The image that came up on the screen made Rob cringe.

"Oh, crap," said Rob.

52

"Is that what it looked like? The thing in the blacksmith's shack?"

"I couldn't see much of it except for the eyes and the fangs," said Rob, "but I gotta say, the fangs look right." Rob tore off another sheet of paper and sketched rapidly, glancing occasionally at the image on the computer screen.

"Unpleasant," said Phoebe.

"You could say that," said Rob. "But these guys all died out, right? They don't exist anymore, they went extinct—Sid and Stinky both."

"Yeah," said Phoebe.

"Two hundred and fifty million years ago."

"That's what the books say."

"So . . ." Rob dropped his voice back down to a whisper. "What are we talking about? That was a two-hundred-and-fifty-million-year-old ghost we met on the mountain this morning? Or are the books wrong and these critters *didn't* go extinct? They just hung around and learned how to talk like someone on Masterpiece Theatre?"

Then they realized that Ms. Philippa Larson was standing

right over them, staring over their shoulders at the images on the monitor.

"Fascinating," she said. "Whatever sort of creature is that?"

"Whatever happened to privacy, is what I'd like to know," said Rob hotly.

"But I wasn't trying to pry, I was just—"

"Let's go, Phoebe. I guess academic freedom is dead in this town."

"But I wasn't . . ." Two pink spots appeared on the librarian's cheeks.

Rob stalked out of the library indignantly. Phoebe, avoiding Ms. Larson's hurt gaze, switched off the computer and followed him.

"We gotta find Sid before all those yahoos blow him to smithereens," said Rob to Phoebe as they moved along the corridor. "We're ditching school."

"I couldn't," said Phoebe automatically. And it was true, she didn't do things like that.

"Yes, you can," said Rob. Grabbing one of the straps on Phoebe's backpack, he guided her through the crowded corridor to Faith Middle School's least-watched exit, near the back loading dock by the cafeteria kitchen.

9
DRIVING
LESSON

Phoebe and Rob ducked through town, heading for the foot of Stair-Master.

"If we can find Sid," said Rob, "maybe we can hide him or something. Take him home with us, even."

They picked up their pace.

"Rob . . ." Phoebe hesitated, glancing over at him. "I've been waiting for you to tell me, but I guess I've got to ask."

Rob gave her a blank look.

"When you touched Sid, what happened? You looked really strange all of a sudden."

Rob looked straight ahead as they walked abreast, and he was silent for a moment.

"You can't laugh," he said at last.

"I won't laugh."

"I think . . . I think I went somewhere," he said.

"What?"

"Somewhere hot and wet and loud."

"Loud?"

"Well, yeah, in a way. Phoebe, it was like I was in a jungle movie or something. There were things all around me making a lot of noise."

"What kind of things?"

"I was moving too fast to see anything—it was a blur."

"Rob, you were standing still, right next to me. And I didn't hear a thing."

"I'm just saying what I saw, all right? And what I heard," said Rob. "There was Sid's head, and his big eyes looking at me, and a green blur everywhere else, and all these wild cries. And I jerked my hand back and everything stopped—the blur, the noises, all of it."

They were about to cross the last bridge over the flume, the one at the bottom of town, near the Conoco, when a 1970s gray Oldsmobile station wagon lurched toward them. Through the windshield they could see old Adelaide Parsons gripping the steering wheel and squinting ferociously over it at the road ahead, while on the passenger side Wynola rolled down her window and waved Rob and Phoebe over frantically.

"Oh, no," moaned Phoebe. "Adelaide's driving again."

"We don't have time for this, Phoebe!"

"Wynola needs us!"

"So does Sid!"

The Oldsmobile rolled to a stop, and Adelaide leaned out her window and said cheerily, "Would you two like a lift, dears? I'm only going as far as the bank."

Twice in the past year Adelaide had taken it into her head to get the old family car out of its musty garage, even though both Adelaide and Wynola had given up driving years earlier. Once

Sheriff Pete saw her weaving up Main and flagged her down. The other time Adelaide had been found in Arenoso, forty miles down in the Valley, without any clear idea of how (or why) she got there.

"Hi, ladies," said Rob in a strained voice.

"Hi, Miss Adelaide, Miss Wynola," said Phoebe.

Wynola muttered under her breath, "Please get in. You have to talk her out of this—she won't listen to me."

Adelaide honked the horn and giggled like a schoolgirl. "Hop in, kids," she chirped gaily. "The meter's running!"

"Oh, I don't know, Miss Adelaide," said Phoebe loudly, leaning in the back door. "We could always *walk* to the bank."

"Nice day for walking, I say," shouted Rob, holding open the other back door of the old car.

"Nonsense," said Adelaide. "I'll have you there in a jiff." And before Rob and Phoebe had fully entered the backseat the station wagon was jerking up Main as the kids struggled to pull the rear doors shut.

"We've already been up Rat Creek," said Wynola in a furious undertone from the front seat, "because she wanted to see Rat Creek again before she died."

"And it was lovely, was it not?" said Adelaide, sounding a little irritated. "I wonder how it got that awful name. It's such a pretty spot."

"Then we had to drive out to the old well and fill gallon jugs with water from the pump. What for? The water from the tap in our home has always been good enough for me."

"It's perfectly fine, as *water* goes, but water from the old well opens your eyes to life's great mysteries," said Adelaide archly. "Also it keeps you regular."

Wynola just shook her head.

"And now Miss Drives-a-Lot has to go to the bank to ask her

weekly question," said Wynola, "even though we did all our banking on Tuesday, walking there and back just fine, thank you very much!"

Phoebe, suddenly horror-struck, cried, "Look out for Nancy Sweet!"

"Nancy Sweet? Where?" asked Adelaide.

"Twelve o'clock!" shouted Rob, pointing at the old post-mistress, another of Faith's hangovers from an earlier era, who happened to be crossing Main.

Out on the road Nancy Sweet looked over her shoulder in disbelief and stepped up her pace, but Adelaide kept going.

"Adelaide!" shrieked Wynola. "What on earth are you doing?"

"Just going to give Nancy a lift, dear," she said, accelerating a little. "She's not as young as she used to be, poor darling. She'll be happy for a ride."

At this point Nancy Sweet broke into a flat-out run, which, given she was seventy-eight years old, was pretty impressive.

Rob vaulted into the front seat between the twin sisters and grabbed the steering wheel.

"Hiya, Miss Adelaide. Maybe I can help a little?"

Rob edged the car to the right, away from Nancy Sweet and back into the right lane.

"Men!" said Adelaide, taking her hands from the wheel and turning to look at Phoebe in the backseat with a chuckle. "Always got to be in charge."

Phoebe nodded numbly.

"Never mind," Adelaide said, relenting with a smile. "A young man needs his practice."

Adelaide suddenly seemed to lose interest in driving. She pulled a compact from her purse, opened it, and stared at the little mirror critically. To the immense relief of everyone else, Rob eased the car over to the curb and it very gradually rolled to a stop—just outside the Faith National Trust, as it happened.

"Well," said Adelaide, "here we are. All ashore who's going ashore!"

She made a final check of hair and makeup in the rearview mirror and stepped daintily out of the Oldsmobile. The others seemed to start breathing again all at once. Wynola got out of the car, muttering, "Hopeless, hopeless." Phoebe got out and ran back to check on Nancy Sweet, and Rob took the keys from the ignition and joined Wynola on the sidewalk.

"She's obsessed with it," said Wynola, looking at the bank and shaking her head sadly.

"What's that, Miss Wynola?" asked Rob.

"My sister's obsessed with the man who owns Faith. She keeps checking at the bank to see if he's come back."

"The man who owns Faith?" said Rob, puzzled.

"She's got a bone to pick with him. So do we all, of course, but I keep telling her Mr. FitzHugh is long dead. The man has to have been dead for decades now."

Phoebe approached the Parsons sisters' car with Nancy Sweet on one arm.

"Sorry about that, Nancy," said Wynola.

"I'll live. That was some pretty snappy drivin' on Adelaide's part, I must say," said Nancy Sweet. "She's in the bank lookin' for FitzHugh, I imagine."

"Oh, yes, nothing changes with us."

Rob pulled the car keys from his pocket and offered them to Wynola.

"Here you go, Miss Wynola," he said.

"Oh, no," she said. "That's the last thing I want. You hang on to them for now, Robert. We'll just leave the old crate parked where it is, and my sister and I will walk home when she's done with her 'banking.' This way I can tell her I don't have the car keys and I won't be lying."

"Say," said Nancy, suddenly turning to the kids, "why aren't you two in school?"

"See ya," said Rob brightly, pretending he hadn't heard and pulling Phoebe by the straps of her backpack. The two of them hurried off down Main, Rob waving goodbye to the old ladies over his shoulder.

Glancing up at Stair-Master, they saw tiny figures spread all across the upper reaches of the mountain. There was an organized line of hunters moving step by step up the mountain's flank.

"Oh, Rob, it looks like a church social up there. We're too late, aren't we," Phoebe said, sagging with both disappointment and exhaustion.

Rob nodded. "Way late."

"Should we go back to school?" said Phoebe.

Rob looked at her with wonder and pity. "Go back to school? You are so incredibly strange," he said.

Phoebe was trying to think of a comeback when her mother stepped out of the post office onto the sidewalk right in front of them.

Phoebe and Rob stopped stock-still, and so did Jane Traylor.

"Hey, guys," said Jane finally. "Why don't you come back to the shop with me? We'll have some mint tea and a little talk."

★ ★ ★

It wasn't as bad as Rob had expected, at least at first. Unlike his own mom, Jane Traylor wasn't the freaking-out type. She wasn't loud, ever, and right now she didn't even seem particularly angry, just a little solemn. The two kids sat silently in the

60

back room of Jane's little shop, the air pungent with herbs and oils, while Jane poured hot water from a kettle into a little brown teapot.

"You guys have had kind of a busy day," said Jane finally.

"It was my idea to ditch," said Rob gallantly. "Phoebe didn't want to."

And then Phoebe launched into the story of how they'd come to the rescue of Adelaide and Wynola, and how Rob had probably literally saved Nancy Sweet's life, so it had turned out to be a good thing, actually, that they'd left school a little early, although Phoebe swore that it was the first time she'd ever done it and she'd certainly never do it again.

Jane blew on her tea to cool it.

"What an exciting life you two lead," said Jane drily. "But I was actually talking about this morning."

Rob and Phoebe were very still now.

"Early this morning." Jane sipped her tea. "Like, say, four-thirty this morning."

There was an awful silence in the room.

"When I heard you leaving, I didn't stop you and—Phoebe, I want you to know this—I didn't follow you: I'm not a spy. I'm your mom. Which isn't always two different things with moms, but with this mom it is, and always will be."

The two kids were staring at the tabletop.

"So I don't know where you went or what you did. But I assume, whatever it was, it was with you, Rob."

Rob felt this was turning out to be way worse than his own mom yelling.

Jane got up from the table and carried her teacup to the sink. She paused a moment to look out the window that faced out back, across the alley toward the big old opera house from the mining era that was now the town's summer stock theater.

"I know what happens when kids get to be your age."

Oh, no. A terrible shape blossomed in Rob's mind.

"I know all about raging hormones, believe me," said Jane.

No! This was a thousand times more awful than Rob had imagined. This was worse than "Hygiene—Physical and Moral"! He glanced at Phoebe: her mouth was open in disbelief, her hands clapped over her ears.

"The two of you have been so close for such a long time. You both had a tough time when your dads left, and it was your friendship back then that helped you get through it all. So it's natural for you to have special feelings for each other."

"Mom, shut up!" cried Phoebe.

"No, Mrs. Traylor, really, it's not like that!" said Rob at the same time.

"Feelings like that are nothing to be ashamed of," said Jane, resolutely staring out the window. "But you're just so very young, I worry about you."

"Shut up, shut up, *shut up!*" Phoebe's freckles were darker than Rob had ever seen them, and her eyes were wide with horror.

"We don't use that expression, actually, Phoeb," said Jane, a little sharply.

"Shut up!"

"Okay, that's enough," Jane snapped.

"I'm not . . . We're not . . . You're ruining everything!" shrieked Phoebe.

"I just think you guys should cool it a little bit, okay?"

"There is nothing to cool!" Phoebe shouted. Rob had never heard Phoebe yell at her mother before. "Oh, I hate you!"

There was a sudden silence in the room. When Jane turned from the window to look at her daughter, there were tears standing in her eyes.

"Wow," she said. Jane looked stunned and so did Phoebe, and Rob's stomach was tied in knots.

"Seems like there's a lot of that going around," Jane said in a quavery voice, looking from Phoebe to Rob and back.

Phoebe burst into tears. "I'm . . . I'm going home," she sobbed, and ran back through the store and out onto the street, leaving Rob standing there, frozen. And then, to his dismay, Jane Traylor sat down heavily at the table and burst into tears herself, covering her face with her hands.

If Rob could have dematerialized, he would have done it, then and there. Instead he racked his brain for something comforting or apologetic or at least neutral to say, to get himself off the hook and out the door.

"Honest, Mrs. Traylor, I'm not the least bit . . . And I really don't think Phoebe is at all . . ."

Jane went on sobbing. Rob eyed the door, but he felt he couldn't just leave her like that.

"Mrs. Traylor," he said after a moment, "who's the man who owns Faith?"

Jane looked up at him with red eyes.

"*What?* Oh, do go away, Robert," she sniffed, and Rob left the store feeling basically lower than a worm.

10
CREATURE IN THE HOUSE

Tears stung Phoebe's eyes, her own angry words ringing in her ears. She put her head down, hoping no one would see her, and quickly walked the three blocks home.

Phoebe and her mom had always been closer than close. To Phoebe, her mother represented safety in a world that, when her father left them, had seemed a suddenly dangerous, uncertain, unhappy place.

In the early years of their marriage, while Jane Traylor worked in the front of their shop on Main, selling herbs and teas and homeopathic medicines, Jerry Traylor had holed up in the back, fiddling with his computers. The software program he created had to do with inventory tracking or bookkeeping or something equally boring. Jerry sold it for millions. Suddenly life in Faith seemed too small-scale for him, what with the loom in the living room and the tofu and the sprouts.

And the wife. And the daughter.

It was the biggest wound in Phoebe's life, and she could hardly bear to think of it, even though Phoebe, thanks to the funds that Jerry had set up for her, became stunningly rich.

You'd never know it, of course. Jane Traylor felt that too much money almost always had a bad effect on people, and both Jane and Phoebe had fought like tigers to rebuild their lives after Jerry left. They'd decided they didn't want to live it up— they wanted to live.

And so the wood-burning stove remained, and the loom. They still made their own clothes, and Phoebe and her mom rented time from the Mitchelsons on their beloved horses when, with the deposits that were made each month to Phoebe's accounts, they probably could have bought a whole stable. Of course, they did make occasional concessions to Phoebe's wealth. One evening, standing at the kitchen sink piled high with dirty dishes after supper, Phoebe and her mom had looked at each other significantly. The next week workers installed a nice, energy-efficient European dishwasher. That must have given them a taste for Europe, because the next summer the two of them went to Paris for a couple of weeks, and stayed in a lovely hotel and went to as many museums and galleries as they could. Phoebe ate really well, and Jane ate as well as a vegetarian could eat in Paris. The highlight of Phoebe's trip was a horse race at a track called Longchamps, just outside of the city.

Together mother and daughter had made their home a refuge, a little castle in Phoebe's mind, one that was unassailable by the forces of hurt. The size of her bank account was a secret, thank goodness, from the town and even from Rob. When other kids made fun of Phoebe's look, her homespun clothing, her book-ishness and love of grammar, or—not the least—her deep friendship with Rob Gates, Phoebe could look down from the castle keep, as it were, and know that she would be okay.

Now all that was over, she felt.

Phoebe went into her bedroom, closed the door, and flung herself down on her bed, the better to suffer.

Did the whole world think she and Rob were an item? Ugh!

Did her mother honestly think they'd sneaked out together to . . . what? Kiss? Worse? The possibilities made her absolutely squirm with embarrassment.

If only she hadn't grabbed Rob's hand that one time! Why ever had she done that? She might have been able to laugh off all of her mother's suspicions if it hadn't been for that one strangeness.

A couple of weary tears leaked from her eyes and then, suddenly exhausted by all that had happened since four-thirty that morning, Phoebe slept.

★ ★ ★

"You'd think you encounter creatures from the dawn of time every day, you take it so lightly."

The words came into her head in a gravelly, British-accented voice. Phoebe sat bolt upright in bed.

She'd forgotten all about Sid!

What time was it? The sun was setting outside her window, and she could hear her mother moving about the kitchen, preparing supper. Automatically she reached for her walkie-talkie to call Rob, but then she stopped herself, remembering all the painful stuff of the afternoon.

"Honestly, what *are* you doing?"

Phoebe looked around, startled and suspicious.

"I know you've had a long day, but I've been traveling for

66

nearly two hundred and fifty million years—*I'm* a little tuckered, too!"

The voice was distinct. Was it just in her head? It seemed to be coming from the floorboards of her bedroom, just as it had the other time.

"If it seems like I'm talking from the floorboards, it's because I'm talking from beneath the floorboards. Use your head!"

Phoebe jumped out of bed, staring at the broad wooden planks. Through a knothole she saw a single large eye staring up at her. It blinked, and Phoebe gasped.

"You're really here?" she said.

"What an odd question," said the Last Synapsid.

"Phoebe?" said Jane Traylor, knocking tentatively on the other side of the bedroom door. Phoebe caught her breath. "Are you awake, honey?"

Phoebe glanced from the door back to the floor and the keen dark eye at the knothole.

"Do you want to talk at all?" said Jane through the door.

"Maybe later," said Phoebe.

"Okay, fair enough. Supper will be ready in about an hour."

"Okay," said Phoebe in a strained voice.

"Okay," said Jane in an equally strained voice. And from below Phoebe's feet came the strange chortling that seemed to pass for the creature's laughter. Quickly Phoebe stooped and clapped one hand over the knothole.

"What did you say, honey?" said Jane from the other side of the door.

"Nothing," said Phoebe. And then she realized that her hand on the knothole was vibrating, and her long thick braid was flying straight back behind her as though she were in a gale-force wind. Phoebe let out a little frightened shriek.

"Phoebe! Are you sure you're all right?" said Jane anxiously.

Phoebe took her hand away from the knothole, and her braid dropped down her back again, the wind ceased, and her hand stopped vibrating.

She did her best to calm her voice. "I'm fine. I just want to be alone for a while, okay?"

"Okay," said Jane unhappily, and her footsteps receded down the hall toward the kitchen.

Cautiously, Phoebe reached her hand to the knothole, and as it neared the eye beneath, the wind began to blow again, warm and wet against her face, and her ears rang with strange cries.

"Careful, dear," said the voice beneath the floor. "It's not a game." Phoebe snatched her hand back and the wind and the noises died.

"What *is* that?" she whispered.

"It's where I come from, Phoebe, I told you this morning. I take my time with me wherever I go. So do you, for that matter. But this is not comfortable for conversation, me down here and you up there. If you'll stand back I'll pry up a board or two and join you."

Phoebe stood and backed away, and the creature brought its head up sharply. *Bang!* The floorboard with the knothole in it flipped up with a squeal of wrenched nails. *Bang!* A second head butt brought up the adjacent floorboard. The synapsid's head appeared in the room. Its front feet, or paws or whatever they were, appeared with a clattering of claws and braced themselves on the lip of the opening, and with an agile spring Sid was standing in Phoebe's bedroom, grinning like a dog grins.

"Pardon my mess—the crawl space beneath your house is filthy," he said. "How long has it been since you and Rob played down there?"

Phoebe stared in wonder at the miracle that stood before her in her own bedroom, panting a little and drooling and glancing at the posters of horses, Nelson Mandela, Matt Damon, and a young John Lennon.

"We used to play down there a lot, but it's been years," she said. "How did you know about it?"

"You left toys down there—a slate with the names Rob and Phoebe in chalk and a row of numbers beneath the names, an old rusted telescope, and I don't know what else."

"So that's where the telescope went," said Phoebe numbly. "It was Rob's and he just about went nuts looking for it 'cause it was something his dad gave him."

"Well, it's there, along with a lot more of your history—yours and Rob's. Had you forgotten?"

Phoebe nodded, and suddenly she was crying.

"I'm sorry," she sobbed, suddenly filling up with memories of Rob. "Sorry. Oh, I'm so embarrassed."

"What a gift," said the Last Synapsid. "To be able to cry like that. We can't cry, you know, as much as we might wish to. I'm afraid it's strictly a human thing."

Phoebe turned away and found a handkerchief in her top drawer. She wiped her eyes and blew her nose. "I don't think it's such a gift," she sniffed.

"You will," said the creature.

He was moving observantly about the small bedroom as he spoke, his claws clicking on the wooden floor, his head sweeping from side to side, looking at everything.

"Nice," he said, looking around. "Very nice, your sleeping hole. We built ours on the double-helix model."

Phoebe looked at him blankly.

"My mate and I. My spouse, my partner. All diictodons did. We dug two interlocking spirals down to the sleeping hole and general living quarters. They came in handy when we needed

69

to use one or the other or both in a hurry. Generally to evade the Gorgon and his kin."

The synapsid must have noticed Phoebe's look: mouth open, totally lost, trying to understand too much at once.

"Sorry," he said. "Ancient history. I miss my mate. She was a dreamer. She saw things, if you know what I mean."

The synapsid lowered his head for a moment, and Phoebe noticed a few drops of something wet hit her bedroom floor before he raised it again.

"You're crying now, aren't you?" she said gently.

"No. It's just a little saliva, darling. Call Rob with that black electric thing of yours and tell him to come join us."

"I . . . I'd rather not," said Phoebe.

"Why not?" said the Synapsid. "We need him right now. Your lessons have got to begin."

Phoebe blew her nose again. "What lessons?"

The synapsid looked a trifle impatient. "For the traveling," he said. "Now call Robert."

"I don't know," she said doubtfully. "He may hate me by now, after the things my stupid mother said about us."

The synapsid's eyes were suddenly stern.

"Phoebe. Question. Do you honestly think your mother is a person of low intelligence?"

"No. But she said such stupid things!"

"Exactly," said the creature. "There's a big difference, you know. Smart people are quite capable of saying stupid things. It's easy to hang ugly labels round people's necks, but difficult to get them off, if you'll forgive me saying so."

Phoebe regarded him in silence for a moment. "Who *are* you, Sid?" she said finally. "And why are you here?"

"What did you call me?"

"Oh, Sid. I hope that's okay. It was Rob's idea—short for *synapsid*."

The creature snorted. "It'll do," he said. "Who am I? Almost the last survivor of a great nation. The forefather of many greater ones, unless we fail. I've been seeking two human children for an extraordinary length of time. Together we have to do our best to make sure that a class of animals called Mammalia come into being with all their genes intact—warm blooded, vertebrate animals, blessed with sweat glands, milk glands, three middle ear bones and a four-chambered heart! That, my dear, would be you."

11
JENKINS' KILL

Earlier that afternoon, as Rob was walking slowly home from the confrontation in Jane Traylor's shop, confused and seriously downhearted, a beat-up SUV pulled over to the curb beside him. Janet Bright rolled down the passenger-side window and spoke to him in the distinctive way deaf people have of speaking.

"Hunting it," she said. "Want to come?" Her husband, Nick, was in the driver's seat, grinning at Rob and nodding.

Suddenly Rob had a vision of these decent people tracking down the Last Synapsid and shooting it dead.

"No!" he said. Janet looked at him quizically. How was Rob ever going to explain this to them? Janet and Nick were in their late twenties, Janet with thick bushy black hair and Nick with buzz-cut blond hair. Both of them smelled a little like horses, always.

Rob spoke distinctly. "I mean, we don't want to hunt the wrong thing, right?"

A voice from the backseat startled him. "Don't be a nervous Nellie, boy," said Jenkins from El Paso. "Climb in! Plenty of room back here!"

Rob felt a knot in his stomach. He decided the best thing he could do for Sid was to join the hunting party. Maybe he could warn Sid off somehow. Despite his instinctive dislike of Jenkins, Rob opened the back door and got in.

Nick drove them west out of town, past the RV park and the airstrip, up into the hills behind town, and finally onto the dirt road that paralleled Rat Creek. Eventually, as the road turned into a rough path, Nick slowed the car to a stop.

The four of them got out of the SUV quietly, shutting the doors as gently as they could. The spring sunshine had warmed the earth here. The long grass by the banks of the creek moved silkily with the breeze, and the cedars were giving off a delicious warm cedary smell. Nick and Jenkins moved to the gun rack on the car's rear gate, each taking a rifle. Nick was loading his rifle and Janet was loading her Minolta with film.

Rob touched Janet's shoulder and she looked at him attentively.

"Nick will be careful what he shoots, right?" said Rob in a clear low voice, doing his best to articulate so she could read his lips.

"Won't shoot anything," she said. "Unless he has to." The four of them set off, Nick and Janet in the lead, moving quietly and quickly up the eastern bank of Rat Creek.

★ ★ ★

Phoebe tried half a dozen times to reach Rob on her walkie-talkie but had no success.

"I have a bad feeling," said Sid, peeling one of the bananas Phoebe had sneaked into her bedroom, along with a bunch of grapes.

"I can't put my mom off anymore," said Phoebe. "I've got to go into the kitchen and eat supper with her."

"Of course," said the synapsid, reaching for the grapes. "Go on with you."

She paused at the bedroom door, staring back at Sid, fascinated.

"You have opposable thumbs," she said.

"Well, not exactly," said the creature. "But diictodon digits were unique in my world, and capable of quite a lot. That's just one part of our legacy to you, dear, but do you humans acknowledge it? Oh, no! Humans were the first at *everything!*" Sid snorted indignantly.

"Okay, then," said Phoebe meekly.

Sid took a bite of the banana and chewed thoughtfully. "I must say, though," he added, just as Phoebe was about to open the bedroom door, "I seem to be able to communicate with you from a distance. You seem to hear me—you sometimes seem to hear my thoughts. But with Rob, communication goes in the other direction: I seem to hear *him*. You remember when he was stuck in that shed with the Gorgon?"

"You heard him then?" asked Phoebe.

"Oh, yes. I heard his heart. I can talk to *yours*, it seems, and I can hear *his*."

Phoebe nodded as she gently shut the bedroom door, leaving the Last Synapsid popping grapes into his mouth, one at a time.

★ ★ ★

Nick and Janet almost bounded up the creek, while Rob did his best to keep up with them, and Jenkins of El Paso stuck uncomfortably close to Rob. Jenkins carried his rifle in his right hand and a long aluminum walking stick in the other, stabbing the earth with it every other step.

Cowbirds looked at them askance with their big eyes, and fluttered alongside, keeping up with them from branch to branch. Ravens hoarsely shouted their disapproval.

Jenkins sometimes walked just ahead of Rob, sometimes just behind, and sometimes, when the trail widened, right by his side, which was the worst. It seemed to Rob that Jenkins kept glancing at him, and Rob, up since 4:00 A.M. and almost stumbling with exhaustion, wished that he'd gone home to supper and bed instead.

Before long Rob lost sight of Nick and Janet around a bend in the creek. That's when Jenkins started talking.

"*You* know what we're looking for, don't you, little buddy," he said in an ingratiating way.

Rob just glanced at him darkly and kept walking.

"More likely to find it by sense of smell, don't you think?"

Rob paused. Did this guy know about the Gorgon somehow? "I don't know what you're talking about," he said.

"No," Jenkins said with a big grin. "No, of course you don't."

They continued on in silence for a few moments.

"I considered warning you that day I saw you wandering up to the old mines. But then I thought it might be good for you to encounter our friend face to face. The one with the body odor problem. After all, what doesn't kill us makes us stronger."

Jenkins glanced at him hungrily, and Rob considered turning around right there and walking back to town.

"And hey," said Jenkins, "I was right—you survived, didn't you? But mercy, don't that thing have a scary appetite?" Jenkins bared his teeth in a macabre grin.

"I think I'm gonna head back," said Rob, stopping.

Jenkins stopped, too.

"You've been up close and personal with *both* of them, haven't you. I envy you that, little buddy."

Rob's mind was racing. Jenkins not only knew about the Gorgon, he seemed to know about Sid! How? Rob didn't know, but something about the man's tone unsettled him. Rob started to ease himself past Jenkins on the trail, but Jenkins blocked his way with his walking stick.

"Wait a minute. Take a look at this thing."

Jenkins laid his rifle down gingerly by the side of the trail and started unscrewing the top of the aluminum walking stick. "See, I've been tracking these old critters for months, working on the whole problem for a long time," said Jenkins. "Way before the unpleasantness with the horses, way before I came to Faith. I knew they'd been to these parts before. Question was, would they come again?"

Jenkins took a thin cylinder, about a foot and a half long, out of the walking stick, inverted it, and screwed it back into the aluminum rod. The cylinder had switches, meters, and an LCD display built into it, and at the end of it was a fine mesh of copper wire.

"This is brilliant, if I do say it myself," said Jenkins, throwing a switch. "See," he added, winking, "I invented the dang thing."

Jenkins pointed the stick directly at Rob's head and Rob froze. The walking stick emitted a low, slow beeping sound.

"You see?" said Jenkins, glancing at the LCD readout. "It's a critter detector. You're a hundred percent human—don't ever let anybody tell you different."

The man pointed the aluminum tube down toward the creek

running alongside the trail and the pitch dropped very low, with slow, drawn-out burplike beeps.

"That there, that's amphibians, right? Frogs, toads. Nothing special, nothing to write home about—unless you're another toad, I guess."

"What is that thing, Jenkins?" said Rob, fascinated in spite of himself. "How does it work?"

"It's Dr. Jenkins, as a matter of fact, little buddy. Dr. Richard Jenkins, paleontologist, University of Texas, El Paso." Jenkins looked at the device in his hand with pride. "There's a lot crammed into this little package, son. You got a spectrometer, you got sonar. You got a kind of sniffer, measures the oxygen content of the air. Plus it can distinguish 'twixt *kinds* of oxygen molecules, the variety of oxygen *isotopes,* you follow?"

"Not really," said Rob.

"Well, let's just say there's young air and there's old air, and there are molecular differences between the two. Air trapped on the underside of a glacier, for instance—air that's three, four, five hundred years old—is different from the new stuff made fresh this morning. Also there's percentages . . ." Jenkins broke off suddenly, reading the LCD.

"Oh, by gosh, by golly," he whispered. "Christmas come early this year. No wonder them crows are going nuts."

He was pointing the walking stick up at the wooded ridge above them, and the beeping had changed to a throbbing musical tone.

Jenkins stooped, picked up his rifle, and started quietly up the slope. Rob followed. Off the trail, the brush and foliage were thick and the going was slow. At one point, when Jenkins had to climb over a large fallen tree, he switched off the critter detector, handed it wordlessly back to Rob, and made it over the log with his rifle held high above his head.

Ravens were wheeling just above them, screaming, and other smaller birds were flying frantically this way and that, chirping and scolding. Jenkins stepped up onto the breast of the ridge, followed by Rob.

There, only a dozen feet ahead of them, two beasts stood facing off, frozen except for a tense trembling in both their bodies. One was a mountain lion, low, muscular, sinewy, crouched to spring. Its ears were flattened back against its sleek head. It was beautiful, noble, majestic.

Opposite the lion stood a horror.

The gorgonopsid was maybe four or five feet long from its oblong head to its heavy tail, and its hide looked hard, like an alligator's. It had a chunk of bloody flesh dangling from its mouth, and it was chewing slowly as it faced the lion. Out of the corner of his mind, Rob glimpsed what he guessed were probably gopher bits lying in the grass.

The Gorgon swung its head round and its yellow-eyed gaze rested first on Jenkins and then Rob. When it saw Rob it stopped chewing and its eyes narrowed, and Rob just about stopped breathing. The monster's jaws were running with blood and drool. A low growl came from somewhere within the beast, and Jenkins slowly raised his rifle and sighted down the barrel.

Shoot it. Shoot it now. The voice in Rob's head was silently, desperately begging Jenkins, but Rob himself couldn't speak. And then there was an explosion in his left ear, and he glimpsed Jenkins recoiling and fire and smoke bursting from the barrel. The mountain lion flipped halfway backward and dropped like a rock.

The Gorgon stood unmoved, still chewing.

"Help yourself," said Jenkins, and Rob wondered what he was talking about. "Help yourself," he said again, and Rob realized that Jenkins wasn't talking to him.

The monster dropped whatever it was in its jaws. It slowly began to walk, stepping warily in an arc, ignoring Jenkins entirely, the muscles in its shoulder joints rippling beneath its leathery hide, steadily closing in on Rob. Rob looked up at Jenkins with a dawning terror, and Jenkins smiled back.

"Good luck, little buddy," he said.

Rob ran.

★ ★ ★

Phoebe and her mother ate their supper in near silence, their forks making unnaturally loud and lonely sounds on the plates.

Jane cleared her throat. "I think I was out of line today, Phoeb," she said. "I know the attack up at the stable was a real trauma for you, and probably for Rob, too, and you two probably were just . . . I don't know what, Phoebe, but believe me, I'm not accusing you of having some dark secret."

A part of Phoebe wanted to tell her mom that yes, actually, she did have a dark secret, and he was in her bedroom right this minute, lying on the floor beneath her desk with a worried look on his face, eating grapes.

Instead she just said, "It's okay, Mom."

"I think maybe it's time you had a horse of your own. What do you think?"

"You don't have to do that, Mom," said Phoebe. "You don't have to apologize by letting me buy something. In fact, you don't have to apologize at all—I *did* sneak out of the house, I *did* cut classes with Rob, and you were doing your duty busting me for it—you were just being a mom."

"Oh, Phoeb . . ."

Phoebe was out of her chair and hugging her mother, and both of them were teary and sniffing and relieved.

"But you were totally wrong about the details!" she added hotly.

Jane said, "Okay, okay."

"And yes," continued Phoebe, "I would like to buy a horse. Do you think we could get one delivered to the Mitchelsons' without them knowing who did it? You know . . . in case Johnny B. Goode doesn't come back. Donna's just so sad. Nobody needs to know we bought it."

Jane looked at her daughter for a long moment, her eyes shining. "Yeah," she said, "I think we could manage that."

Suddenly Phoebe heard a distinct gravelly voice in her ear. "Come!" it said.

Phoebe blushed.

"What is it?" said Jane.

"You didn't hear anything?"

"No."

For a moment Phoebe considered telling her mother everything. But only for a moment.

"Listen, I've got a ton of homework. I think I'll go get started," she said, slipping out of the kitchen.

When Phoebe opened the bedroom door, Sid was waiting for her. He said, "It's Rob. He's in mortal danger. We need to go to him."

"But my mom—" began Phoebe.

"It's his life that's at stake, Phoebe," Sid interrupted, and she nodded. "Put one hand just here, on the back of my neck."

As Phoebe's hand neared the creature's head, she felt herself falling from a great height, and then the whole world was a blur of green and a roaring in her ears.

★ ★ ★

As he ran, he could hear the Gorgon pursuing him, crashing through the underbrush behind. Rob's toe caught on a root and he somersaulted forward through the air, still clutching Jenkins' aluminum walking stick. He landed almost feet first with a flash of blinding pain in his right ankle. He used the stick to right himself and in a second he was running again, wondering if the ankle was sprained. It didn't matter. All that mattered was that he keep on running.

The brush was thinning now, and he was on the downhill slope of the ridge, racing through a glade of aspens. Dark spots were swimming before his eyes and there was a jabbing pain like a knife in his side, but then he was off the ridge and down into the meadow, slicing through the tall green spring grass, with the lip of the ravine in the distance ahead of him.

Suddenly he thought he saw his friends Billy Springer and Aran McBell ahead of him in the distance, disappearing down into the ravine. It couldn't be, he thought. People from the real world couldn't be here where he was. Rob had crossed into an unreal world, he thought, inhabited by monsters—and monsters in human form.

Crossing the meadow, he couldn't hear the Gorgon behind him anymore, and that was actually worse than hearing him. Rob fought the temptation to look over his shoulder, to see how close on his heels the beast might be.

Don't look back, he said to himself. *The second you turn, it'll get you. Just keep running, just keep running.*

A moment later he couldn't help it; Rob turned and looked back, braced for the quick hot slash of claws and fangs.

There was nothing there! The meadow was empty! Wasn't it?

Rob stumbled to a stop and leaned on the aluminum rod, trying to catch his breath as the pain from his ankle shot up and down his leg. He scanned the horizon. Maybe the beast didn't dare show itself in the open. Maybe it had gone back to its kill, to finish eating.

Rob thought he saw a row of men in the distance, coming toward him from the opposite end of the meadow, and the tallest of them made him think of Billy's dad, Keith, the deputy sheriff. And wasn't that Ernie, from the volunteer fire department? There was Kevin Scudder, Chad's older brother, and a couple of others—maybe they were real after all.

Suddenly inspired, Rob switched on the critter detector. The device emitted a low, slow beeping sound, very faintly, and the words HOMO SAPIENS scrolled across the LCD. Then the beeping gave way to a throbbing musical tone, which grew suddenly louder. Rob looked to his left and there, galloping toward him along the rim of the meadow, not twenty yards off, was the Gorgon.

Rob turned and leapt, tumbling down into the folds of the ravine. He dropped the walking stick, which clattered down behind him. He scrambled on his hands and knees across the sandy soil, fell and rolled down another rib of the ravine, and finally lurched to his feet and threw himself into the dark opening of an abandoned mine.

Instantly the warm spring day was gone, replaced by a damp, cool, musty darkness. Rob flattened himself against the wall just inside the entrance. He wasn't about to go deeper into that dark world with a monster on his heels; he'd take his chances right here, where a bit of the daylight still penetrated. In a matter of moments, his nose told him that the gorgonopsid was just outside.

He heard the crunch of gravel as the creature moved cautiously back and forth in front of the broken-down entrance. He saw its shadow pass and re-pass the door. Through a chink between the old upright timbers that formed the door frame, he saw a sliver of the Gorgon, peering into the darkness of the mine. The stink was stomach-turning.

The creature crossed the threshold—and then it was inside the mine, not four feet from Rob. Rob held his breath. The beast took another step, and another, looking about and sniffing. A minute passed. The Gorgon moved farther into the narrow mine passage, and hope rose in Rob's heart—maybe he could dart out of the mine without the creature noticing.

"Keith, over here!" A voice from outside penetrated the mine. "Here's where the stink's coming from."

The beast whirled around quickly and planted itself defensively, looking out the door.

"Dad!" It was Billy Springer's voice. "Dad, Rob Gates is in there with a monster!"

"It's huge!" shouted Aran McBell.

"You boys step away from that mine." It was Deputy Keith Springer talking.

That's when the yellow eyes of the Gorgon came to rest on Rob. They flickered and narrowed, like a cat's when it's just been given a dish of milk. Neither moved. There were more voices from outside, muffled and somehow irrelevant now.

"Robert," said the Gorgon in a deep voice, "you're mine." Its tail thrashed behind it, and the creature moved toward the boy.

Rob stooped, picked up a handful of gravel, and hurled it into the beast's eyes. The Gorgon yelped and swatted at its face like a bear in a swarm of bees, and suddenly there was a roar of color and wind in the mine, and the Last Synapsid was there, shouting, "Get back!" The other voice was Phoebe's, saying, "Rob, I'm right here!"

Phoebe crouched beside Rob, staring in shocked horror at the beast. Sid put himself between the kids and the monster, and then the Gorgon leapt on Sid and the two beasts snapped and snarled and bit like two dogs on a street corner.

"Sid and It" by Rbt. Gates Jr.

Phoebe grabbed Rob's hands and flung them onto the back of Sid's neck. Rob was plunged into a rushing river of light and sound, traveling farther and faster than he'd ever traveled before.

But when Deputy Keith and the others cautiously entered the mine just moments later, guns at the ready, there was nothing there but a bad smell.

12
FIRST TRIP

The moment Rob's and Phoebe's hands made contact with Sid's neck, the world around them changed. In a blinding flash, the entrance to the mine was teeming with men and machines and horses pulling wagons. Without warning there was a deafening explosion. Phoebe and Rob instinctively ducked and covered their heads as a wave of black dust engulfed them, and for a few moments they were lost in a darkness darker than any night.

"Oh, dear." Sid's gravelly voice seemed to come from nowhere. "I seem to be off by a moment or two."

"Where are we?" cried Phoebe.

"We haven't moved, at least not geographically. Rob, are you there?"

"Uh-huh." Rob's voice was small, exhausted, and bewildered. "Where's the thing? The Gorgon?"

85

"I think we left him back in the future," said Sid. "Or present. Whatever."

"*What?*"

"Let's get out of the way of these miners. Try to follow the sound of my voice. This way, this way."

As the dust began to settle Rob and Phoebe moved cautiously behind the synapsid, whom they could just barely make out.

"They're miners?" whispered Phoebe.

"We don't want them to see us."

"Where'd they come from? What are they doing here?"

"Phoebe, this is a *mine,* they're *miners.* This is a very busy place. At least, in the early nineteen hundreds it is."

"The early *whats?*"

"Hush!"

Now they could dimly see the outline of the mine entrance, and vague figures moving outside. Sid paused while one man carrying a lantern led a large horse past them into the mine, and another man followed. As soon as they passed, Sid darted quickly out of the mine, Phoebe and Rob just behind him.

It was nighttime in Faith.

"Up here!" Sid commanded, and they made their way up the side of the ravine, scrambling up the sandy ridges, and finally climbing up and over the lip into the meadow. Rob felt dizzy from the pain in his ankle, and he leaned heavily on Phoebe until she was practically carrying him.

The two kids collapsed onto the grass, and the synapsid looked at them with his big black eyes, his brow wrinkled with concern. Phoebe was looking down on the town of Faith, a dazed expression on her face, while Rob just lay on his back, his eyes open but glassy.

There were lights lit in town, but they weren't the lights Phoebe had known all her life—these flickered with a dim orange glow. She could barely make out buildings in the darkness, but they looked to be wood-framed and unfamiliar, and there didn't seem to be any paving on the streets; it appeared to be a lot of rutted mud. Raucous piano music drifted up from the town.

"It's 1902, I'm guessing, or thereabouts," said Sid, looking down on the town. "I overshot my mark."

Phoebe nodded numbly.

Sid gently put the side of one of his paws on Rob's forehead for just a moment.

"Rob?" he said, and the boy moaned.

"Jenkins," Rob mumbled.

"What's that?" asked Sid.

"He tried to feed me to the thing."

Sid turned to Phoebe. "We need to get this boy home," he said.

Phoebe nodded again. With one paw resting on Rob's brow, Sid extended his other paw to Phoebe and she grasped it, feeling the hide and the long, slender front digits fully for the first time, feeling the life beneath the skin. Sid squeezed her hand, there was a dropping, roller-coaster feeling in Phoebe's belly, and then the three of them were falling from her bedroom ceiling, landing on her bed with a sound of cracking bed frame. In a flash the synapsid leapt down and disappeared beneath the open floorboards, and when Jane Traylor rushed into the room, Phoebe said, "Hi, Mom. Rob hurt his ankle."

★ ★ ★

In the weeks that followed, the citizens of Faith breathed easier, believing that Jenkins, by killing the mountain lion, had rid them of the animal that attacked the horses. He became something of a local hero, and even more so when he announced that he was making a geological study of Faith and finding hopeful signs there might be new ways of locating untapped mineral deposits under the feet of its citizens. Faith just might have a future, people said, instead of only a past.

The night Rob and Phoebe got back from the old mine, Rob slept for nearly forty-eight hours straight. He woke up to a sprained ankle and a pair of crutches that he had to learn to walk with. He had been in such bad shape that night that there was no possible lie he could tell to cover it all up. So Rob told his mother everything, just blurted it out, and Lucy Gates got on the phone to Jane Traylor instantly. Phoebe, confronted by *her* mom, realized she had very little room left for improvisation, so she confessed the whole story, too. All about Sid and the gorgonopsid and Pinkie and the horses and Jenkins and the time travel: everything.

The two moms discussed it all with each other, and the upshot was that Rob and Phoebe each met with a psychotherapist in Arenoso once a week. There was a kind of freedom to it. The two kids could say absolutely anything they wanted with no consequences, because no one believed them.

"And the three of you—this talking animal and you and Phoebe—have a mission to accomplish?" said Louise Barnett, Rob's therapist.

"I guess," said Rob, sitting in a big black leather chair and looking at the floor. "We have to help Sid. I'm not sure how."

"That's your friend—Sid?"

"Short for *synapsid.*"

Louise nodded. "And he smells bad, you say?"

"No, not Sid. It's the gorgonospsid that stinks. Sid's a diictodon."

"I thought he was a synapse."

88

"*Synapsid*," said Rob. "They're both synapsids. One's a di-ictodon, the other's a gorgonopsid."

"What wonderful names!" said Ms. Barnett. "Did you come up with them or did Phoebe?"

"I didn't come up with anything—they're real! They existed! Millions of years before the dinosaurs!" Rob saw that his thera-pist was nodding with a patient smile on her face. *Look it up!* he almost shouted.

"And if you don't succeed, there will be no human race?"

"Or our genes won't be right. Us and all the other mammals."

"I see," said Louise, not looking as though she did. "And you and I, we two mammals sitting here, we don't actually exist?"

"We can't be sure," said Rob, wishing he were somewhere else.

"Fascinating," she said. Louise was forty-something with black hair streaked with pure white. She had a gentle, compassionate voice.

"Do you know what a mammal is, Robert?"

He looked at her blankly.

"It's any creature that gives birth from the mother's womb," she said, "and who suckles its young from its mother's teats."

"I have to go now," said Rob.

"We still have a couple of minutes left," said Louise, glancing at her watch.

"Sorry," he said, clambering to his feet with his crutches under his armpits, moving toward the door. "Ankle hurts. Helps if I move around."

Louise looked at him thoughtfully as he managed to open the office door.

"Why is it, do you think," she said, "that talk of teats makes you uncomfortable? And wombs? And suckling?"

Rob smiled and shrugged awkwardly as he eased the door shut behind him.

Lucy was waiting outside in her elderly Subaru, reading the want ads in the Arenoso paper. Therapy wasn't cheap, and neither of her jobs offered health benefits. She jumped out of the car when she saw Rob approaching on his crutches, and went around to the passenger door and opened it.

"How was it?" she said, tousling his hair.

"Good," said Rob, not looking at her. Passing his crutches over into the backseat, he folded himself into the car and forced himself to smile up at his mom. "Really good."

Phoebe *loved* therapy. Unlike Rob, she wished her sessions could go on for *hours*. Her therapist was a youngish blond man named Sven who wore sandals and T-shirts and clothes made of hemp, and Phoebe thought he was a major hottie. Once she got over the initial awkwardness, she let everything spill out—not so much about Sid or her adventures, which was okay, since Sven thought all that was just symbolic of thrilling words such as *id* and *libido* and *superego*—but mainly she talked about her own feelings and her relationships with her mom, Rob, her school friends and enemies, her absent dad, and horses.

The mysterious delivery of a fine young stallion to the Mitchelson stables was big news in Faith. The Mitchelsons (and the entire town) were stunned. There had been a card hung by a ribbon round the stallion's neck that said, "In Hopes that Johnny B. Goode May Be Well and Happy Wherever He Is." With Janet Bright's help, Sally May had survived massive blood loss and a very tricky infection, and was slowly recuperating. Donna named the stallion Junior, and he and Sally May quickly seemed to develop a special relationship.

Both Phoebe and Rob had changed since the day Sid rescued Rob from the Gorgon in the mine. For one thing, Rob, with the memory of the flesh-hungry Gorgon still vivid in his mind, astonished his mother by announcing that he didn't want to eat meat anymore.

"I beg your pardon?" said Lucy Gates, standing at the stove, where she had just dropped a couple of hamburger patties sizzling into a pan.

"I'll just have the french fries," said Rob. "And the lettuce and tomato, and a piece of cheese. Two pieces. And the bun. And ketchup and mustard. And chips."

"Robert, you're scaring me," said Lucy. "Your entire lifestyle is based on the burger!"

Rob shrugged.

"I am this close to calling 911. I mean it!" said Lucy.

But it was more than that. There was a difference their mothers and friends and teachers couldn't define. They both seemed older somehow. They seemed a little distant. And they seemed quietly and acutely alert. As if they were waiting for something. Something they knew was coming.

★ ★ ★

School was school. You could travel to the ends of the earth, or even through time itself, and when you arrived back at school nothing would be any different. Classes droned on, chalk scraped across blackboards, and long division grew ever longer while students gazed yearningly out the windows.

In the first few days after the mine incident, Rob's mom drove him to and from school. After that, Rob and Phoebe generally walked slowly to school together, Rob on his crutches, both of them alert and watchful. They didn't really expect the Gorgon to leap out at them in the middle of town in daylight, but hobbled as he was, Rob felt really vulnerable. A couple of times Aran McBell and Billy Springer walked with them, neither of them talking very much but looking somehow as though they'd like to.

Phoebe took what Rob thought was a big chance by writing a short story for English class about a dog-sized prehistoric talking beast. Mrs. Peabody praised it to the rest of the class, causing Phoebe to blush.

"The writing is so vivid," said Mrs. Peabody enthusiastically, her jewelry jingling. "You have the feeling you're actually in the presence of this magical creature. Now *that's* the power of imagination."

Later, in the cafeteria, Phoebe overheard Arabella Giddens impersonating Mrs. Peabody for the kids at her table.

"The writing is so *vivid!*" said Arabella, and all the kids cracked up, laughing and glancing over at Phoebe's table, where she sat with Donna Mitchelson and Angela Cruz. Phoebe pretended to be engrossed by her cole slaw, and was grateful when Angela muttered, "Arabella is actually *proud* of not being able to do anything well—she thinks it's cool." Phoebe looked up and smiled gratefully at Angela, and realized that both Angela and Donna were watching her intently, questioningly. Phoebe went back to her cole slaw and grilled cheese, her face reddening again.

Philippa Larson, the librarian, got used to the sight of Rob and Phoebe hunched over the school's computers, grabbing every chance they could to study the creatures of the Permian era. They studied artists' impressions of long-extinct animals and Rob drew his own versions of them: beasts with strange names like "estemmenosuchus," "moschops" and "eryops." They read everything they could about the terrible disaster 250 million years ago that almost ended life on earth altogether. They learned that huge volcanic activity had put a massive amount of greenhouse gases into the atmosphere. The earth's temperature rose globally and everything began to die. Within a relatively short period of time something like ninety percent of all animal forms perished forever, very nearly leaving the earth a barren, lifeless rock.

The kids also did a search for Dr. Richard Jenkins, University of Texas at El Paso. "Rob, look at this," whispered Phoebe. "There's an article in the *El Paso Times.*"

Rob looked over her shoulder at the screen.

"Controversial Paleontologist Missing," ran the headline of a small article in the paper's back pages.

"He stopped showing up for classes just before the end of the spring quarter, and no one's seen him since," said Phoebe, scanning the article. "You see the date? That's about the time he arrived in Faith, isn't it?"

Rob nodded. He didn't like talking or thinking about Jenkins. He was more scared of him than he was of the gorgonopsid. In Rob's dreams Jenkins was everywhere, always ready with a big grin and the promise of death.

"I'm going to order one of his books," she said. "And here's a paper he read at a paleontology convention this past winter."

Phoebe downloaded the article and hit the print command just as the bell for the next class rang.

"I'll save the printout for you, Phoebe," said Ms. Larson with a smile. "You can pick it up after your next class."

Rob and Phoebe had become the librarian's favorite students. They seemed so earnest in their pursuit of knowledge, they actually valued the library, unlike so many. There seemed also to be something about the sight of Rob on his crutches that sparked a memory for her of something dear, something lost.

In their out-of-school hours, Rob and Phoebe were getting personal instruction from the Last Synapsid himself. Sid would travel between the two homes in the dead of night, and when the kids woke in the morning they'd know if the creature was beneath their bedroom floor by his coughing. Sometimes it was a hacking, wheezing cough that went on and on, but when the kids asked if he was all right, Sid would wave them off with a paw. "Just feeling my age, I guess," he'd say.

There were moments when Rob and Phoebe were overwhelmed by the inconceivable lengths of time involved in the lifetime of their new friend. The very shape of land on earth had changed, again and again. According to articles they read in the library, the continents had drifted and collided and split and reformed; entire mountain ranges had burst up out of the earth and disappeared within it again. When Sid and his kind lived, there was only a single massive continent, which scientists today call Pangea.

One afternoon in Rob's bedroom, Phoebe was sitting on the floor, paging through a book on the Permian era. The synapsid was looking over her shoulder at a map of Pangea, and Rob was lying on his bed, bouncing a tennis ball against the wall, *pock, pock, pock.*

"Sid, you're drooling," said Phoebe, wiping the page of her textbook with a handkerchief.

"Sorry."

"What are those tusks for, if you're a vegetarian?"

"Herbivore, according to your people," said Sid. When talking about contemporary human science and scientists, Sid always used the term "your people," a little condescendingly.

"What do you need tusks for if you don't eat meat?"

Phoebe was genuinely curious, and also maybe a little defensive, since she was the only omnivore in the room.

"The tusks?" said Sid. "They're a sign of what your people call sexual dimorphism."

"Eww," said Rob. "I don't think I want to know."

"Life wasn't always divided into male and female, you know, and among thousands of creatures it still isn't, to this day. But diictodons were among the first species to be clearly one or the other, and only males like me had tusks."

"So only the males killed other animals and ate flesh?" asked Phoebe.

"No, no, no, the tusks aren't for killing—they're for *show!* They're for attracting the ladies! They're for knocking your rivals out of the running! Tusks are *so much fun,* I can't tell you!"

"Attracting the *ladies?*" said Rob with a wicked gleam in his eyes.

"Well, you know what I mean," said Sid, looking a little abashed. He had come to know Rob's sarcasm and was wary of it. "I used to be considered quite the looker, as a matter of fact," he continued.

Rob nodded. "I can see that," he said somberly, and then stepped into his closet and shut the door, exploding with laughter as he did.

The synapsid shook his head. "Thinks he's funny," he muttered. Sid moved to the closet door and growled through the keyhole: "All right! If you're well enough to make fun, you're well enough to start your traveling lessons!"

The closet door flew open. "It's about time!" cried Rob. He stood framed in the door, holding an old skateboard from when he was a kid.

"Exactly," said Sid. "It *is* about time."

Rob tried to launch himself back into the room by flipping his skateboard, but he was less than successful and crashed to the floor.

"So?" he said, all in a heap. "Let's get started."

From the other side of the door, Lucy Gates called, "Robert, please don't destroy the house. It's not paid for yet."

"Sorry, Mom."

"I'm going back to work. There's a stew you can microwave," said Lucy. "Is Phoebe still there?"

"Hi, Mrs. Gates," said Phoebe to the bedroom door. There was no answer—just the sound of Lucy leaving the house. Things had been a little tense between Lucy and Phoebe, ever since Rob had injured his ankle while supposedly traveling in time.

"You're going to get us caught, Rob," said Phoebe.

In a high-pitched singsong, Rob said, "You're going to get us caught, Rob!"

The Last Synapsid cleared his throat and regarded them both darkly.

"Are you two quite finished?" he said.

"Sorry, Sid," said Phoebe. She closed her science textbook and sat up straighter.

"Lessons, right, yes, sir," said Rob, standing the skateboard on end and spinning the wheels.

"Phoebe, Rob, you may have noticed that things can get a little . . . jiggy at times when you touch me." Sid's black eyes twinkled. "Is that the right word, *jiggy?*"

"It sure as heck isn't," said Rob. "But yeah, we noticed."

"Well, that's because I'm not altogether here."

"So . . ." Phoebe hesitated. "Where are you?"

"Flesh is mortal. Nothing organic could survive two hundred and fifty million years, and I assure you, I am one hundred percent organic. In one way, Phoebe, I am still living my life at the end of the Permian era. My mate has just sent me out to search the ages for the allies who will help me keep the last hope of life on earth alive."

"And what *is* the last hope for life on earth?"

"Well, the gorgonopsid, of course."

"We have to kill it?"

"Oh, dear me, no! Without the Gorgon, we're lost! I've been struggling to keep him alive for a quarter billion years, and you're the help I've been looking for all this time. Phoebe, Rob—we've been brought together to *save* his life, not end it!"

13
BEFORE FAITH

Phoebe and Rob were appalled.

"No!" said Phoebe, shocked to her core.

"Get out!" said Rob. "Never, no way!"

Sid cleared his throat and fixed them both in his big-eyed gaze, and suddenly they were clearly children and he was very much their senior.

"I mean, *come on!*" said Rob.

"It killed Pinkie!" said Phoebe.

Sid cleared his throat again.

"It tried to kill Sally May, and it probably killed Johnny B. Goode," said Phoebe hotly.

"It was gonna kill *me!*" said Rob. "It's a killing machine!"

Sid looked at them both steadily. "Yes," he said, "and you're descended from it."

The thought was so repulsive to Rob and Phoebe, they were speechless.

"I need to get the Gorgon back where he belongs, so his offspring can survive the Permian. I need your help to do it. Do you want to travel? If so, you have to practice traveling. And you have to trust me."

"Are you sure *we're* the ones who need the practice?" asked Rob. "The first time we went anywhere with you, you landed us in the wrong century."

"I'll ignore that," said Sid.

"*I'm* ready to travel, Sid," said Phoebe.

"So am I. I hate it here," said Rob with feeling.

"You do?" said Sid.

"Everything about this town sucks."

"You think so?" said Sid.

"Absolutely."

The diictodon sat up on his haunches and extended his forelegs.

"Take a paw," he said. And, after a moment's fearful hesitation, they did.

★ ★ ★

Stair-Master rose above them on their right. The ragged toothy half circle of cliffs stood before them, lit with a golden light, and the gap between the cliffs led up into the mountains. All around them was an upward-sloping field of grass—long, silky grass, rippling like water, glowing the same shade of gold as the cliffs in the afternoon sunlight. The breeze was sweet-scented, fresh. On the steep rise above, the leaves of the aspens fluttered, glittering like emeralds.

Rob moved like a sleepwalker through the grass, still holding his skateboard, up the grassy slope toward the cliffs. Phoebe watched him in wonder, as though she'd never seen him before, or any creature like him. She looked at the diictodon by her side, and he looked up at her with kind eyes and nodded. A laugh burst out of her, and immediately she covered her mouth: her laugh had sounded loud and harsh in the purity of the world she'd just discovered.

They were in Faith, they knew that much, but there *was* no Faith. No town, no buildings or roads, no flume, no abandoned mines in the hills. No people. Just earth and sky and air and a crystal-clear stream of icy water meandering through the grass, running down from its mountain home above to the valley below.

Sid lowered his head, bit off a mouthful of grass, and began to chew, savoring the flavor, his eyes narrowing with pleasure. Looking at him, Phoebe laughed again—she couldn't help it—and Rob turned back to her and laughed as well. The synapsid, still chewing, started a low, raspy chortle deep in his throat.

Suddenly Phoebe took off running, for the sheer joy of it, and Rob dropped the skateboard and took off after her. First, she made for the spot where their school would someday stand, Rob shouting from behind, "There! Right there! You're on top of it!" Cedar trees and aspens grew there, and Phoebe ran in and out among the trees, and Rob jumped up and down on what he thought had to be Mr. Brinkley's classroom.

"Down with Brinkley! Down with Brinkley!"

It was all a little crazy and childish and they knew it, but they didn't care: they *did* feel like children, brand-new people in a brand-new land.

From there Phoebe and Rob zigzagged through the town that wasn't there, shouting like idiots.

"The Conoco!"

"My house!"

"Billy Springer's!"

"Post office!"

"The bank!"

Phoebe took off running for the western slope, opposite Stair-Master, up toward what would someday be the cemetery where the miners would bury their dead, her long legs pumping through the grasses, Rob racing after her. Up they flew into the meadow, Phoebe's braid flying behind her, and then Sid flashed between the two kids, speeding like a greyhound across the meadow to the lip of the ravine—which hadn't been a ravine at all twelve thousand years ago, but the steep lush bank of a mountain stream.

The synapsid made a broad U-turn back, skirting the edge of the meadow's rim, down toward "town" again, and Phoebe was close on his heels, sprinting for all she was worth, but now Rob, below them, had the advantage and cut the other two off, all three of them finally stumbling and laughing to a breathless, panting stop.

"Not bad . . . for a diictodon my age," said Sid, his body quivering like a terrier's.

"I like it . . . here," said Rob between breaths.

"I thought you hated it here," said Sid.

"I do," said Rob, looking up at the diictodon. "I mean . . . not here, *there!* I mean, I wish I lived here."

"But you do," said Sid, but Rob shook his head.

"No, I don't. Believe me." Rob moved up the slope again, while Phoebe walked to the edge of the little stream, knelt, and plunged her hands into it.

"Ow!" She pulled her hands back fast. "Oh, that's cold!" The synapsid joined her at the stream and very gingerly lapped up

101

a sip of water with his long pink tongue, his eyes getting very wide in response to the iciness of the stream.

"Guys?" Rob's voice above them was suddenly urgent.

Phoebe looked and saw Rob standing motionless, his back toward them, looking up at the most incredibly huge creature she'd ever seen, standing in the meadow maybe twenty yards from him. Her first thought was that an elephant had somehow got onto the mountain, but she quickly realized that it was twice the size of any elephant. It was covered in long, shaggy fur and had a pair of upward-curving tusks. Two other gigantic creatures, just like the first one, appeared from the other side of the meadow and approached ponderously.

"Oh, golly," said Rob in a small voice.

"Don't worry," said the synapsid.

"Why *not?*" whispered Rob angrily.

"They're just mastodons."

Rob took that in for a moment. "How is that supposed to be good news?" he said finally, but Sid didn't answer.

The mastodons made the earth shake perceptibly as they approached, and then they were side by side, all three of them staring down at Rob.

"They've never seen anything like you," said Sid.

"Yeah, well, ditto," Rob whispered.

The three mastodons shifted their gaze from Rob and seemed to see Sid for the first time. Suddenly one of them trumpeted, and the noise of it was just short of deafening. The other two mastodons trumpeted, and then all three of them were trumpeting at once and Phoebe put her hands over her ears and Rob dropped to his knees.

The Last Synapsid sprang up the slope and placed himself between Rob and the great beasts. He raised one paw and they went silent instantly. All the kids could hear now was the sound of the mastodons' breathing, heavy and rasping. And then the strangest sight of all: the three gigantic beasts, towering above Sid, slowly bowed their great heads before him.

Sid said something in a strange voice. It sounded like just one word, but it wasn't English. He reached up and briefly laid a paw on each of the mastodon's trunks, walking from one to the other. And then he stepped back and the great creatures rose. They took a final look at Rob and Phoebe, turned, and walked slowly back across the meadow. They paused on the edge of the pine forest at the meadow's end, looked back, and trumpeted. And then they were gone.

Rob got up, his face pale. "Cool," he said. "Very, extremely, hugely cool."

"What did they say to you?" said Phoebe to Sid. "What did you say to them?"

But before Sid could answer, Rob pointed past them, down into the valley. "Look!"

Phoebe and Sid turned.

Far below them, moving slowly across the broad valley floor along the banks of the great river, were entire *herds* of mastodons, groups of one or two dozen each, and between these, tens of thousands of buffalo. From this distance, none of the creatures seemed to make a sound. They just moved, like the sea moves.

"Are there people?" Rob whispered, staring at the vast herds.

"Not here, not quite yet," said the synapsid. "Humans are migrating, and they'll be here soon, in maybe a thousand years or so. They'll form tribes in the valley. They'll revere this mountain—it will be one of their holy places."

"It's my holy place now," said Phoebe quietly.

Rob nodded in agreement. "Mine, too."

"Try to remember that, Rob, when you think of your town," said the synapsid, looking out over the valley. "They'll kill the mastodons, of course," he continued with a sigh. "And, eventually, all the bison."

The two kids looked at Sid, suddenly pained, and Sid nodded sadly.

"Not one mastodon will survive the coming of men."

"How do you know all these things, Sid?" asked Phoebe. "Do you . . . I mean . . . sort of know *everything*?"

Sid chortled. "Actually not, although my mate used to say I acted like I did."

"This is all so strange, it wears me out," said Phoebe. "It really does."

Sid looked at Phoebe and Rob for a moment in silence. Then he said, "I need to tell you a story."

Instinctively, the two kids sat down in the long grass. Sid made a rumbling sound in his throat, and began.

"The continents move. We know that. They float around the earth's surface like chunks of ice on a half-frozen river, and as they do, every once in a while, a sort of snag will form. A catch. The earth keeps moving, and time along with it, but bits of time and place get caught, linking one era to all other eras that follow or precede; and making a nonsense of our ideas of past and present and future.

"One dark day, toward the end of the Permian era, when the rain of hot gases and ash was at its worst, a diictodon— let's call him Sid—was running for his life. He was fleeing his longtime enemy, the gorgonopsid—we'll call him the Gorgon, shall we? Sid was very quick, but the Gorgon was relentless, and the pursuit was quickly becoming desperate. On the upward slope of a low hill, Sid spotted a dark opening. He ducked into the cave and froze, his heart pounding in his chest. Before long, the telltale odor of the Gorgon made itself known. The monster was approaching. The diictodon turned and plunged deeper into the utter darkness of the unknown cave, running blindly.

"Sid certainly didn't know it then, but this cave happened to be a snag, a link to another place and another time. It was, in fact, the door to Faith."

"This 'Sid' is you, right?" said Rob.

"Don't interrupt," said Sid. "I knew the Gorgon had entered the cave; I heard him behind me. I had no choice—I had to keep going, deeper and deeper into the darkness. Every now and then I'd run right into a wall, and then I'd grope frantically until I felt another opening, another passage. There seemed to be a lot of them; I could feel drafts coming from my left, my right, from above and below, some cold, some hot, some stinky, some pure. Suddenly there was a glimmer in the distance before me. The cave had a back door, I thought! I sprinted for it, the sound of the Gorgon's pursuit ever gaining on me. The light grew dazzlingly bright and I was out.

"I found myself on a high stony mountain peak. You must understand, my own homeland was a hot marsh, a riverbank surrounded by wetlands beneath a range of low hills. Now here I was, high on a huge mountain. It didn't make sense. The air here was colder and sweeter than any air I'd ever breathed—and the view! I didn't know what snow was, but it covered the peaks around me. I'd never seen a bird. They didn't exist in my world, and wouldn't exist until the dinosaurs' era—but here were miraculous little creatures, flying and singing with remarkable voices. I stood stock-still for a moment, bewildered, forgetful of the danger behind me. When I finally glanced over my shoulder, there was the Gorgon, standing motionless, looking cautiously about, blinking in the sunlight, clearly confused. He took a tentative step out into this alien world, but then thought better of it and retreated to the mouth of the cave. He gave me one long, searching look, almost as if he wanted to ask me a question, and then he turned and retreated. I waited on the mountainside until I thought I might be safe, and then I, too, followed the cave's passages back to the Permian era, not realizing what had just happened.

"Back home, the air was foul and stifling. The earth was dying. The few diictodons and gorgonopsids in our region were among the very last of their species. It wasn't a happy place or time.

"As for my particular Gorgon, I kept my eye on him. Evidently the memory of cool, clean air haunted him (as it did me, to be honest), and finally he decided to return to the cave. Cautiously, quietly, I followed.

"This time, when the Gorgon emerged at the end of a long, twisted series of passages, he was looking out onto a reedy meadow. He made his way guardedly out of the cave and into the meadow, while I hung back, watching. I think we both saw them at the same moment: creatures larger than any we'd ever seen or imagined, a herd of gigantic beasts, each twenty or thirty feet long, with narrow heads mounted on long thin necks and massive bodies, dragging tails behind them that were as big as trees. Flying above them were huge creatures, screaming with loud, harsh voices. We didn't know it, but we'd traveled into the midst of the Jurassic era, the age of the dinosaur, a hundred million years after our own. The place was Faith—and it wasn't.

"The herd of brontosauri turned their gaze on the gorgonopsid, their jaws moving slowly as they chewed. They wouldn't hurt him, but the Gorgon didn't know this—nor did I. He turned in terror and ran back into the cave. He saw me there at the mouth of the cave, and once again our eyes locked for a moment. Then he plunged past me, running backward in time. And I followed.

"Back home, no time at all seemed to have passed. But the Gorgon, at home in his own era, among his own kind, felt oppressed. The air was bad, his kin were sickly, and all about him was the stench of death. He came to despise his lot in life; he came to despise himself and all creatures who shared his fate. He became obsessed with his glimpses of what seemed to be other worlds. And so, again and again, the Gorgon returned to the cave's many tunnels, to journey wherever they'd take him. Again and again, I followed him.

"So it was that I pursued the Gorgon through the ages. I saw mountains appear where once there had been plains, and deserts which became oceans. I witnessed the births of countless species and the deaths of countless others. As the Gorgon grew more comfortable with traveling, he began to hunt and kill and eat the creatures he discovered, if they were small enough. It was awful, somehow. Back home, it was his nature to hunt and kill—he *needed* to eat the creatures of my world to survive, even diictodons! But to stalk and devour the beasts of other worlds? It felt very wrong, and I think he felt it, too, in spite of himself.

"I don't think I paid much attention when I glimpsed my first human, except to think that moving on two legs instead of four didn't seem to be an improvement. And upright? That made no kind of sense. They used weapons to kill; that, too, was new. Human beings were, and are, the most confusing of all the creatures I've ever encountered, thrilling one moment, terrifying the next, and merely annoying the next. The *noise* they make! Talk, talk, talk! Spindly little beasts, yapping at each other, climbing into metal boxes that cough and shoot smoke out their back ends and jerk across the landscape—so unlike anything else that lives, and yet, of course, descended from us older beings. From these, our children, the Gorgon and I slowly acquired language."

"He *talks*?" said Phoebe.

"Oh, indeed," said Sid.

"That day in the mine," said Rob, "I thought it was just my imagination when he said my name."

"No, he's actually *most* articulate," said Sid grimly, walking to the top of the hill overlooking the valley. "He and I have spent countless thousands of years debating life's big questions. I had to be wary of him, always—there was always the danger of him turning in a flash and devouring me. At the same time, a strange bond grew between us. He did not love me; rather the opposite. But he seemed to need me. We shared a great mystery, he and I.

"Through the ages, the Gorgon hid and watched the humans closely. They both fascinated him and repelled him. He learned from them, and at the same time he resented them. They were everything he wanted to be, with their language and learning and achievement, and at the same time, with their wanton cruelty and thirst for blood, they were everything he hated most in himself.

"Some of our trips had very strange destinations. I came to realize that some of the snags led to bizarre worlds—worlds that seemed unreal, with red skies and boiling seas, or vast deserts of purple dust with no visible life whatsoever. It finally dawned on me that some of the tunnels were merely passages to *possible* futures.

"As I say, each time I returned home it was as if hardly any time had passed at all. Still, the days *were* passing in my era, and among my own kind more and more were dying. There came a day, finally, when I returned to our burrow to find my beloved mate feverish, lying on a bed of dry grasses, her breathing labored and irregular. She looked up at me with her deep dark eyes.

" 'Where do you go?' she said. 'Where do you keep disappearing to?' "

She had always wanted offspring more than anything, but so far we had none. Her beautiful eyes were often sad, but now I saw hurt in them. I was ashamed. I told her everything: about the Gorgon, the cave, the tunnels to strange destinations, the strange creatures on the other end.

" 'Take me with you next time,' she said.

" 'You're not well,' I said.

" 'Take me,' she said. And I did.

"We kept our distance from the gorgonopsid, moving slowly and quietly, but I think he knew we were behind him. My mate seemed to gain a little strength the farther we traveled, but I feared it was only delirium. I feared the journey would be the death of her. When I begged her to turn back, she turned to me with shining eyes and said, 'I'm having an adventure'—and so we kept on. But suddenly the Gorgon, and then we, were falling from a great height in a cascade of water!

"The waterfall must have dropped us forty or fifty feet, plunging us into a deep, icy pool. I thought my lungs would burst. I could just make out my mate above me, underwater, her arms flailing as she and I struggled to swim to the surface. We finally burst up into air within moments of each other, and found ourselves surging along in a trough of fast-moving water. I feared we would drown or freeze to death, but my spouse got one of her paws round a rusted old pipe sticking out from the cement water chute, and I grabbed on to one of her rear legs, and the two of us crawled, half dead, out of the frigid waters of . . . the flume."

"*Our* flume?" said Phoebe.

"Your flume. We sat, shivering and wet, under a little wooden bridge that spanned it, looking around anxiously for the Gorgon. He was nowhere to be seen. But this is where the story gets a little strange."

"It's already a little strange," said Rob.

"Don't interrupt," said Sid. "Sitting down there, we heard voices, very near, just above us on the bridge. 'What's that?' my partner asked me. I said in a whisper, 'Humans. I told you about humans, remember?' She nodded. 'Two young ones,' I said, 'a female and a male, maybe six or seven years old.'

"The girl was crying—a brand-new thing for my spouse, she'd never encountered crying before—and immediately she wanted to rush up onto the bridge to see what she could do. She actually crawled out from under the span to see the creatures for herself. I held her there while she trembled with excitement.

"The boy was doing his best to comfort the girl. 'Now we both got dads who went away,' he said. 'They'll come back. Don't worry.' The girl shook her head and blew her nose. 'Mine won't,' she said. The boy scooped up some white stuff from the railing—snow, it was—and packed it together into a ball and dropped it down into the rushing water, where it shot past us. 'In that case, we'll have to stick together,' he said. 'You and me. Okay?' And the girl said . . ."

110

Phoebe cleared her throat and spoke, very quietly. "And I said, 'Okay.' "

Sid nodded.

"What?" said Rob. "That was us?"

"Don't you remember?" said Phoebe.

"No."

"Oh, my God—the marmots!" said Phoebe. "They were Sid and his mate!"

"Huh?"

"There were a couple of critters on the edge of the flume— you pointed them out just before they disappeared under the bridge. You thought they were marmots and I thought they were beavers. Later that day you sketched them. Don't you remember?"

"No."

"Anyway," said Sid, "she fell in love with you. My mate. All the way back home, she was beside herself with excitement. 'They're very special!' she said, and I agreed. 'Human children can be wonderful,' I said.

" 'No!' she cried. 'You don't understand! *These* two! They're going to be *needed*!'

" 'For what?' I said.

" 'I don't know! I had an adventure, and now I've had a vision! Neither one comes with instructions!' She was quite put out with me, and I feared it was the fever talking.

"A difficult time we had of it, making our way back up the mountain without being seen by the citizens of Faith. We never managed to find the opening beneath the waterfall where we'd emerged, but finally we came upon a crevasse, just behind those horse stables up on the hill. It was a snag, and from there we made our way home again to the dark latter days of the Permian era. She was still unwell, my mate. The

111

memory of her two human descendants—her 'children,' she called you—became her most precious possession. Even as she grew weaker in those terrible days, the thought of you two kept her going."

Rob and Phoebe looked at each other—and quickly looked away.

"From that trip, the Gorgon never returned. We didn't think much of it until one night my spouse shook me awake. She'd had a dream, she said, of all that might or might not come to be if synapsids did not survive the Great Dying—not only diictodons, but all of us synapsids, gorgonopsids included. A dream of glorious worlds that might never come into existence if our particular gorgonopsid did not live to return. She woke up fearing that the Gorgon was already sick and dying, just like all the other gorgonopsids at home. If so, the children of men might never be born. The route we'd taken through time would turn out to be merely one of the tunnels of possibility—not reality. Her own two children of Faith would not live to 'stick together' as friends.

"So she sent me forth to search for the Gorgon—and you two. I had to bring him back, and our 'children' would help me. That's what they were needed for! Well, it wasn't easy to find my way back to Faith. When I finally did find the Gorgon I could tell that he'd been up to something. He was more dangerous than ever, and very unwilling to hear talk of going back. He wasn't well—I could see that—his eyes were sick and he was clearly running out of time. He's getting old, after all, for a gorgonopsid—he must be thirteen or fourteen!"

"*What?*" said Phoebe. "Hasn't he been alive for millions of years?"

112

"No, he hasn't," said Sid, "and neither have I. We've *traveled* for millions of years, but we're *living* in our own era, where I've reached the great age of twelve—very old for a diictodon."

"You mean you're just my age?" said Rob.

"Yes and no, stop interrupting," said Sid. "When I found him again, I discovered that he no longer needed a cave through which to do his traveling. There is a stickiness about time—everyone feels it eventually, not just me and the Gorgon. But for us travelers, it seems that by passing *through* a snag, you also *become* one, in a sense. Bits of you cling to the times and places you visit, and bits of *them* stick to *you*. He and I had become snags, so to speak, with links to eon after eon of earth's history."

"And your mate? How is she?" Phoebe asked.

"I don't know," said Sid simply. "I haven't seen her since we last said goodbye. I hope, where she is, she's still hanging on. What can I do but hope?"

He hung his head for just a moment, then raised it again. "Anyway, I couldn't go back without the Gorgon. It would put everything she cares for in jeopardy. Do you think you two could persuade the Gorgon to go?"

"*What?*" said Rob.

"*Us?*" said Phoebe.

"*Persuade?*"

"*Him?*"

"We were having a nice moment here, Sid," said Rob. "Don't spoil it with crazy talk."

Sid shook his head. "The Gorgon has got to choose, and choose soon. According to my mate, you two have a part to play in his decision. He's got to want to be who he is, and that seems to be the last thing he wants. You see that trait all the time in humans, but the gorgonopsid is the first example of it in the animal kingdom."

Both Rob and Phoebe had personal experience of wishing they were someone else, somewhere else, so they just chewed on that for a moment while Sid stared down at the various herds in the valley.

"Phoebe, Rob," said the synapsid, "we need to leave. Take a paw."

"No!" said Rob. "Please!"

"We just got here!" said Phoebe.

"I'm sorry," said Sid, "we can't linger."

"I *never* want to leave," said Rob.

The synapsid looked back at him intently.

"Never? That sounds lonely. What would you do for company?" he said.

Rob dropped his head.

"I understand, I think," said Sid. "No Mr. Brinkleys. No Chad Scudders." The synapsid paused, then continued gently. "No missing fathers, either."

Rob looked at him again, his brow furrowed.

"Rob," said the synapsid, "what you've seen today will always be a part of you, and you will always be able to return to it, one way or another. Think of it as a *snag*."

"Sid," said Phoebe, "what did the mastodons say to you?"

Sid hesitated for a moment. "They called me 'father,' " he said. "They asked me for my blessing and I gave it to them. Come now, you two—side by side."

The three of them stood looking out over what would someday become Faith, where one day, with luck, many thousands of years later, Rob Gates and Phoebe Traylor would be born.

They each put a hand on Sid's shoulder and were gone.

★ ★ ★

"Oh, dear," said the Last Synapsid.

The three of them were sputtering and gasping for breath when they came to the surface. The flume carried them nearly a block downstream before they managed to climb out, cold and shivering, onto the cement banks and the streets of Faith.

"Sorry, sorry," Sid was saying as they darted toward Rob's home, which was nearest. "I was *so close.* I mean, I really thought I had it *spot-on* this time."

The kids' teeth were chattering as they moved through town. The only person to see them was Angela Cruz, passing fast on her bicycle. She waved and said, "Hi! New dog?" And she was gone.

Rob and Phoebe were cold and wet, but they were home in their own Faith again, and happy to be there. Lucy Gates was out at a PTA meeting, fortunately, and the house was empty. Sid was silent and thoughtful while the kids toweled off and heated some mac and cheese in the microwave.

"Oh, my God!" said Rob suddenly. "My skateboard! I left it back there!"

"Rob, how could you!" said Phoebe. "What if you change everything in history just because you can't keep track of your things?"

The two kids turned to Sid, fear on their faces, but he just shook his head.

"That's not been my experience. In terms of changing history,

I'd worry more about a species going extinct than the odd skateboard here and there."

Rob and Phoebe breathed a sigh of relief.

"I need to know what's keeping him here, the Gorgon," Sid said distantly. "There's something I've missed, and I've got to figure out what it is or we won't get the Gorgon back to the Permian before it's too late."

But the kids were too excited to share the synapsid's gloom. They'd seen and done amazing things. Phoebe, wearing a big fluffy robe, opened a fresh page in her diary and wrote and wrote. Rob dug through boxes of his old drawings, one after another.

"Phoebe, look!" he said finally.

He held up an old yellowed page of drawing paper.

The two kids looked at Sid. He nodded, a sad smile on his old face.

"Marmots by the Floom"
Robbie Gates

14
CONFRONTATIONS

"It's still out there, people!" cried Mickie Pine. He was up in the gazebo in the little park near the town hall, hollering at the passers-by like a preacher on a street corner.

"It weren't no mountain lion attacked that horse! The danger's not gone away! You're not safe, you just *think* you are!"

Mickie's eyes were bloodshot and staring.

"There's a monster out there, folks. I seen it myself, up close and personal!"

There were amused smiles among the people who passed by. Some of them paused beneath the gazebo steps to listen. Nick and Janet Bright stopped with Phoebe Traylor, who did her best to translate what Mickie was saying into sign language. Rob Gates was with them. Billy Springer and Aran McBell were there, and Sam and Emma Decker, who ran the summer stock theater, were listening, too. Gary Dirks slouched around with

Chad Scudder, smoking and smirking. Wynola and Adelaide Parsons were sitting on a park bench, looking as though the Mickie Pine show had been arranged solely for their benefit, and enjoying it immensely.

"I seen it, and not only that—I heard it, too! It *talks,* people!" A ripple of chuckles spread through the crowd. "It does! It speaks English like a man, out between its long, curved tusks!"

People were grinning and shaking their heads and moving on.

"I swear it!" Mickie's voice was rising and a little desperate. "Hey, there's some here who could tell you the same! There's some right here who seen the beast just like I did!"

Phoebe stopped signing to Nick and Janet and just listened.

"There's some standing right here, right now, *who talked to it*!" The veins in Mickie's forehead and temples were bulging. "Folk right here amongst us . . . who are *in league with it*!"

The chuckles turned to outright laughter. Suddenly Rob was standing on the bottom step of the gazebo, glaring up at Mickie Pine.

"Who is it, Mickie?" asked Rob in a low, angry voice. "Some kids, maybe? Kids you were shooting at with your rifle, for instance?"

Mickie Pine hesitated and sort of drooped. He ran his hand across his face nervously.

"Forget it," he said, looking down at the little crowd. "Just forget all about it."

Rob rejoined Phoebe, and Mickie sat down abruptly on the gazebo steps, looking as though he'd forgotten why he was there in the first place. The last of the crowd moved on, shaking their heads. *Poor Mickie. Off his meds again.*

Phoebe and Rob were heading out of the little park when Rob stopped.

"Hey, Chad," he said. "Where'd you get that thing?"

Chad Scudder made a show of turning slowly to address Rob, and Gary grinned at the prospect of a confrontation.

"What thing?" said Chad, leaning on Jenkins' aluminum walking stick.

"That metal stick thing. It's mine."

"I beg your pardon?"

"Well, it's not exactly mine, but—"

"You're right about that much, Gates. It's not exactly yours 'cause I found it and it's mine."

Rob took a step toward Chad, who turned and thrust the pointed pole at Rob like a rapier.

"Don't even think about it," Chad said. Everyone was watching now, including Billy and Aran, who looked like they were ready to jump into it all. But Rob, after a moment, took a deep breath and turned away.

"Come on, Phoeb," he said.

"Come on, Phoeb!" mimicked Chad. "Tell me—is that short for *feeble*?" The sound of laughter followed Rob and Phoebe as they walked stiffly away.

★ ★ ★

Rob and Phoebe didn't realize at first that Aran and Billy were following them. It was a Saturday, and they were headed down to the Conoco at the bottom of town, where Lucy Gates was working her weekend shift. She could generally be counted on to let the kids take a couple of ice cream bars from the freezer or a big bag of chips, and there were a couple of tables crammed into the back where you could eat, behind the shelves of motor oil and air fresheners and antifreeze.

"What was that thing you wanted from Chad?" said Phoebe as the two of them walked south on Willow.

"God, nobody ever listens to me!" Rob kicked a rock on the road and it went skidding halfway down the block. "I told you—it's something Jenkins invented. It's hidden inside the aluminum walking stick. You point it at an animal and it tells you what kind of thing it is. The critter detector. He used it to find the Gorgon."

"So why does Chad have it?"

"*I* don't know. I dropped it and Chad must have picked it up that day at the old mine. That's not the point. The point is, Sid needs to know about it. Is he back yet?"

Phoebe shook her head. The synapsid had left the day before, "traveling," he'd said, searching in time for the missing something that would allow them to complete their quest. Sid swore he wasn't being evasive when they quizzed him about it—he said he simply didn't know what he was looking for, but was hoping he'd recognize it once he saw it.

Phoebe and Rob heard a crunch of gravel behind them and turned around fast.

"Hey," said Aran McBell.

"Hey," said Phoebe.

"Hey," said Billy Springer.

"What's up?" said Rob.

"Not much," said Billy.

Billy was a tallish twelve-year-old with hair so blond it was almost white, pale skin, and watery blue eyes. Aran McBell was short and sharp-tongued, with reddish hair and a pair of ears that stuck out from his head in a way that was comical to everyone but Aran.

As they walked, Billy reached into his backpack. "Ms. Larson said to give this to you if we saw you on the weekend." He held out a manila folder, and Rob took it. "She was looking all over for you guys yesterday afternoon. Where'd you go?"

"It's the article about Dr. Jenkins that was about to print out when the bell rang," said Rob, briefly glancing inside.

"Thanks, Billy," said Phoebe.

Instead of taking off, Billy and Aran kept walking alongside the other two, glancing sidelong at each other. The four of them turned in to the Conoco without a further word and took the table at the very back.

Lucy Gates greeted Billy and Aran enthusiastically, pleased to see Rob hanging out with someone other than just Phoebe.

"Where in heck have you two been?" she said, wiping her hands on the bottom of her apron as she approached their table. "A couple of total strangers! Listen, let me zap a couple pizzas for you guys, my treat."

She started back to the counter.

"No meat on mine, Mom," said Rob, and Lucy sighed audibly.

When the kids were alone again, Billy cleared his throat and sort of nodded at Aran, and Aran cleared *his* throat and looked at his lap.

"Okay, what's going on?" said Rob finally.

"You tell us," said Aran, looking up at Rob.

"We saw you," said Billy.

"We saw the dragon thing follow you into the mine," said Aran.

"We were afraid it was going to eat you," added Billy.

"What *was* that thing?"

Rob and Phoebe were too stunned for a moment to say anything. Then the bell at the door jingled, and Donna Mitchelson and Angela Cruz walked into the Conoco. They headed directly for the back, and both Billy and Aran looked like they were expecting them. The girls pulled up a couple of chairs and sat, and Rob and Phoebe each had an uncomfortable, trapped sort of feeling, like all this had been planned in advance.

121

Donna turned to Aran and Billy and said, "Have you asked them yet?"

"*Have* you?" echoed Angela stridently when the boys hesitated.

Aran and Billy nodded, a little intimidated by these two powerful girls. Donna was a brunette, and what people call "big-boned." She wasn't fat—she spent much of her life on horseback and she was very muscular and fit—she was just built on a broad pattern. Angela was slight and dark, and passionate about most everything she said or did.

"Okay," said Donna to Phoebe and Rob. "What about it? What's going on?"

"We've been watching you," said Angela.

Phoebe and Rob were still speechless.

"You can't pretend, you can't play innocent with us," continued Angela. "We've *seen* you with it."

"I saw it crawl under your house one night," said Donna to Phoebe, "and then the light went on in your bedroom and you pulled the blinds! I nearly freaked, Phoebe!"

"I saw you both climb out of the flume with that . . . thing!" said Angela. "What were you doing in the *flume*? With a *thing*?"

"What *is* it?"

"We know it's not a dragon, like these idiots say, 'cause dragons don't exist, *obviously,* but what is it?"

"A dog?"

"A kind of lizard?"

"We're *not* idiots!" said Aran hotly. "It's too big to be a dog!"

"It's not big at all!" said Angela.

Rob and Phoebe watched the kids arguing back and forth like they were watching a tennis match, Rob flipping the manila folder open and shut.

"How many dogs do you know that are five feet long?" Billy almost shouted.

"Five feet? You're crazy," said Donna. "It's no bigger than a boxer or a German shepherd."

"Yeah," said Aran, laying on the sarcasm. "A German shepherd from the Planet of Giant Dogs!"

"Why are boys like this?" asked Donna. *"Why?"*

"Oh, God," said Rob suddenly, and the squabble came to a sudden stop. Rob was staring at one of the color printouts inside the folder.

"What is it?" asked Angela.

Rob and Phoebe stared at the photo.

"It's . . . footprints," said Rob, with a stunned look on his face. "Animal footprints, and human ones."

"Human?" said Phoebe. "Where? I don't see it."

In a reddish clay bank were the partial impressions of large, clawed pawprints, from what seemed to be a four-legged creature. Near it on one side was the print of what might have been a naked human toe. On the other side, difficult to make out, seemed to be a slight heel-shaped dent.

"Read the caption!" said Rob with an edge in his voice.

The caption said the fossilized prints, human and beast, were between 240 and 260 million years old, and pointed out that since the first humanoid didn't appear until about 3 or 4 million years ago, Professor Jenkins' photograph represented either an "astonishing impossibility" or, much more likely, a blatant hoax. Rob looked up at Phoebe across the table.

"So?" said Phoebe defensively.

"You know whose footprints these are, don't you?" he said.

"What footprints?" said Phoebe. "I'm not sure they're really—"

"I'm guessing this one's you, the toe, and this heel thing is me."

"Rob, you don't know that! These are fragments! You can barely tell what they are!"

"You're in denial," said Rob.

"You got *that* from your *therapist*!" said Phoebe.

"Guys?" said Angela.

But Rob was focused on Phoebe. "He said we were gonna help him, maybe talk to the thing—he never said we had to go all the way home with him!"

"Guys?" Angela said again.

"Do you think?" said Phoebe. "Back to the Permian? All two hundred and fifty million years . . . ?" She trailed off.

"It's too much! It's too far! I don't want to, and he can't make me!"

"Guys!" Angela was red in the face. *"What is going on?"* Phoebe and Rob seemed to realize suddenly that they weren't alone. Phoebe glanced at Rob.

"Be my guest," Rob said.

Phoebe turned back to their friends. She took a deep breath and said, "I guess there's some stuff we better tell you."

★ ★ ★

It took a while to explain that there were *two* beasts, not one; that what Billy and Aran had seen going into the old mine was very different from the creature Angela had glimpsed scrambling out of the flume with Phoebe and Rob. That these animals were a quarter billion years old, well, that was just altogether too much for Phoebe and Rob's friends to absorb.

The gang finished their pizzas and thanked Lucy Gates and went out to sit in the old rusty swings they had used when they were little, in the park next to the ball field at the bottom of town. The high school varsity boys' baseball team was playing an intramural game, and Mr. Brinkley was behind home plate in a baggy sweatsuit, serving as umpire. The thwack of the ball into the catcher's glove and the occasional crack of the bat became the background for the strangest story Donna, Angela, Billy, and Aran had ever heard.

While Phoebe did most of the talking, Rob borrowed Angela's notebook and started sketching.

"Mastodons?" Danna interrupted when Phoebe got to that part of the story. "In *Faith*?"

"Mastodons are kind of the least of it, actually," said Phoebe. "Basically we're trying to help Sid save the human race and all other mammals and life on earth as we know it."

None of their story was easy to believe, but for Rob and Phoebe it was still a relief to talk to someone other than their therapists about the whole thing. At least their friends didn't try to interpret what they were saying. If their friends decided that Phoebe and Rob were just plain crazy, it wouldn't mean quite the same thing than if their therapists said it.

Rob showed them his drawing, and the others looked at it in confused silence.

The kids looked up from the sketch, glancing at each other

"Mastadons in Faith"
by Rbt. Gates Jr.

doubtfully. Just then there was a crack from home plate and a ball streaked foul, past the swing sets, right past their feet, and a dog appeared from nowhere, racing like a greyhound after it.

At first the kids paid no attention. Angela was asking if it had just *felt* like they had traveled through time or if they were saying it was literally true when Phoebe stood up, watching the dog. Then Rob stopped swinging and stood, too.

The Last Synapsid turned back to the kids, the baseball clenched between his teeth and tusks, grinning like a happy hound, drool dribbling from his lower jaw. Billy and Aran and Angela and Donna all got up from their swings and stared. Sid trotted toward them proudly, but Rob dashed to his side, crouching beside him and doing his best to shield him from view.

"The *ball*, Gates!" yelled Mr. Brinkley. "The *ball*!"

Rob grabbed the saliva-soaked ball from Sid's teeth and threw it back to Brinkley, who caught the soggy thing bare-handed and said a four-letter word. Brinkley hurled the ball away, wiped his hand on his pants, and scowled back at Rob.

"That your dog, Gates?" he shouted.

Rob was quite pleased to have gotten diictodon saliva all over Brinkley's hands, despite his annoyance with Sid.

"Just a stray, sir," said Rob. Mr. Brinkley suddenly put one hand on the catcher's shoulder, as if to steady himself from a wave of dizziness. Then he put a new ball into play and the game resumed.

Phoebe joined Rob, hiding Sid from the baseball team as best she could.

"What on earth are you thinking?" she hissed into his ear opening.

"Have you lost your mind?" Rob whispered into Sid's other ear.

But Sid just grinned at them both.

"It's broad daylight, Sid, with lots of witnesses," said Rob through clenched teeth. "In case you hadn't noticed."

Sid chortled, looking past Phoebe and Rob to the other kids who stood, frozen, staring at him with their mouths open.

"Well, you've already told this lot about me, if I'm not mistaken," said Sid. Almost in unison, Donna, Angela, Aran, and Billy each took one horrified step backward.

"We didn't tell 'em you could *talk!*" hissed Rob furiously.

Sid glanced up at Rob and Phoebe.

"Odd," he said. "I should have thought that would be the first thing you'd mention. Anyway," he continued, looking back at the others, "aren't you going to introduce me?"

Donna, Angela, and Aran each grew pale, but Billy Springer turned a faint shade of green, dropped to his knees, and sicked up his portion of the mushroom and mozzarella pizza.

15
THE GANG OF SIX

The kids and Sid were in an old disused equipment shed at the lower end of the ball field, Sid grooming himself after his travels and Rob and Phoebe sitting on the floor nearby, quizzing him. The others stood, ill at ease, huddled at the opposite end of the room, watching and listening. They were experiencing the warm, humid dizziness that came with proximity to the diictodon. Rob and Phoebe had become so used to it, they barely noticed it anymore.

It had been Billy Springer who had got them into the shed, after he'd put his head under the stream from the drinking fountain and recovered somewhat. Deputy Keith didn't know it, but Billy possessed a copy of his dad's master key and could get into lots of places around town that otherwise would have been out of bounds. It was Billy's most treasured possession, and in terms of his popularity with the other kids, it went a long way toward making up for his frequent puke attacks.

"So what put you in such a good mood, Sid?" said Rob with a little edge.

"Where have you been, anyway?" asked Phoebe.

"Why shouldn't I be happy?" he said. "Life is a gift."

"Yeah, right," said Rob suspiciously.

"Life's a gift, friendship's a gift, and here I am, back with my two best friends in the whole new world and *their* best friends. It's all wonderful!"

Sid got up and stretched, and the other kids nervously retreated a step. Their universe was still spinning, and their sense of reality was being put to new and frightening tests. Sid beamed at them reassuringly and then walked right up to the group, his claws clicking on the shed's wooden floor. He stopped directly in front of Billy Springer.

"Don't worry about it, Billy. The first time I saw a human I thought *I* was going to throw up, too. Talk about *grotesque*! I've become accustomed to your species by now, of course, but at first you all came as quite a shock."

"Thank you," said Billy faintly.

"Angela," said the synapsid, "you've got beautiful eyes and they don't miss a thing. I've watched you watching us for some time now."

"You have?" she said, fighting off the dizziness she was feeling.

"Oh, yes," said the creature. "You too, Donna. You spotted me at Phoebe's, coming and going, didn't you?"

Donna nodded, her eyes very wide.

"You're saying you *knew* these guys were spying on us?" said Rob indignantly. Sid grinned back at him. "Well, why didn't you say something?"

129

"I don't feel a need to tell you *every* little thing, Robert."

Rob's scowl deepened, but Sid seemed oblivious.

"Aran, I'm pleased to know you. These two call me Sid; I hope you will, too."

"Yes, sir, me too. I mean, Sid, sir. Can I?" said Aran, tentatively extending his hand toward Sid's head.

"May I," said Phoebe automatically.

"No, don't!" shouted Rob. "Aran, stop!"

"But I want to travel in time, too," said Aran.

"No!" Rob's face was red all of a sudden.

"What's up with you?" said Aran.

The synapsid winked at Aran and said, "Later."

"Why is it suddenly okay for the whole world to know about you, Sid?" Rob continued with growing heat.

"Not the whole world—by no means," said the synapsid, amiably shaking his head.

There was something about his attitude that was making Rob crazy. "You're up to something," he said.

"Maybe I am, Rob," said Sid, smiling slyly. "Maybe I am."

"Okay, cut the crap!" Rob stood up angrily. "What's going on?"

There was a shocked silence in the room. The other kids were still in a state of shock over the whole Sid thing, but even they could sense that Rob had crossed a line. It was sort of like yelling at your grandpa—it just wasn't done. Sid blinked silently, his black eyes very big.

"Rob!" said Phoebe. "What's wrong with you?"

"What? Oh, nothing! I just had my whole life hijacked by a creature from another world, no problem! I just got put in charge of saving the human race, that's great, life's a gift!"

Rob was pacing angrily as he spoke.

"I don't understand," said Phoebe. "Where is all this coming from?"

Aran McBell spoke up hesitantly.

"I think he's jealous," he said.

"*What?*" said Rob.

Aran looked Rob full in the face, took a deep breath, and said, "I think you had the synapsid all to yourself, but now you've got to share him."

Rob just about detonated.

"Idiot!"

Rob gave Aran a shove, and Aran shoved him back.

"I'm not an idiot!"

"You are too, and you always have been and always will be!"

"Will not!" Aran shouted back. "And wasn't!"

"And won't be!" added Billy helpfully, taking Aran's side.

"Anyway, what do you know about it?" Rob shouted. "About any of it?" He turned in a half circle, facing each of them. "Nothing! Absolutely nothing!"

"Rob, please," said Phoebe. "What's got into you?"

"I just saw a picture of my footprints alongside yours, fossilized two hundred and fifty million years ago, and you're asking me what's *wrong*?"

"No, you didn't!" said Phoebe. "There weren't necessarily *our* footprints in that picture. You just read that into it!"

"What picture?" said Sid.

Rob tilted his head in Sid's direction. "This little genius can't transport us across the street without landing us in the wrong century or the middle of the flume! Now he's gonna send us back two hundred and fifty million years? He doesn't know what he's doing, he just pretends he does, and I want it to stop! I want things to go back to the way they were!"

There was a deep silence in the equipment shed. The sounds of the baseball game outside continued, faintly.

"So do I, Rob," said the synapsid quietly. "I want to go back to

131

my burrow in the old world. I want to find my mate and be with her before our kind vanishes forever from the world. I want to lie down beside her before I die, and listen to her tell me about the children of her dreams, the children of Faith. I want to stop all this traveling. But I can't do any of that if I don't think you have at least a chance of coming into existence. Because, of course, you *are* my children. And you mean the very earth to me."

Rob's eyes were troubled. He didn't speak for a moment, but then he said in a barely audible voice, "You're not my father."

Sid clicked across the floor to Rob's side and looked up at him with compassion in his eyes. Rob hung his head, caught somewhere between regret and resentment.

"Not to worry," said the synapsid. "Now listen to this—I've got news. Do you remember the Faith we stumbled into a few weeks ago, more or less by accident?"

"Entirely by accident," said Rob under his breath.

"More or less by accident," repeated the synapsid, choosing to ignore him. "The Faith that existed a hundred years ago? I just went back there, and I found something I think you'll find rather interesting—you especially, Rob. The way back to the Permian for the Gorgon and me does indeed lie through Faith—but *that* one, not this one. I believe I found what's been keeping the Gorgon here."

Sid looked at each one of the kids, engaging them in turn with his deep black eyes. The kids glanced at each other apprehensively.

"You *have* told them about the gorgonopsid?" Sid asked Rob and Phoebe.

"Yeah, a bit," said Phoebe.

"Well, you're all going to have to be most careful from now on. Not timid, mind you—but careful."

"So what was it you discovered back there?" said Phoebe.

The synapsid looked at the six kids appraisingly, and then seemed to make up his mind.

"It's not a what, it's a who. Now then, who wants to become a traveler?" he said, excitement glittering in his eyes.

"Sid—no!" said Phoebe. "Are you sure you're feeling okay? You seem a little out of control."

"Crowd round," said Sid, paying no attention to her. "Put your hands just here, on my shoulders."

Phoebe was seriously alarmed. "No, Sid, it's too soon. These guys just met you, they're not ready to travel yet!"

"Just a quick trip, there and back."

"All six of us?" said Rob. "What if you screw up?"

"I won't dignify that with a reply," said Sid.

"It's not fair to them, Sid!" Phoebe pleaded.

"They're just kids!" said Rob, which set Aran off completely.

"Forget you, Rob Gates!" he said, thrusting his hands toward Sid's shoulders, and Angela followed suit, along with Billy and Donna. Then all six of them were falling, falling through a blazing spectrum of light and wind.

★ ★ ★

"Oh, dear," said the synapsid with dismay.

All you could see was his snout poking up from a massive drift of snow and his front paws making futile swimming motions in the blindingly white landscape. The kids were too shocked to register the intense cold at first, but they also were buried almost to their shoulders in snow, the six of them scattered in a semicircle around Sid, high on a mountain slope, and they were gasping to catch their breath. The air was crystal clear. There was no wind. The mountain peaks that surrounded

133

them looked vaguely familiar to the kids, but the light was so bright it almost burned their eyes.

"I'm guessing this isn't what you wanted to show us. Am I right, Sid?" said Rob. "Or am I wrong?"

The synapsid said nothing but looked around nervously.

"This was seriously irresponsible, Sid!" said Phoebe, her teeth starting to chatter.

"Well, let's try to keep a sense of perspective here," said the creature.

"Perspective?" It seemed to be Phoebe's turn to be angry with the synapsid.

"Where are we?" said Aran.

"That looks like the top of Mount Argento," Donna said in a daze, pointing to a nearby mountain, "but where's the valley?"

"There isn't any valley," said Phoebe acidly. "*Is* there, Sid?"

"Well, technically . . ."

"Because *technically,* where the valley should be, there's a big honking *glacier*! Am I right, Mr. Act-Before-You-Think?"

"Glacier?" said Billy, awestruck. "But there aren't any glaciers in . . ."

"Twenty-five thousand years ago there were!" said Phoebe stridently.

"Cool," said Aran.

"You think?" Phoebe was so angry, her freckles would have been dark red if she hadn't been so incredibly cold.

"Come here, all of you, and put your hands on my back, and we'll try again," said the synapsid.

"I can't move," said Angela. Her voice was small and frightened.

"None of us can move, Sid, actually," said Phoebe.

It was true. They had all dropped into the snow with enough force to drive them in like tent stakes. They wriggled and thrust

134

with their arms, but their legs especially were firmly planted. Angela's breath began to sound labored, and Billy Springer, who was nearest her, realized she was going into one of her infrequent asthma attacks.

"I feel . . . like I'm . . . sinking," she whispered.

"Put out your hand," he said, and when Angela thrust her right hand up above the snow, Billy grabbed for it, but there was a gap of just an inch or two. Billy yanked the lanyard from around his neck, the one that held his master key. He wrapped the bottom end tightly around his fist and flung the looped end toward Angela.

"Grab on to the loop," he said, and she did. Billy's crush on Angela was well known, but he hardly dared to speak to her, as a rule.

"I've got you," he said. "Don't worry. You're not going anywhere."

"That's what I'm afraid of," said Angela.

"Well, anyway," Billy said, only slightly abashed, "you're not alone."

"No, as a matter of fact," said a strange, deep voice. "You're not."

The kids looked up the mountain slope and to their horror saw a long black snout emerging from a snowdrift about 20 or 30 feet above them. It wriggled up and out, just the head and neck, and then it was looking down at them. The creature's lips drew back in a macabre grin, revealing long sharp fangs, and a nasty odor drifted down over them.

"Go . . . back!" said Sid hoarsely. He seemed to be caught off guard.

"Oh, I don't think so." The voice was low and musical. "Not, at least, without a souvenir or two."

A hissing noise came from its jaws, which may have been what passed for laughter with it. One black razor-clawed paw appeared above the snow, and then another.

Donna gulped back a sob, and Aran said a four-letter word very quietly, and Billy Springer for once in his life didn't throw up but turned anxiously to the others and said, "Angela's fainted."

"Sid," whispered Phoebe. "Please—what do we do?"

The Last Synapsid was still making urgent movements with his paws, straining to climb out of the drift and not making much headway. He clearly wasn't built to navigate Ice Age snow. He turned his head and glared at the Gorgon and made a sort of barking, angry yelping noise, and the Gorgon answered with a bark that seemed to turn into a nasty snicker. It sounded like language, one Permian-era creature speaking to another, but the kids had no idea what was being said.

With a sudden lurch, the entire Gorgon was up out of his drift, onto the crusted surface of the snow. For the kids, it was like looking into the darkest corner of a nightmare, the part that's so awful you don't remember it in the morning, you just know that it was there.

The Gorgon's long snout turned this way and that, its yellow eyes taking in each kid in turn. "What a treat—Popsicles!" he said.

It took a tentative step toward them, and then another, making crunching noises in the snow, and the foul smell grew in their nostrils. The kids all struggled helplessly against the snow.

"Angela," said Billy urgently. "Come on, wake up!"

"We need to touch," said the synapsid in a low voice. The Gorgon took another step and broke through the thin snow crust but righted himself in a moment. He raised his head and opened his jaws, and the silence of the mountain was broken by a fearsome, roaring bellow.

"Oh, golly," said Rob under his breath.

Sid looked round at the others, gauging distances with his eyes.

"Billy," he said, "can you try again to touch Angela's hand? Just a fingertip would do."

Billy thrust his legs downward against the snow with all his skinny might and yanked on the lanyard at the same time.

"Okay," Billy said, "I'm touching one finger."

"Good," said the synapsid. "Just keep contact with her, and grab Aran's hand. Phoebe, take Aran's other hand. Donna, can you reach Phoebe? Now then. Rob, if you can touch Phoebe's hand, and get your other paw over here to me, we'll complete the circuit, so to speak."

"What's that noise?" said Rob, and the kids all looked up at the blinding white vastness above them. They heard a deep rumbling.

The Gorgon cocked his head to one side, listening intently, and Sid cocked his. The rumbling intensified and surrounded them.

Donna whispered the word that had suddenly formed in each of their minds.

"Avalanche."

"Shh." Phoebe put a finger to her lips, which were rapidly turning blue. "Everyone, stay very, very still."

"No," said the synapsid in a low voice. "We need to leave this instant, no matter what it takes, and we need each other to do it. In unison, grasp hands on the count of—"

It began, the avalanche, just above them on the mountain. The rumble suddenly became a roar.

"Now! Now! Now!" shouted Rob.

The kids all shot their hands toward each other, grasping, some of them only just barely touching, and Rob slapped Sid's neck with his right hand just as their side of the snow mountain detached itself and began to plummet.

The Gorgon was suddenly frantic, his yellow eyes rolling, his massive head swinging back and forth, his paws scrambling, and then—bizarrely—he seemed to be levitating, his legs dancing in midair.

They were all screaming without knowing they were screaming, the noise of the avalanche drowning out all other consciousness. And then the screams faded to nothing, and there was only the falling.

★ ★ ★

Angela was surprised to wake up in Billy Springer's arms. The six kids were sprawled across the floor of the equipment shed near the ball field, along with Sid, who at that moment was almost looking his age, lying flat on his belly, paws outstretched and eyes glazed, in a patch of melting bluish glacial ice and snow.

"Why are you holding me?" asked Angela, and Billy shrugged and smiled sheepishly. Angela noticed the lanyard in her hand and didn't seem to recognize it. Suddenly she put her hands to her mouth and puked into Billy's lap—pizza, of course, not a lot, just a little—and because it was Billy, there was a kind of poetic symmetry to it. Billy didn't freak at all—he just nodded sympathetically, like he was an old pro at all this. He pulled a tissue from his back pocket, and along with it some packed Ice Age snow, and he started cleaning himself, still smiling at Angela, as if this sort of thing happened all the time among close friends.

"Sorry!" said Angela, deeply shocked and embarrassed. Angela didn't even glance at Sid as she got to her feet and made her way, a little wobbly, to the door.

"I'll walk you home, if you like," said Billy.

"No, thanks," she said. "I'm really sorry about the . . . you know . . . in your lap and all." Angela's crush on Billy was known to absolutely no one but herself.

"Not a problem," he said, brushing himself off with the soggy, snowy tissue.

"Is that snow?" said Angela incredulously.

"Well, yeah," said Billy.

"Where on earth did *that* come from?"

Billy and the others just looked at her, at a loss for words.

The synapsid lifted his head from the floor. "I deeply regret the whole time mix-up on the mountain," he said, "and I'm sorry about the gorgonopsid scare, and I am *truly* sorry about the avalanche. . . ."

Sid's voice trailed away. But Angela acted as though she hadn't heard or seen him; she just made her way to the door, leaving snowy footprints behind her.

"Angela," said Phoebe, "are you sure you don't want one of us to walk you home? I think you may be in shock."

"Why would I be in *shock*? I'm just feeling a little sick, that's all. I think it must have been the pizza," she said, stuffing the lanyard into her cardigan's pocket. She pulled her hand out: her pocket was filled with snow. "It must have been the pizza," she said again faintly, and left.

In the silence that followed, the kids glanced around apprehensively.

"Where is it?" whispered Aran.

"The Gorgon?" said Sid. "Probably making his way from the last Ice Age to the present. We're all right for now. But we *will* have to go back."

"Where? Back where?" said Billy, Donna and Aran, almost in unison.

"To the Faith of the silver boom, which is where I meant to bring you all along," Sid explained. "I'll get it right next time, I promise."

Phoebe spoke in a low, ominous voice. "Not today."

The other kids got up and brushed themselves off and started to leave. They barely said a word. Probably they were afraid Sid was about to transport them in time again, and they weren't quite up to it. They shuffled wordlessly out of the equipment shed and headed individually for their homes.

The baseball game was over and the field was empty. Rob and Phoebe walked together, while Sid trailed behind.

"You gotta admit," said Rob, "that was pretty cool with the Gorgon hanging in midair and the mountain collapsing and all. I think I'll do a watercolor."

"Rob, do you think Sid's all right?" said Phoebe quietly, glancing over her shoulder at the diictodon.

"What do you mean?"

"I'm worried about him. He doesn't seem to be himself sometimes."

"He did say he was old for a diictodon," said Rob.

"Rob, what if it's not just the Gorgon who's running out of time?"

Rob turned and looked back at their friend. Sid was clearly moving slower than usual, his head hung, looking at the ground before him. Usually he paced ahead of the kids, eagerly looking at everything around him. Rob called back to the creature, "Hey, Sid, how's it going?"

His head rose. "I'm afraid I was a little reckless today," said Sid. "I'm very sorry. I don't know what got into me."

"I wish the vet could give you an exam," said Phoebe. "But I'm afraid you'd accidentally send her back in time somewhere."

"No, no, I'm feeling much better, thanks," Sid said, trotting to catch up with them.

"So what was your big discovery?" said Rob. "What's keeping the Gorgon from going back to the Permian?"

"Simple," said the diictodon. "Greed. Human greed."

16
TRICKY PITCHES

Life can, and does, throw some pretty tricky pitches. You think you've got a bead on what you should be worried about, and then from somewhere way off you hear a little noise that turns out to be the universe snickering. That's when you need to duck, and fast.

When Phoebe got home after her adventure on the glacier she was surprised to find her therapist sitting on one of the sofas in the living room. *What have I done?* she thought in a panic. And then she remembered exactly what she'd done in the past few hours, and where she'd gone, and she almost shuddered with guilt. Thank goodness Sid had gone off with Rob, to sleep at his house.

Oddly enough, though, it seemed to be Sven, her therapist, and Jane, her mom, who looked most uncomfortable.

"Hey, kiddo," said Jane in a strained voice. "Sit down, why don'tcha, and let's talk."

Phoebe squinted, first at her mom, then at Sven. She slowly sat on the facing sofa and waited for it.

"Phoebe, hello," said Sven in that calm, reassuring voice of his, as smooth as sandalwood. He was *such* a hottie. "We've talked in our sessions about how things in life are always evolving and growing and changing."

Phoebe didn't like the sound of this.

"Yes?" she said.

"It's a process that governs all of life, really."

"In fact, it's a big part of what it means to be alive," said her mother with what looked like a forced smile.

"Exactly," said Sven, also smiling and nodding.

"Exactly," chimed in Jane, sort of idiotically.

"Yes?" said Phoebe with increasing suspicion.

"Phoebe," said Sven, "I'm afraid I can't be your therapist anymore."

Phoebe stood up. "*What?* Why not? What have I done?"

"Nothing, nothing—Phoebe, please, it's not you. I think we've made some wonderful progress together, and you can be very proud of all your hard work in therapy."

"But . . . ?" asked Phoebe.

"Sven and I . . ." Jane hesitated, then plunged forward. "You know that Sven and I were friends long before you started your sessions with him . . . and now we find our friendship has deepened."

"Your mother and I . . . Well, we want to start dating, Phoebe, and I can't be both your therapist and your mom's boyfriend. It wouldn't be right."

She sat down again, numbly. Boyfriend? As she looked at him, Sven was transforming right before her eyes from a hottie to an old hemp-clad man with a sloppy rope belt. This was almost more confusing than being transported to the last Ice Age.

143

"It's actually good news, right?" Jane said. "I mean . . ." Her voice trailed away.

Phoebe looked at the two of them wordlessly, and Jane tried a different tack.

"Listen—Sven has found you a really great new therapist!" she said.

"I think I've had enough therapy, thanks very much," said Phoebe icily.

"Phoebe, come on," Jane begged.

Phoebe shrugged. "It's just an example of how things in life are always evolving," she said, laying it on kind of thick.

"Hey, give us a break," said her mother.

"I think I want to be alone right now," said Phoebe, rising.

"Okay, okay," said Jane.

"We'll talk later," said Sven.

As Phoebe moved toward her bedroom, Jane was staring at a melting little white heap on the floor.

"Phoeb?" Jane said. "Is that snow?"

Phoebe's stomach did a backflip, but she just kept walking. "Snow?" she said indignantly. "*Snow?* How utterly ridiculous."

Later that night, Angela's mother called Donna's mother, who called Rob's mother, who knocked at Rob's bedroom door. Rob shouted, "I'm talking to Phoebe on the walkie!"

Lucy pushed open the door and said, "Great. Now you can talk to *me*, in person."

"Phoebe's quitting therapy, Mom—can *I*?"

The walkie-talkie squawked and Phoebe's voice crackled into the room. "*May* I," she said automatically.

"No," said Lucy to Rob, "you may not. Say goodbye and turn that thing off."

It seemed that Angela was sick in bed with a fever of 103

144

degrees, muttering stuff about mountains and monsters, and Mrs. Cruz was seriously worried about her.

"She didn't seem sick to me when you kids were all together in the Conoco," said Lucy. "Did she show any signs of coming down with something later?"

Rob, trying to hide the guilt he was feeling, said, "Well, she did kind of throw up a little in Billy Springer's lap."

"Wow," said Lucy. "Usually it's Billy Springer doing the puking."

"Actually, he threw up earlier, too."

"Oh, my God," said Lucy, suddenly horrified. "What if I poisoned you guys with those microwave pizzas?"

"Mom, you didn't."

Lucy anxiously felt Rob's forehead. "You're warm," she said. "Get into bed."

"Mom . . ."

"Do you feel nauseous?"

"No!"

"Get into bed anyway, and I'll bring you some hot tea."

"Mom, it's Saturday night!"

"What?" said Lucy sarcastically. "You were going dancing, maybe? Get to bed!"

Rob shook his head and said, "Mom, you are seriously weird."

"You think so?" she said. "Why don't you get back on that walkie-talkie thing and tell Phoebe I'm calling her mom—using the *telephone*, like *normal* people. I think you guys should all stay in this weekend—make sure you're all right."

Rob slammed his pillow with his fist. "God!"

Lucy stopped on her way out the bedroom door.

"Oh, yeah," she said. "I got a job. I start tomorrow night."

"If you let me quit therapy, you wouldn't have to get another job," said Rob.

"Nice try," she said as she walked away.

Rob opened the door to his bedroom closet and whispered angrily, "Thanks a lot, Sid!" The diictodon lay in a nest of towels. He blinked up at Rob, his eyes glittering, and he seemed to be trembling a little.

"Hey, buddy, are you okay?"

The creature nodded. "I'll be better in the morning," he wheezed.

And he did, in fact, seem to be himself the next day, so Rob decided not to worry.

★ ★ ★

Dr. Richard Jenkins gave a public lecture at the theater that Sunday night, when Rob and Phoebe and the others were, in essence, grounded. So they didn't have the shock of seeing Rob's mom, Lucy Gates, onstage with Jenkins, beginning her new job as his assistant. Quite a number of townspeople had showed up to listen. Jenkins was popular with the public ever since he'd shot the mountain lion.

The lecture was about the geological history of Faith and the possibilities of vast untapped mineral deposits beneath the town, which with today's new mining technology could generate huge profits. Jenkins was setting up a new corporation, Faith Mining Enterprises (or FAME), and the smart citizens would be the ones who got into the action now, merely by making available to him any old mining records they might still have—maps, deeds, titles, family records moldering away in safe deposit boxes, that sort of thing. By plotting these old mining claims, Jenkins, with today's technology, would be able to pinpoint many lodes of precious minerals that the old-timers had missed. The citizens of Faith wouldn't have to invest a dime.

Lucy Gates sat at a little table onstage with the forms people would fill out if they wanted in on the new enterprise and had records to share. Judging from the murmurs and frequent applause, the audience in the theater was eating it up. But one woman wasn't buying it.

Philippa Larson, the school librarian, stood up and cleared her throat. "Dr. Jenkins!" she said. "Excuse me, sir! Excuse me, but I have some questions for you!"

She was standing up in the fourth row, clutching a bunch of file folders to her breast, with papers dropping out of them and fluttering around her.

"Yes, ma'am?" said Jenkins uncertainly.

"Is it not true, sir," she went on, "that you are absent without leave from your position at the University of Texas, El Paso? Is it not true also that the authorities are even now searching for you? Is it not true that your work in paleontology has been held up to ridicule throughout the academic world?" Ms. Larson, trembling, dropped another sheaf of papers from her folders. A murmur spread through the audience, along with a few titters.

Jenkins cleared his throat and the house went silent. "Let me see," he drawled. "No, no, and yes and no."

Renewed murmurs and laughter.

"No, I am not absent without leave, and no, nobody is searching for me, leastwise not anymore. My colleagues at the university are well used to my sudden departures—my work often demands my presence around the globe at a moment's notice. There was a glitch in communications for a minute there, and some overzealous police officer got it into his head that I

147

needed finding, but I soon let them all know that I was found, found, found."

The audience laughed at this, and Ms. Larson turned several shades of red.

"Now then," continued Jenkins. "As to my standing among other so-called academics? Guilty as charged, sort of. There are some in this world who *do* respect the work of a pioneer when they see it, but there are always many others who are happier to offer ridicule than respect."

"Dr. Jenkins," said Ms. Larson, "forgive me, but there is a difference between a pioneer and a crackpot. You call yourself a geologist, and yet you claim to have evidence that the earth is only a few thousand years old and that human beings coexisted with dinosaurs and even older creatures, do you not?"

"I did, indeed, ma'am, and I'm sure there are others right here who believe as I did."

"I'm sure there are, and no disrespect," said Philippa, "but they're not miners, nor descended from miners. Those of us who are, those of us whose kin went down into the earth, know how very old this great earth is—they know *real* geology, not the made-up kind. It's not only how our fathers made their living; their very *lives* depended upon the science of geology."

An uncomfortable murmur went through the crowd. This was getting into tricky territory—couldn't the librarian just pipe down and let the man go on talking about how rich they were all going to be?

But Jenkins was unfazed. "You're not payin' close attention, ma'am," he said. "Those *were* my beliefs, once upon a time. I even wrote some papers and articles to the effect that the earth was thousands of years old instead of billions. Since then I have altered my views, ma'am. Experience has shown me my errors."

Philippa flushed red.

"Don't you worry about it, ma'am," he said, "I want to thank you for your interest. You've obviously been looking into my life and work, and I find that highly gratifying." A wave of titters spread throughout the house.

"Then you won't mind if I *continue* looking into your life and work, will you, Dr. Jenkins?" said Philippa defiantly.

For one brief moment, if the audience had been watching Jenkins closely, they would have seen the flicker of murderous rage that crossed his face. But they were watching Philippa Larson instead, wishing she'd go away.

"Ma'am, I respect your intellect," Jenkins said. "Folks, let's have a big hand for scientific curiosity!"

The whole audience responded. The poor librarian looked (and felt) like a nut job. She ducked down into her seat and gathered up her papers and folders from the floor. Clutching the papers tightly, she edged out of her row and stumbled out of the auditorium, to a huge round of applause.

★ ★ ★

Angela was home sick on Monday, but the other five got together as soon as they could, which turned out to be lunchtime at a table in the cafeteria.

"It all feels unreal," said Donna first thing. "I guess it actually happened, but when I think about us on that mountain, and the monster and Sid, and the avalanche, it feels like it's something I read in a book, you know what I mean?"

"Yeah," said Aran, "but when I took my shoes and socks off

149

Saturday afternoon, my toes were, like, frostbit, you know? You don't get frostbite from a book."

"And I tracked ice and snow into the house," said Phoebe, "and I had to pretend to my mom it just wasn't there."

Billy nodded and said, "It was weird, how long it took for that stuff to melt, but then I looked it up on the Internet and it's true—it takes longer to melt because the crystals in glacier ice are built different."

"Built differently," said Phoebe automatically.

Billy and Aran and Donna had each spent the weekend on their computers, checking out the creatures of the Permian era and reading about the terrible global extinction at the end of that period caused by greenhouse gases, melting ice caps, and worldwide warming. The extinction was so complete that scientists call it the Great Dying. Rob didn't have a functioning computer (he spent much of his life begging Lucy to replace their ancient, forever-crashing PC, but it never happened), and Phoebe and her mom didn't own one on principle—they'd had more than enough of computers with Phoebe's dad.

The gorgonopsid was very much on their minds. Donna had read that gorgonopsids were the main predators of the late Permian era.

"Yeah," said Aran. "And also just about the largest."

A momentary silence fell as they all internally reviewed their memories of the beast.

Once the kids started talking about Sid, though, they could hardly stop. They agreed that even though some of the artists' representations of what a diictodon might look like were pretty good, none of them captured the aliveness that radiated from him. To be in the same space with the synapsid was to be almost dizzy with life, with the pulsing surge of blood beneath the skin.

"He makes me feel like I'm on horseback, galloping," said Donna, her eyes looking off into some distant, horsey landscape of her soul. "There's the same rush or something—the wind, the pounding . . ." Her voice trailed away.

"Yeah," said Aran. "Or you're downhill skiing and no one's ever been on that snow before you."

"Or you just woke up in some kind of Garden of Eden," said Billy.

"It's his eyes that get me," Phoebe said. "They're so deep, they've seen so much."

"He makes me want to draw better. I don't know why," said Rob.

"Hey," said Aran, "all of us who met Sid and traveled in time can be, like, the Gang of Six!"

"Lame," said Rob.

"Feeble," said Donna.

"Sad, really," said Phoebe.

"Jerks," said Aran, trying not to laugh.

"Where is Sid?" Billy asked.

"He wanted to come to school with me," said Rob, "but I told him he couldn't."

"He's becoming completely reckless. It's not safe," said Phoebe.

"He was kind of quiet all weekend," Rob said. "I think he felt like he embarrassed himself in front of you guys, and he was definitely worried about Angela."

"Has anybody heard from her?" asked Donna, but no one had. They decided to meet after school and head to Angela's to say hi.

Just then, Ms. Larson approached, holding a sheaf of file folders.

"Phoebe? Robert?" she said. "Might I see you in the library, please?"

★ ★ ★

Ms. Larson sat at a library table, placed the folders in a neat stack in front of her, and with a nod and a hesitant smile, invited Rob and Phoebe to sit.

"You've been doing research," she said. "Well, so have I."

She glanced around almost furtively at the half dozen or so other students who were using the library. "I hope you won't think I'm just a busybody or a snoop. It's simply a part of my job nowadays, in the Internet era. Before I go home each night I have to check the history files of the three library computers; it's required of me, and it's *necessary*—as you doubtless know, there are aspects of the Web that can be distasteful at the least and even dangerous for young people, very dangerous. It's for your own protection. I hope you'll understand." She looked from Phoebe to Rob, and they both nodded soberly.

"All this . . . paleontological material . . ." Ms. Larson opened the file folder at the top of the stack and then the one beneath it. "It's fascinating, isn't it?"

Rob and Phoebe glanced silently at each other.

"I had no idea that the earth had come so close to total extinction. It makes one think about the earth *today,* and Antarctica melting and frogs and bees dying, and where will we be without *them,* and rain forests vanishing, and the only people who seem to be interested are Hollywood *movie* stars, but they and everybody else in America are driving these enormous cars, regular greenhouse-gas-mobiles, although I have heard some of them—movie stars, I mean—drive cars powered by vegetable oil, which is *something* at least, but what is anyone actually *doing* about any of it besides fiddling merrily while Rome burns to cinders?" Two spots of pink appeared on Philippa Larson's cheeks, and she blinked rapidly behind her bifocals.

The kids nodded, a little confused.

Ms. Larson took a deep breath and the two pink spots began to fade.

"Right now that's not my concern. It's all this material you've been gathering by and about Dr. Richard Jenkins that concerns me. I know that folks around here think he's the cat's flannel pajamas, but I frankly do not. All you have to do to make folks admire you is to tell them they're going to be rich, rich, rich. Well, this town was unfortunately founded by a bunch of confidence men who were promising basically the same thing back in the 1890s, and the only folks who got rich were a very few of the con men, and most of *them* ended up on Shotgun Hill with bullets in their backs." Shotgun Hill was the old name for the miners' cemetery above town.

"Didn't the early miners make absolute fortunes here?" asked Phoebe.

"No, they did not! They should have, for all the risk they took and the work they put in, but they didn't," said the librarian. "When they went to cash in on their claims, they found that most of them had already been bought up by a fellow named FitzHugh, just the year before. The miners of Faith eventually woke up to the fact that they weren't working for themselves, they were working for Patrick Mulcahy FitzHugh—they were tenants, as it were, instead of landowners. The millions of dollars in silver they dug out of the earth with their own toil and

153

sweat, and often at the cost of their lives, went straight into FitzHugh's bank account, while the laborers themselves didn't make much more than just a living. But that's not what I brought you here to talk about."

FitzHugh, thought Rob, doodling as he listened. *I've heard that name before. . . .*

Ms. Larson opened a third file folder, adjusted her bifocals on her long, thin nose, and scanned the pages of an article. "As for Dr. Jenkins. A person doesn't just up and disappear, not if he's respectable. He doesn't walk away from a professorship and show up in a remote town, which is what Faith is—I'm sorry, but there you have it—claiming to be doing research, and shooting what I'm convinced was a perfectly innocent mountain lion, and, according to a little-birdie friend of mine at the bank, setting up bank accounts all over the place! Something's wrong with this fellow, I just know it. I've decided to contact the authorities in El Paso; I've got an appointment to speak by phone with an officer there on Wednesday. Maybe I'm way out of line here, but I urge you not to trust this man."

"We don't," said Rob.

"We don't," said Phoebe.

Ms. Larson looked as though someone had just pulled the emergency brake cord on the train she was riding, and she came to a very abrupt stop.

"Oh," she said, sounding oddly disappointed. "Well. That's all right, then. It's just that when I found the two of you had been collecting a little dossier on this fellow, and then learned that he's actually hired your mother to be his assistant, well, I just had to put my sixteen cents in and hope you don't take offense, but I *had* to say something."

154

"Excuse me," said Phoebe.

"Pardon me," Rob said at the same time.

"Whose mother?" they both said in unison.

Ms. Larson looked at them in surprise. "Why, yours, Robert, *yours.*"

17
GOOD DOG/ BAD DOG

After school that day the Gang of Six (minus one) headed out to visit Angela. Rob and Phoebe were a little somber. For Rob's mom to be employed by Jenkins was so unthinkable, Rob could barely stand to talk about it.

Angela Cruz lived with her parents and two little sisters on the other side of the flume from the old opera house. Vidal Cruz worked for the Forest Service, and Nicoletta Cruz worked at the hotel. The whole family spoke English, Spanish, and Portuguese (because Mrs. Cruz's parents were Brazilian), making Angela the only trilingual student in Faith Middle School.

When the kids approached, Mrs. Cruz was hanging newly washed sheets on a clothesline and three-year-old Lily was toddling around her ankles, while Angela's snow-white pet goat, Whiskers, was cropping the stubby grass. Nicoletta looked up at them and gave them a wry smile. Whiskers bleated and trotted across the little yard to greet them personally.

"Hey, guys," said Mrs. Cruz. Lily ran to Phoebe and hugged her around her knees.

"Hey, Lily," said Phoebe, picking her up and holding her with one arm while stroking Whiskers' silky white fleece with the other. "Hey, Mrs. Cruz, how's Angela?"

"Better. She goes back to school tomorrow," said Nicoletta. "But honestly, guys, what *have* you been up to?"

The kids silently flicked glances at each other.

"Did you rent some horrible movie? Or were you trying to scare each other out of your heads with monster stories? 'Cause I'm here to tell you, it worked."

Angela appeared in the doorway, wearing a fluffy white bathrobe that contrasted beautifully with her jet black hair, or so thought Billy Springer.

"Mom," said Angela, "don't."

"Well, it's true, *mi'ja*. You were talking some pretty scary stuff when the fever was on you."

"I don't remember," she said, staring fixedly at her friends. "I don't remember anything."

"But you're feeling better?" asked Billy hopefully.

"I guess."

Mrs. Cruz picked up her half-full laundry basket and walked around to the side of the house, where there was a second clothesline.

"Can we come in for a minute?" Donna asked. "I brought you some romance novels in case you were still laid up."

"*Romance* novels?" said Aran with disgust.

"Donna," said Rob, picking up on Aran's cue, "we want Angela to feel better, we don't want to make her *sicker*."

"You are such an idiot, Rob," Donna said. "These are best sellers!"

"News flash, Angela," said Phoebe. "Rob hasn't gotten any less obnoxious since you saw him last."

"I don't remember when I saw him last," said Angela, just a little bit zombielike, and the Gang went suddenly quiet.

"Angela, sure you do," said Phoebe gently after a moment.

"No, I don't," said Angela woodenly.

"Hey," said Billy, grinning shyly, "you remember *me,* don't you? Billy Springer? I pulled you off the glacier?"

"I want you all to go now," Angela said, her eyes brimming, and Billy turned even whiter than he always was and looked like he was about to sink into the earth then and there.

"Hey, we're your friends, Angela," said Aran.

"Mom!" shouted Angela.

"Come on, Ange," Rob pleaded, "what's up?"

Lily, sensing her sister's distress, started to cry, and even Whiskers the goat started bleating. Nicoletta Cruz came around the side of the home at a trot, her face creased with concern.

"Mi'ja!" she cried, and ran to her daughter and put her arms around her. "You guys go on now," she said. "You're good kids, I know you are, but you gotta stop scaring each other, okay?"

Rob started to protest. "But we didn't try to—"

"Just go!" said Mrs. Cruz, and Phoebe put Lily down, who ran to her mother and clung to her legs, and Whiskers raised her white-bearded face and let out a piteous bleat. The Gang of Six (minus one) left, feeling highly depressed.

Billy walked with the knuckles of both hands pressed hard against his forehead.

"I made her cry. I can't believe I made her cry," he moaned as they crossed the bridge over the flume.

"It wasn't you," said Donna. "She's just not herself."

"Maybe it was too much for her, traveling in time like that, and she just had to block it out," offered Phoebe.

"What's up with that?" said Aran. "I can't wait to go somewhere with Sid again."

"Bull," said Rob. "You were scared stupid on that glacier."

"You're full of it, Rob, I was not!"

"Do you two think you two could possibly stifle all that?" said Phoebe grimly. "Here comes trouble."

Sid was racing toward them up Willow for all the world to see. At the same time, Chad Scudder and Arabella Giddens were just coming out of the diner, opening bags of chips.

Phoebe sprinted toward the synapsid, followed by the others.

"Hullo, hullo," said Sid, "what's all this then? How's Angela?"

Phoebe crouched down beside the creature and whispered in his left ear, "Have you gone nuts? People will see you!"

She scooped Sid up into her arms and carried him like you'd carry a pet.

"Bad dog!" she said in a loud voice as Chad and Arabella stared. "Naughty dog!"

"I beg your pardon?" said Sid indignantly.

"Be quiet!" hissed Phoebe. Arabella was pointing at her and Sid, and Phoebe assumed they'd been busted totally. The others had gathered round her by now, and she looked at them helplessly.

"They've seen Sid. What do we do now?" she whispered, but then Arabella and Chad burst out laughing.

"Bad *dog*?" said Arabella. "Try *bad hair day*!" Chad and Arabella moved off, digging into their bags of chips.

"I never saw anything like it!" Chad said, trying to chew and laugh at the same time, and spraying potato chip bits all over.

"Score another one for the Earth Mother!" said Arabella.

It was only then that Phoebe realized her arms, holding Sid, were vibrating, and her thick blond braid was standing straight up from her head like a flagpole.

Rob clapped Phoebe on her shoulder as Arabella and Chad disappeared round a corner. "That was incredibly lucky," he said. "You were great."

"You think?" said Phoebe, still cradling Sid in her left arm and trying unsuccessfully with her right hand to pull her braid down.

"Excuse me . . . ," said Sid, but no one paid any attention.

Aran and Billy and Donna offered Phoebe their congratulations, too, and everybody wanted to touch her upright braid, and Rob said, "Honest, Phoeb, I think you've finally found your look," so Phoebe finally had to laugh.

"Excuse me, my dears," said Sid in a strained voice, "I am delighted you're all having such a fine time, but I'm afraid I can't hold on much longer."

"What do you mean, Sid?" Aran started to say . . . but before he even got to the question mark they were all engulfed in color and noise and a great rushing wind.

★ ★ ★

"Oh, dear," said the synapsid.

The five kids stood knee-deep in a shallow icy stream, Phoebe still holding Sid in her arms. After the first instant of total shock, they were dancing with the cold and the wet. Sid jumped down out of Phoebe's arms and they all scrambled up onto the bank of the stream with a lot of grunts and cries, their sneakers making squelching noises. They found themselves shivering in a muddy lane that ran between the stream and the backside of a ragged row of one- and two-story wooden buildings. On the other side of the creek was a stand of massive weeping willow trees, trailing their branches down into the water.

"I am never gonna get used to this," said Billy.

"Where are we?" asked Donna. "It looks a little like Faith, or at least the mountains do."

"Oh, it's Faith all right—but when?" said Phoebe.

Aran looked up at the willow trees on the opposite shore. "Maybe this is how Willow Street got its name!"

"Of course it is," snapped Sid huffily. "Names aren't just arbitrary sounds, names *mean* something."

"Is this what the flume used to be?" asked Billy, nodding toward the little stream they'd just emerged from.

"Oh, I think it just might be," said Rob, stomping his sneakers to make the water squirt out, "since it's one of Sid's very *favorite* places to land."

Sid snorted and said nothing.

"Sid, let me ask you," Rob said, enjoying himself immensely. "Has anything *ever* worked out the way you planned? *Ever?*"

"I didn't plan this! I didn't ask to be picked up, and I didn't ask to be chided like some errant *pooch,*" he said indignantly, his dark eyes flashing between Phoebe and Rob. "But no, dear Robert and Phoebe, this is not entirely a mistake—we are precisely where and when I *would* have brought you next had I been given the chance in the *normal* way of things, thank you very much."

"Sorry, Sid," said Phoebe, "but there were people looking at you—I had to do something. And okay, I'm sorry, but what exactly do you consider to be the *normal* way of things?"

All Phoebe got by way of an answer was another irritated diictodon snort.

In the gaps between the few buildings, the kids could see a muddy, rutted dirt road that ran up through the middle of the village. Smoke rose from tin chimneys, and there was an acrid, burning smell in the air. A few mules and a couple of old sway-backed horses were tied to hitching posts that lined the road. A building on the opposite side of the road had a painted wooden sign above the door: WILLOW CREEK TRUST & DEED.

"That's the bank," said Sid. "In 1890 the town was called Willow Creek, not Faith, although they might as well have called it Blind Hope, which was the only thing the place had going for itself. At this moment the town consists of little more than a handful of prospectors hoping to strike it rich, but so far no one has. We're standing behind the saloon, which was almost the first thing they built here."

Peering between the ramshackle buildings, they saw two prospectors emerge from what seemed to be a general store, carrying bulging burlap sacks. They moved with a weary stoop to two of the mules. The men were scarecrow skinny, their hair was matted, and their beards were grizzled and streaked with gray.

"That's Lemuel Parsons and his brother, Willis," said Sid.

The kids looked at Sid blankly.

"Wynola and Adelaide Parsons' great-grandfather and great-grand-uncle," said the diictodon.

The two men stuffed the burlap sacks into the saddlebags on their mules and then crossed in their direction, toward the saloon.

"In less than a year, those two and a couple of others will discover vast silver deposits in those mountains. This whole place will explode. Suddenly there'll be ten or fifteen thousand here, digging like maniacs. They'll put up an opera house, and a bawdy house, and a few more saloons. They'll rename the town

Faith, which was old Jeremiah Sweet's mother's name—I believe you know her great-great-granddaughter, Philippa Sweet Larson? Jeremiah Sweet and the Parsons brothers will be among the first to stake claims, but it will already be too late."

"What do you mean, it'll be too late?" said Rob.

"Because there's a fellow who's here in town right now, buying up every piece of land where the silver will be discovered."

A sharp bark startled them all. They turned and saw a yellow labrador across the stream chase a squirrel into tree. The squirrel raced safely up to a branch and sat there scolding, while the flea-bitten dog danced and barked furiously below.

Suddenly the rear door of the saloon swung open. "Hide!" hissed Sid. He ducked into a woodshed nearby, and the kids followed.

A young woman, about seventeen years old, pushed through the swinging door, carrying a large tin pan. She stepped gingerly through the mud down to the edge of the stream and threw what looked like a panful of dirty dishwater into the water.

"That's Lemuel Parsons' daughter, Serenity," Sid whispered. "Since her mother died, she's had to manage their household, cook and clean for the saloon, and raise her younger brother, all by herself."

"She's beautiful," whispered Donna. "She looks like Adelaide looks in those old pictures in Town Hall."

At that moment, Serenity headed for the woodshed.

The kids and Sid scurried to the rear of the shed, each one scrambling to find a hiding place behind the stacks of firewood. The young woman entered and stopped suddenly, silhouetted by the daylight behind her. She stared into the dim slatted light of the woodshed. The kids held their breath.

Then Serenity set the large tin pan on the floor and began

filling it with kindling and small logs. She picked it up again and left, and everyone exhaled.

Aran put his hand on Sid's shoulder to get his attention, and Sid said, "Careful, son."

"Oh, right," said Aran, quickly withdrawing his hand, which had already begun to vibrate. "How do you know what's happening here?"

"Because it was happening the last time I came here, Aran, a moment or so before I first met you at the ball field. I wanted you to see it for yourselves, so here we are."

The kids' faces showed the strain of trying to understand it all, and Sid responded with diictodonic frustration.

"Time gets *snagged,* I keep telling you. Everything that ever happened is still happening . . . Oh, never mind, just try not to think too much."

"Excuse me," said Phoebe. "I think somebody's spotted us."

The yellow lab stood on the opposite bank of the stream, his nose working, his sharp eyes focused on the woodshed. He advanced slowly to the edge of the water, his head sunk low, sniffing all the while. His upper lip lifted in a menacing ripple, revealing his teeth, and they could hear, even from where they were, a low growl.

"Oh, dear," said Sid. "There's something I want you to see, and it's not this pesky dog. You need to witness it because then you'll understand much more of what this is all about."

The yellow lab lifted his head sharply and cocked his ears. A dog's version of doubt furrowed his face. He tilted his head to one side, then the other. He stopped growling and his tongue came out, panting.

"I'm not sure," said Donna, "but I have a feeling Old Yeller likes us." The dog's tail had begun to wag slowly, tentatively. He trotted forward toward the stream, stopped, sniffed again, and looked keenly across at them. Then his tail went mad with wagging, and the yellow lab was racing eagerly back and forth at the water's edge, glancing down at the water with just a bit of apprehension.

"There it is," said Sid. "There's the joy gene kicking in."

The yellow lab took a running leap, splashing into the flume, swimming earnestly, head up, and then crawling up out of it onto the bank. He waited until he was in the woodshed with them before he shook himself off, splattering them all with icy water. Then he jumped all over them in a state of total dog ecstasy.

"Bark! Bark! Bark! Bark!" said the yellow lab, and Sid said, "Hush, son!" The dog immediately stopped barking, but the rest of him was still going kind of nuts. He hopped and leapt and thrust his black nose into their crotches and up to their faces and generally slobbered all over them, but always came back to Sid, who seemed to be his favorite.

"The joy gene?" said Phoebe.

"As you see," said Sid, watching the capering lab. "The joy gene comes in a direct line from we diictodons, I'm proud to say."

"From us diictodons," Phoebe said automatically, and Sid's eyebrows went up. (He didn't have eyebrows, *per se*, but it was like that).

"Really?" he said. "Funny, it doesn't sound right. Never mind. It's a big part of our quest, to ensure that the joy gene survives the Permian so that hundreds of millions of years later you mammals can inherit it, you humans especially, so you won't be quite as entirely murderous as you might have been, or might become. It runs purest, of course, in the common dog, but humans have a bit of it, and it would be just about disastrous if they didn't."

By now the yellow lab was challenging the others to play, darting at the kids and going into that "I dare you" stance that dogs do with his front end low and his rear end high, with a tail like a metronome set at *accelerando.* Sid heaved a fond sigh.

"It's a wonderful gene," he said. "There's the anti-joy gene, too, of course. And the mine-all-mine gene, the grabber gene, and the awful snapper gene. Your scientists haven't isolated them yet, and when they do they'll give them other, more scientific names, I suppose, but that's what I call them. When they do locate the joy gene, they'll probably try to sell it in pill form, and people will pay money to buy what they already have in them. You humans are actually enough to break an old diictodon's heart."

Sid looked so sad all of a sudden that Rob reached down to pet him sympathetically, and then jerked his hand back when it started to tremble.

"Right," said the diictodon. "The bank's just across the way, and its windows are open. If we can make it across the road without attracting attention, you'll be able to hear it all, I think. I have a feeling there's a transaction going on right now in the bank that I want you to witness."

"Too late, old-timer! It's already done."

A man in his forties stood in the opening of the woodshed, pointing a rifle at them. Serenity Parsons hid just behind him. The man's hair was thin and black and slicked back, and he looked like he wanted to sell you something.

Rob and Phoebe gasped, and the yellow lab growled.

"Jenkins!" whispered Rob.

"You got the wrong fella, son. I'm Patrick Mulcahy FitzHugh, and I'd like to know what you all are doing scaring my friend Serenity."

The young woman touched Jenkins' shoulder and pointed to the very back of the shed. "What is *that*?" she whispered.

Jenkins took a moment, still smiling. "Turtle, honey," he said. "Big dumb snapping turtle, crawled up outta the stream. These kids must have found him. Listen, darling, I want you to run back into the saloon and get some food into your pappy and his brother before they head back up the mountain, y'hear? There's nothing to be scared of here."

Serenity looked doubtful.

"Git!" said Jenkins sharply, and Serenity left. Then he turned back to the time travelers.

"You brought the kids!" said Jenkins to Sid pleasantly. "What fun!" His gaze rested on Rob. "Travel expands one's horizons, don't you think, little buddy?"

The yellow lab's low growl turned into an angry snarl.

"Shut that dog up and do it quick, or I'll shoot him."

"Hush, boy!" said Sid. The lab's snarl became a suppressed whine.

"How do you like my new lady friend?" said Jenkins. "I promised to take her away from all this, give her a new life, and she bought it! Sadly, I'm going to have to leave her for a spell. Got unfinished business back where you came from."

Sid padded forward. "How did you come by your new identity?"

Jenkins looked at the kids and shook his head. "Don't it just creep you out when they *talk*?" he said.

"How?" said Sid.

"Tragic, really," said Jenkins. "Seems there was a young fella out here from the East Coast, little Irish guy, looking to make his fortune. Lost his identity papers moments before he went off one of these here cliffs above us. Sad, sad, sad."

"Murderer!" said Phoebe.

"Don't like that word, missy. Don't use it again, y'hear?"

The yellow lab's hackles rose and he bared his teeth, his entire body trembling. Suddenly a terrible stench filled the woodshed. Phoebe screamed and pointed.

The Gorgon stood just outside the shed. He opened his vast mouth and belched, and the odor was awful.

"You can't take this one *anywhere*," drawled Jenkins. "But he takes me *everywhere*!"

Jenkins turned to the Gorgon. "No snacks, handsome, not this time—you behave."

The gorgonopsid hesitated, then slowly turned and dragged his massive tail toward the stream.

"Come on out here where I can see y'all." Jenkins motioned with his rifle, and the kids moved out of the shed, followed by Sid.

"I feel like celebrating!" said Jenkins. "I just went from being a low-paid teacher to a rich silver baron!"

Just then the Gorgon turned and lunged, fast as a snake, right at Rob's ankles. Rob stumbled and fell, and was scrambling frantically backward on his butt when suddenly the yellow lab was right there above the boy, snarling and snapping fearlessly at the beast's snout. The Gorgon recoiled a bit, surprised, and Sid was on the monster in a flash, his tusks coming down like spikes on the Gorgon's flank. The Gorgon yowled. That's when Jenkins hissed, *"Heel!"* with a viciousness that made the kids all take a step backward.

To everyone's wonder, the gorgonopsid *did* heel, eventually creeping back to the stream like a whipped cur.

It paused on the bank, its entire body quivering, and then it spoke to Jenkins in a low voice, barely audible. "Heel?" said the Gorgon. The kids all shuddered to hear it speak. *"Heel?"*

"You got a problem with that?" said Jenkins. "If so, go on back to your own era with this old fool and die out with all the rest of them."

The Gorgon's massive head turned back toward Sid for just a moment, and then he slipped back into the water. There he swam in slow serpentine circles, his ghastly yellow eyes eyeing Jenkins all the while.

"You can't tame him," said Sid, breathing heavily and addressing Jenkins.

"Seems to me I already have," Jenkins replied. "He likes the menu hereabouts. He's fond of dog, he's fond of goat, and he's just crazy about horse."

Jenkins turned his grin on Donna and Phoebe.

"I got a number of other properties I'm interested in purchasing, so him and me, we're gonna be doing a lot of traveling together."

"No, you won't!" Rob suddenly shouted, advancing toward Jenkins. "Don't you understand? You won't even exist! None of us will!"

Jenkins laughed. "I don't like you, son," he said with a big, amiable grin. "From the bottom of my heart, I just don't."

"The boy is right," said the synapsid. "You and all this world of mammals may end up nothing more than the dream of an elderly diictodon, two hundred and fifty million years ago."

"Don't like you either, Gramps, frankly, but you and your smelly friend are coming in *very* handy," said the man.

"Handily," said Phoebe, reflexively, and Jenkins raised his eyebrows.

"Child," he said, "you are simply *strange*." He snapped his fingers. "Come!"

The Gorgon swam sullenly to Jenkins' side of the stream, and Jenkins knelt beside the water.

"Whew! Somebody here needs a little deodorant!" The yellow eyes flicked up at him, but Jenkins didn't seem to notice. He reached out with one hand and stroked the back of the Gorgon's hideous head. The level of the stream rose, and the water turned to steam—clouds of it—and Jenkins, staring at Sid, said, "Last one out, turn the lights off!"

A beastly bellow pierced the air, and man and monster were gone.

The kids stood where they were, dazed and overwhelmed by it all. Finally Billy broke the silence.

"My folks are gonna kill me if I'm late for supper."

Sid glanced at Billy and said drily, "Noted."

"What does it mean, Sid?" asked Phoebe. "Jenkins is using the Gorgon so he can travel in time and buy property?"

"Past tense, Phoebe!" said Rob hotly. "He already did it! And it worked! He bought the mountains that all the silver came out of over a century ago!"

"Just now, you mean," said Phoebe, but Rob ignored her.

"And all the people who ever lived in Faith, all the miners, like my dad and his dad, and Adelaide and Wynola's dad and granddad, they were just working for him! He's the man who owns Faith, and now all he's got to do is go back to the present and get his millions out of the bank. He won!"

"We can't rewrite the whole history of Faith, Sid, can we?" asked Phoebe. "If we could stop him, if we could change that history somehow, is there any guarantee that a person named Phoebe Traylor would even be born? Or Rob, or any of us?"

Sid seemed to sag, looking suddenly old and tired. His big dark eyes were focused on the yellow lab. "I don't know," he admitted. He coughed a deep, rumbling cough.

"In my old heart I feel certain of this," Sid said after a moment. "If we don't change the course of that foolish, grasping man's

170

particular history, the Gorgon will never get back to the Permian, and neither will I. We're running out of time—did you *see* that gorgonopsid? He's not well, believe me." In a whisper he added, "And neither am I."

Phoebe said quietly, "We know."

Sid looked from Phoebe to Rob and slowly nodded.

"If the synapsid line dies out utterly, there will be no history for any of you—for any of your ancestors or descendants, or any other mammal who ever might have lived."

The yellow lab yawned widely and wetly, with a little contented sigh.

Sid seemed to take strength from the sight of the dog. Smiling to himself, he said in a strong voice, "Well, we're not going to let that happen. Come, children. We're going home." He extended one of his paws toward the dog. "You too. Come!"

The yellow lab looked up and grinned. Then his eyes got very big and he started to tremble.

18
TEST, TEST, TEST

When Rob got home that night with Sid and the yellow lab, he quietly guided his two four-legged friends into the crawl space beneath his house. Rob sneaked a couple of old bowls out there for the dog, filling one with water and the other with cut-up wieners from the fridge. For Sid, he brought a couple of onions, a favorite of the diictodon. After they both ate, the dog and the diictodon quietly bedded down for the night.

Rob ate supper with his mom, pretty much in silence.

"What is it, Rob?"

"Your new job. Jenkins is no good, Mom."

"How would you know?" countered Lucy.

"I just know."

"Listen, kiddo, it's a paycheck, nothing more. I've had plenty of bosses I didn't particularly like, okay? And so will you, most likely. So you just try to do your job and pay your bills."

"Mom, what if . . ." Rob hesitated. "What if he's a *really* bad man? Like, say, if he was a thief or a murderer or something?"

"What?" cried Lucy.

"Then would you quit?"

"A *murderer*?"

"Just quit, Mom, okay?"

Lucy stood, opened the window above the kitchen sink, and lit a cigarette, blowing the smoke outside. This generally wasn't a good sign, in Rob's experience, so he just stood there and waited for it.

"Mrs. Barnett thinks you should be seeing her twice a week instead of just once," Lucy said, "and I think she's right."

Rob's face reddened. "Mom, I'm not crazy!"

"Of course you aren't . . ."

"The more I try to tell you the truth, the worse trouble I get into."

"Therapy isn't trouble, honey," Lucy said gently, "it's help."

"Oh, God!" Rob shouted. "I wish Dad was still here!"

There was a silence between them, Lucy staring out into the night. She turned on the tap at the sink and doused her cigarette, and put it in the trash.

"Well," she said finally, turning to him, "he's not. I'm all you've got. Sorry about that."

Rob got up from the table and stalked into his room, slamming the door behind him.

The following morning Lucy Gates could still hear the sound of Rob's bedroom door slamming shut. It was barely 7:00 A.M. and she was opening mail at the little storefront Jenkins had rented on Main, trying at the same time to figure out where the nasty smell was coming from. The shop was on the ground floor of an otherwise vacant two-story building, sandwiched between the theater on one side and the post office on the

173

other. FAME was doing a very brisk business. Townspeople and others from down in the Valley had brought in old family deeds, tattered old prospecting maps, and diaries from the 1890s. In return, they would have a share in any new mineral claims that were discovered—at least according to Jenkins they would.

Jenkins himself had just come in with a cup of coffee from the diner, flicking on his computer and sitting in front of the monitor with a preoccupied look on his face. Lucy knew better than to speak or even say good morning when her new boss looked like that, so she just opened another letter, spread it out on the desk before her, and adjusted her reading glasses.

Wynola and Adelaide Parsons, passing on the street outside, peered in through the plate-glass window and waved, and Lucy waved back at them. Then she realized the old twins were motioning her to come out, with nods and winks. Lucy glanced at her boss, who was still engrossed, and slipped out the door onto Main Street.

"It's him!" Adelaide whispered excitedly with a significant tilt of the head. "It's him!"

Lucy smiled cautiously, wondering what Adelaide was talking about.

"We finally found him, in the Argento County title and deed office."

"We took the bus," added Wynola.

"We'd looked there before, of course, but always for records of FitzHugh, not Jenkins."

Lucy was thoroughly confused.

"As soon as we asked the clerk to search for Jenkins, he came up with a Richard Jenkins, who claimed P. M. FitzHugh as his pen name!"

"Pen name, my fanny!" said Adelaide. Lucy looked from one old sister to the other, totally confused.

"Anyway," said Wynola, glancing through the window at the man inside, "that man in there—that's our grandpa."

Oh, golly, thought Lucy.

"Not a nice man, alas!" said Adelaide, also shaking her head. "He's got a lot to answer for." She took her sister's arm, and the two old ladies moved off. "Have a happy day, dear!"

Those two are getting seriously batty, Lucy thought as the twins walked slowly away. She went back into the shop and took a seat at her desk. Jenkins' chair scraped on the floor, and Lucy looked up to see him staring intently at his screen. She heard him curse very softly, under his breath. He moved the mouse rapidly over the pad and stared again.

"Lucy," he said, switching off the computer, "that woman who spoke up at the meeting the other night. Who is she again?"

"Philippa Larson? She's the librarian at the middle school."

"A librarian, of course. That explains the amount of research she'd done. Always on the Internet, I suppose," said Jenkins.

"When she's not hiking. And she's a big reader—there's nobody in Faith reads as much as Philippa. She just *loves* Shakespeare."

"Who doesn't?" said Jenkins with a thin smile. "Single woman?"

"Yes," said Lucy.

"Does she have any family?"

"Well, not anymore, but the Larsons were one of the oldest mining families in Faith. They were here from the very beginning, along with the Sweets and the Parsons. Why?"

Jenkins looked at her sharply, then relaxed his features and smiled.

"I'd like to win her over," he said finally. "If a person with her

175

family credentials was to endorse me—especially after the ruckus she raised at that meeting—that would be a real thumbs-up, wouldn't you say?"

"I guess."

"I'm gonna do it," he said, standing and grabbing his cup of coffee. "Where can I find her?"

"Well, this time of day," said Lucy, "Philippa's likely not at school yet for another half hour. She's probably on her morning walk up the mountain."

Jenkins nodded thoughtfully and then he was gone. Lucy pushed back from her desk and moved to the rear door, the one overlooking the flume. She had already checked the garbage cans behind the building that morning, but the foul odor wasn't coming from them. She crunched across the gravel to the theater loading dock. Unpainted set pieces for Faith Rep's upcoming production of Shakespeare's *The Tempest* stood just inside the massive doors. Two big Dumpsters held the discarded set of the Rep's last production, a Wild West melodrama. She stood on tiptoe, peering into the big bins. The odor didn't seem to be coming from the Dumpsters (although Lucy and Rob had seen the show and thought it stank).

The loading dock door at the rear of the theater was open, and Lucy put her head into the dark interior.

"Hi," she said, "anybody home?"

★ ★ ★

Philippa Larson hadn't gone for her mountain walk as usual that morning, but had walked briskly from her two-room suite in the Faith Hotel directly to school. She let herself in with her

176

passkey a little after 6:00 A.M. She went straight to the library and sat down before one of the computers and switched it on.

While it booted up she took a piece of soggy, buttered toast from a plastic bag in her purse and munched on it with a preoccupied look in her eyes. The answers to her inquiries had been coming in all week: two of the three universities on Dr. Richard Jenkins' posted resume had reported either no record of such a student or that Jenkins had attended for a semester or two and dropped out. He clearly had gotten his job at the university in El Paso under false pretenses—but what did that matter to her, Philippa Larson? So the man was a fraud—she'd already suspected *that*.

But then she'd seen something that alarmed her on the Internet news the night before, as she was closing up the library. A body had been discovered in a dried-up riverbed on a remote ranch forty miles south of El Paso, Texas. The corpse was badly decomposed, making identification difficult. It could have been anyone, Philippa had told herself. So why did the article connect in her mind with Jenkins, "up from El Paso"?

She'd barely slept all night, and now she was back to see if the story, and her suspicions, could possibly be true.

The screen came to life, Ms. Larson pressed a few keys with buttery fingers, and a page came up that she read and reread. The story had been updated: dental records confirmed that the body was that of a professor from the University of Texas, El Paso. The man's name was Dr. Jerome Nathan, and he'd made an impression in the scientific community through his invention of a device he had called a *zoological spectrometer,* or zoospec.

Dr. Jerome Nathan had gone missing in March. Just before Jenkins showed up in Faith.

Philippa hit the print button and stuffed the last of the toast into her mouth.

"I need my walk," she said to herself as she pulled the story from the printer. "I need the mountain. I need to think."

★ ★ ★

Phoebe and Jane Traylor were on horseback, riding Junior and a mare named Lucky Girl slowly over the mountain in the early light of day (Sally May was still recuperating). When Phoebe had come home the night before from her trip to early Faith, she had found her mother waiting for her. Jane hadn't asked her daughter any questions as she reheated her supper, despite a strange, far-off look in Phoebe's eyes. Instead she proposed a plan: they'd get up at dawn like they used to, and ride and talk.

It turned out to be a glorious spring dawn, and the slanting, pink long-shadowed light touched mother and daughter and horses and mountain gently. It was healing, as Jane had meant it to be.

"I can't lose you, Phoeb," she said after one of their long silences. "Someday I know I'll have to give you up and let you go, but I won't be *losing* you—I'll be watching you blossom and bloom and take flight and any number of dumb metaphors like that, and it'll be a good thing."

Phoebe nodded but didn't speak.

"I wonder if you feel like I'm trading you in for Sven, or something like that."

They rode in silence for a few moments, the horses' footfalls on the trail the only sound. "Are you two getting married?" Phoebe asked quietly.

"I don't know. Maybe someday. We care for each other a lot. But for now, we've decided to put things on hold for a while. I want to get things straight with you before I move in any other direction."

Phoebe thought that over for a while, the horses' hooves making their comforting steady *clop* on the rising mountain trail. "You don't have to do that, Mom. You don't have to stop seeing Sven because of me. You've been really lonely, I know that. I don't want you to be lonely."

"If I felt separated or estranged from you in any way, nothing and no one in the world would cure the loneliness I'd feel."

They were riding single file, with Phoebe and Junior in the lead, so Jane didn't see Phoebe's private smile. Her mom had said the absolute right thing. The castle was rebuilding itself again, miraculously, and soon she and Jane would be safe again in the castle keep. Maybe there'd even be room for Sven there—she didn't know yet.

"Your dad called," said Jane finally, and Phoebe's smile vanished. She turned around and gave her mother a questioning look.

"Honest, it wasn't me calling him, he placed the call."

Phoebe faced forward again. "What did he want?"

"He's suggesting you spend a couple weeks with him and his family as soon as school's out—they're going on a cruise up to Alaska."

"Mom, I can't go to Alaska, I can't go anywhere until—" Phoebe broke off.

"Until what, honey?"

"There's just . . . stuff I have to do."

They rode again in silence.

"Is it to do with this . . . creature?" Phoebe was silent. "Tell me again about him, Phoebe. What did you call him? Sid? Please. I want to try to open my mind to it all."

"That's just it, Mom. When I try to talk about it, even to myself, it sounds completely crazy. *I'd* send myself to therapy, I really would."

"Therapy isn't about being crazy, Phoeb," said Jane. "Therapy is for everybody. Therapy is . . . therapy is better than college!"

Phoebe laughed.

"Mom," she said, twisting round on her horse, "*you're* crazy, actually."

"I beg your pardon!"

"Of course you are! Everyone in town has said so for as long as I can remember."

"You're kidding," said Jane. "Really? *Me?*"

And Phoebe laughed again because her mom looked so innocent and astonished. "Yeah, but you know—crazy in a good way."

That's when they heard the cry. It was very brief, cut off, but Phoebe and Jane both reined in their horses and listened. Was it a bird's shrill call? Or a woman's scream?

There was nothing but silence. Without a word to each other, they urged the horses carefully forward, toward the summit.

★ ★ ★

Lucy walked through the theater set shop, which was deserted. The clean smell of sawdust on the floor was mingled with something else, a nasty, rotten-sweet odor. *There's a trash bin in here somewhere they've forgotten to empty,* thought Lucy. *It's got the leftovers from somebody's lunch in it, a chicken carcass or something like that, and it's gone bad.* She heard voices and passed an open door and saw where everybody was: the shop staff and technicians were ranged around a conference table in the middle of a breakfast meeting concerning their upcoming production of *The Tempest.* Lucy decided she didn't need to interrupt them. She'd locate the offending trash and dispose of it herself.

A sharp, rank draft suddenly eddied down from the spiral iron staircase before her. *Gotcha,* thought Lucy as she started to climb the steps.

★ ★ ★

Phoebe and Jane Traylor dismounted and let their horses graze among the large upright stones at the topmost ridge of Stair-Master. It was the very spot where Mickie Pine had nearly shot Rob, where Phoebe and Rob had first encountered the Last Synapsid face to face and heard him speak.

The breeze up here was brisk. Below them, all of Faith was laid out like a toy town, and beyond the town the land fell away to the broad valley and the winding dark green line of the great river. As Phoebe looked out over the scene, she remembered her glimpse of Faith when the mines were teeming with workers. She remembered the Faith that had existed a year *before* the silver had been discovered, when the tiny settlement had been called Willow Creek. She remembered how it had looked when there were no people whatsover, when mastodons and bison roamed here by the tens of thousands. She remembered how, even earlier, the Ice Age glacier had filled the valley to a depth of hundreds of feet, when there had been nothing in this whole world that wasn't brilliantly, blindingly white. She wondered how many more Faiths there had been, stretching back into the unimaginable past.

"So what was it?" said Jane finally.

"What?" said Phoebe, lost in thought.

"The noise, or the scream, or whatever it was," said Jane. "Remember?"

181

"Oh, yeah—sorry. A bird, probably, I guess."

"What is it, honey? What's wrong?"

"Nothing." She hesitated. "Mom, the world is a miracle, don't you think?"

"Sure is, Phoeb," Jane said, wondering what was going on in her daughter's mind.

"I don't want it to die," said Phoebe quietly.

Jane moved to her daughter and put an arm around her. "No, honey, of course not. The world isn't going to die, Phoeb."

"You can't take that for granted, Mom. There are people who are willing to kill it. And for such stupid reasons."

Phoebe continued to stare out over the Valley, and Jane with her. Neither of them noticed the single sheet of computer print-out paper that the breeze carried along the mountain's crest and off, eddying into the air, spinning and dipping with the currents of wind.

"Come on, kiddo," said Jane. "It's time for school."

★ ★ ★

Lucy Gates was in a pitch-black room, groping frantically for a way out.

She had reached the top of the spiral staircase only to find herself in a narrow corridor that led inexplicably to another, shorter spiral staircase. *This old monster of a building has to have been designed by a madman,* she was thinking as she climbed the second senseless set of stairs. These brought her out onto a little iron-railed gallery, set into the brick wall, that gave a view of the stage, about twenty feet below. Unfinished portions of the set for *The Tempest* were in place;

wooden staircases and ramps that the audience wouldn't see were hidden behind theatrical flats. The deserted stage, lit by a single work light, had a desolate feel.

The foul odor came and went with the drafts of air that swirled down from the heights of the fly loft above. Lucy suddenly felt foolish. *What am I doing here?* she asked herself. *The theater staff can clean up its own mess, whatever it is.* Just as she was about to turn around and retrace her steps, an iron door swung open right behind her, as though a downdraft had pushed it ajar.

Lucy hesitated, then stepped across the threshold. Instantly she found herself in darkness and surrounded by an unspeakable stench.

"Oh, God!" she gagged, one hand over her mouth and nose, but as she tried to back out, the door sagged shut again with a clang, and the blackness was suddenly complete. Panic rose in her like a rocket. She groped for a door handle and couldn't find one, she groped for a light switch and couldn't find one, and the foul air pressed on her all the while like a sodden pillow over her face.

A musical, deep voice from the darkness said, "Finding everything you need?" Lucy just about jumped out of her skin. She whirled around to face the voice, but the voice was faceless and there was no such thing as light.

"Hey diddle dee dee," the voice continued, "an actor's life for me." Then it laughed quietly.

Lucy could see nothing, but she didn't dare turn her back on the voice. Instead she put her hands behind her, feeling the wall, feeling for the door.

"You smell like your son," the thing said, and a whole new landscape of fear spread through Lucy's chest.

183

"Who are you?" she dared to say, fueled by anger now as well as fear.

"I? A distant relative, dearie. I'm your past and your future. I'm your missing husband and forgotten dreams. I'm the piano lessons you stopped taking, and the man you could have married but didn't. I'm your next cigarette, and I'm every single one of your lost hopes."

Lucy struggled to breathe, groping for the seam of the door. "You . . . *creep*!" She tried to shout, but it came out barely louder than a whisper. "Whoever you are, you stay away from my son!"

"Your son needs to stay away from *me,* doesn't he." Lucy felt the sting of tears in her eyes, and was determined not to give way to them.

"They think of me as an inferior, a monster, a beast, a dumb animal, a brute. The old fool, they adore. *Me,* they shrink from. Why? It was I who first learned the languages of men. I learned that all they use those languages for is to lie! I'm not a man, I'm proud to say. I studied man's music and man's art, man's philosophy and science, and now I'm supposed to return to a dying world? Merely to reproduce? *Why?* So all of *you* can come into being? From what I've seen of you, *you're not worth it.*"

Lucy could hear the man breathing (she assumed, of course, that it was a man, no matter what he claimed; in the darkness she had no reason to think otherwise). And then, she heard voices from below, muffled and distant. Maybe people were out on the stage!

"I despise the old fool," said the voice, "and I despise your smart-mouthed boy. I despise you all."

The voices from below, faint as they were, helped orient Lucy,

184

and now she distinctly felt the edge of a door, and then, thank God, a knob. She yanked it open, backed out, and slammed the door shut, all in one motion.

"Help!" she cried, starting to sob uncontrollably. "Help me! There's a crazy man in there! Help!"

The stage crew got Lucy down off the gallery and onto a couch in the greenroom, with Emma, the theater director, holding a warm, moist washcloth to Lucy's forehead. Eventually Lucy stopped sobbing and Emma walked her home. When the tech staff searched the old equipment cupboard off the gallery, they found nothing but the half-eaten body of a large rat.

At least they knew now where the stink had been coming from. It had been a problem in the theater for weeks, so everyone was happy when the rat was carted off to the dump. It didn't occur to them to wonder what had been gnawing on the rat, and later that afternoon the nasty odor seemed to return.

★ ★ ★

At school that day there were end-of-term exams. Phoebe wrote her final essay for her class on Colorado history with an I-wish-I'd-studied-the-book-instead-of-actually-living-the-history feeling. In his math class, Rob sank like a stone, straight to the bottom. His multiple-choice exam paper was smeared with check boxes that had been un-checked, then re-checked, then crossed out again. Eventually, when he had completely mutilated his test, he flipped the sheet over and dreamily filled the page with sketches of the yellow lab that had come back to the present with him.

At the lunch break, kids stumbled into the cafeteria in a

"J.L."
by Rbt. Gates Jr.

kind of daze, headachey and famished. The Gang headed straight for their usual table, everybody talking and moaning at once, everybody convinced that theirs had been the worst test ever.

Billy, always on the lookout, spotted Angela first. "Hey, Angela, you're back!" he said.

She nodded, moving through the milling crowd.

"How're you feeling?"

"Fine," she said shortly. She had already been through the lunch line and was carrying a tray with a grilled cheese sandwich, a pickle, cole slaw, and a carton of milk.

"Hey, Angela," said Phoebe.

"We went on the most amazing trip," Aran said.

"We saw Faith before it existed," added Donna.

"We brought back a dog from over a hundred years ago!" said Billy excitedly. Angela stopped stock-still.

"Will you *leave me alone*?" she yelled, and everybody in the vicinity turned and stared. Billy's complexion went from white to whiter.

"Angela," said Phoebe, "what's going on with you?"

Arabella Giddens came up to the group, carrying a tray.

"Come on, Angela," she said, "sit with us. You don't need the Special Eds anymore."

"Shut up, Arabella," said Aran, who actually did get special-education tutoring because of his dyslexia and was fairly sensitive about it.

Chad Scudder and Gary Dirks suddenly flanked Aran. "You take one ear," said Chad, "and I'll take the other."

Gary made a grab in the direction of Aran's prominent ears, but Aran shoved him so hard he lost his balance and fell back across a couple of lunchroom chairs. Chad jumped on Aran, but Rob got Chad around the neck and yanked him backward onto the floor, the two of them crashing into the legs of chairs and tables. When Gary got up he struck out wildly, and Billy's nose became a fountain of bright red. Girls were screaming, and it all could have ended in a major brawl if the fire alarm hadn't gone off just then. It was deafening, and suddenly teachers poured into the lunchroom and started ushering kids out into the corridors and out of the building. Mr. Brinkley was there, blowing his whistle like an idiot, and it was so completely chaotic that it broke up the fight without anybody getting busted for it.

It turned out that a couple of guys from the high school had pulled the alarm as a prank, and *they* got busted instantly and were out there in the middle school parking lot with Principal Dunne and three male teachers in their faces, the boys looking as though they wished they hadn't done it.

Angela stuck close by Arabella Giddens as they all stood around on the grass across from the school, waiting for the all-clear. She hardly glanced at her friends. Billy Springer stood with his head tilted back, pinching his bloody nose, feeling like a fool whose world has come to an end. Chad and Gary stared daggers at Rob and Aran, and those guys stared back until Phoebe told them to knock it off, 'cause it was exactly what those goons wanted. Mr. Brinkley came out, carrying the aluminum walking stick.

"Who left this in the lunchroom?" he demanded.

Rob shouted, "I did!" a moment before Chad shouted the same thing. Brinkley looked from Chad to Rob.

"Okay, Gates, you can reclaim it from me after the detention you're gonna serve when you finish your exams. You can't bring something like this to school!"

Chad and Gary practically fell over laughing, but Rob thought it was well worth it to get the critter detector back.

Eventually the fire department drove off, a bell rang, and the students all trooped back into school like condemned prisoners for another couple of hours of examinations. At the last moment, Billy realized that Angela was walking right next to him, head down, brow furrowed. To Billy's confusion, she reached for his hand and put something in it and then hurried off into the crowd. Billy looked: it was a white hanky. He stared after her departing form, his bloodied face glowing with hope reborn. If Angela thought Billy Springer was going to use *that* to clean up his bloody nose, she didn't know Billy Springer. He would keep that little bit of lace until his dying day.

As the crowd moved along the corridor, Phoebe heard two teachers talking to each other.

"You're kidding," said Mr. Jackson. "Philippa Larson?"

"I'm serious," said Mrs. Peabody.

"But she hasn't missed a day of school in, what is it now? Fifteen years? Twenty?"

"Well, she's missing today, and she didn't even call in sick."

But there was so much going on that day, with the long afternoon of tests ahead of them, that Phoebe didn't pay much attention to the librarian's absence—at least not then she didn't.

★ ★ ★

When Rob got home after school, the yellow lab raced out of Rob's yard to greet him, leaping up and licking the boy's face and practically wagging himself to pieces. Rob glanced guiltily up at the windows of his house and pulled the dog into the backyard again.

"Hey, boy, how's it going? Where's Sid?" The dog's paws were on Rob's chest, but Rob lifted them down to ground level and asked the question again. "Where's Sid, YL?" (Rob's name for the yellow lab, obviously.) YL's head tilted to one side and then the other, as though he were thinking. He looked off, up at the mountain above them. "Did Sid go up Stair-Master, boy?" The yellow lab grinned, and Rob's first reaction was, *Wow*. Then he thought about it and realized the look on YL's face could mean yes, or no, or feed me, especially feed me, or nothing at all, because this clearly wasn't Lassie.

Rob ran the dog for another few minutes and then used one of the dog biscuits he'd bought on the way home to get him to crawl under the house and lie down. As Rob approached the house he saw his mother at the door, watching him. Lucy opened the door for him and said, "Where'd the dog come from?"

"Aw, he's been around town for about a hundred years," Rob improvised.

To Rob's surprise, instead of getting all upset and saying "No way are we keeping that thing," Lucy didn't say anything; she just looked at her son and blew her nose with a soggy tissue as he followed her into the house. Rob realized she must have been crying, and then he noticed that Wynola and Adelaide Parsons were sitting quietly in the living room, Wynola knitting and Adelaide watching Rob with a benign smile. He turned back to his mother.

189

"What's going on, Mom?" he asked in a whisper. "Are you okay?"

Lucy nodded and stuffed the tissue into a pocket of her cardigan. "Listen," she said, "I need to know if anybody's been bothering you."

Rob immediately assumed she was talking about the big fight at school.

"It was Chad Scudder's fault, Mom, and Gary Dirks. They were being really mean to Aran."

"No, I'm not talking about kids, Rob. A grown-up, I mean—a man. Has anybody been hanging around school or around town, talking to you, maybe?"

Rob was genuinely confused now. What was she talking about?

Wynola cleared her throat. "Your mother had a bad scare today, Robert. At the theater."

"We've been sitting with her since she got home," said Adelaide. "She was going to run straight to school and put you in a car and drive and drive and never stop driving, but we talked it over and she decided to think it through calmly."

"What happened?" Rob was utterly bewildered. "What were you doing in the theater?"

Lucy went on to describe her terrifying encounter with the voice in the darkness.

Suddenly Rob's stomach flipped.

"He *smelled*?" said Rob.

"I've never experienced body odor like that on anybody," said Lucy with a shudder.

"You just haven't had much experience with miners, in that case," said Adelaide. "Oh, my goodness, those men used to come home from a long shift in the mine positively reeking!" She and her sister smiled and sighed nostalgically, as though it were something they missed terribly.

"So, Rob," said Lucy, "is there anything you can tell me about any of this? The crazy man mentioned you—*you* specifically—and it just about scared me to death."

Rob looked at his mom's red eyes. Every now and then, between their frequent skirmishes and all the yelling, Rob realized how much his mother loved him. This was one of those moments. But what could he say? How could he tell her who, or what, she'd been trapped with?

He went to her and awkwardly hugged her, and Lucy sniffed and tried very hard not to start crying again.

"I'm sorry the guy scared you, Mom."

"Any idea who it could have been?"

Rob hesitated. "Doesn't sound like anybody from around here," he said.

Wynola put down her knitting and moved to the kitchen. "I'll make us all another pot of tea," she said.

Rob excused himself, went into his bedroom, and radioed Phoebe. He told her about the Gorgon hiding out in the theater and threatening his mom. Rob was furious and regretful at the same time, feeling it was *he* who had put his mom at risk. "We're going to the theater tonight, Phoeb. We're going to find that thing."

★ ★ ★

She thought she was dead. Then she thought, *If I'm thinking, I can't be dead.* Then she thought, *How do I know the dead don't think? I may have a lot to learn about the dead.*

Philippa Larson, middle school librarian, amateur Shakespeare scholar, and lover of knowledge, lay somewhere between the top of the mountain and the base of the canyon that led to the mines behind town.

She could see sky. She could see fir trees climbing the steep

191

cliffs above her, and could smell pine resin very close to her face. She didn't know how far she'd fallen. She didn't remember falling, precisely, but she remembered the grinning face and the slow Texas drawl that came out of it; she remembered the man's hands. She'd been sitting on a flat stone, rereading the news article she'd printed out about the bludgeoning murder of the professor of paleontology. She had decided she would go directly to Sheriff Pete's office when she came down off the mountain, even if it meant being late for school for the first time ever.

Then someone had sat down next to her. Philippa remembered the fear that had gripped her belly.

"I always had trouble with librarians," said Jenkins, "ever since I was a kid."

Philippa tried to keep breathing steadily. "I'm not surprised."

"Truth is, I never was much of a scholar," said Dr. Richard Jenkins.

"I know you weren't," said Philippa fearlessly. "I've read your work—pure hogwash."

Jenkins laughed. "Ain't you a peach, though," he said. "Maybe it was hogwash, but there were a lotta people who wanted to believe it. No skin off my nose—folks wanted to saddle up a dinosaur? I was happy to oblige."

"And Dr. Jerome Nathan?" said the librarian.

Jenkins sighed. "He wasn't buyin' it. But he was always decent to me—one of the few on the faculty who treated me with respect. He wanted to *talk it all out,* our scientific differences. Then, six or so years ago, we went fly fishing together. There was a little mountain stream full of trout, he said, up in a town called Faith.

"We caught our limit first day, and were doing pretty well on day two. Then we saw something else was fishing that same stream. Floating like a gator, letting the current take it, snapping up trout two, three at a time. And the stink? Mercy.

"Suddenly it saw us, standing in the middle of the stream in our waders. What happened next didn't make sense. It opened its snout, steam rose up off the water, and bingo! We were back where we'd started that morning—there weren't no fish in our basket and our lures were lying there on the grass, waiting to be tied. We'd gone back in time two or three hours.

"Dr. Nathan knew what the thing was; he recognized it. That's what *he* was excited about. Missed the point, if you ask me. Back in El Paso, for the next few years he worked on a gadget that would help him find that stinky beast again. While I was thinking about all the things you could do if you could hitch a ride in time."

"I don't have the slightest idea what you're talking about," said Philippa. "But I imagine you killed this man, the one man who you say was decent to you, for the device he invented."

"Ma'am, if you miss the point, what's the point?"

Philippa remembered the man grabbing her under the arms at this point and dragging her. She'd never weighed much, it wasn't difficult for him. She remembered the brief, vain struggle at the cliff's edge. She closed her eyes.

When she opened them again, the sun had moved across the sky and she lay in shadow and it had become cool. *I would like a drink of water,* she thought. She experimented with turning her head, and gasped.

After a silence, she said, "You look just like the picture in the article."

"You mean the one in the *National Geographic* that Phoebe and Rob found on the computer?" said Sid gently.

"Oh, my word." Philippa smiled, rapturous. "The article didn't say you could *talk.*"

"I'm sorry I didn't get here sooner," said the synapsid. Sid glanced up to the mountain's peak. "I'm sorry I didn't stop him."

193

"But you're here now, and that's wonderful," she said. "My life . . ." Philippa licked her dry, cracked lips. "My life has been, in general, a little quiet. You wouldn't think life in a hotel could be lonely, but it can be, a bit. Now, though, I've seen what so few have seen."

Sid sat beside her, his big black eyes looking into hers. He reached for her shattered glasses, and with his long fingerlike digits he gently took them off her face.

"Thank you," she said. Her breath was labored, but she seemed to savor every taste of the air she drew in.

"They are dear children," she said, "Robert and Phoebe. I'm so glad you found them."

Sid nodded, looking down at her. "So am I."

After a long silence he said, "If you could go anywhere, anywhere at all, where would you go, Philippa?"

She closed her eyes for moment. There were birds nesting everywhere, it seemed, in trees on the steep slopes above them and below, and they made a busy, springtime racket. Finally the librarian opened her eyes. "I'd stay right here in Faith, I think. But it did used to be so much more lively here when the mines were open. I had so much family here at one time, and so many friends." She looked up at Sid shyly, nearsightedly. "And in the old, *old* days," she whispered, "the times I was told of by my elders, it must have been a real *adventure* to live in Faith, and not nearly so lonely."

"Well," said Sid, "there's a coincidence. Because that's exactly where I happen to be going myself."

Sid took one of her hands in his paws and it began to vibrate. Philippa's eyes widened, and after a moment a smile of radiant happiness spread across her narrow face.

19
THE
REHEARSAL

At the theater they were in the middle of a dress rehearsal for the upcoming production of Shakespeare's *Tempest*. Rob and Phoebe had entered quietly through the loading dock doors and made their way into the back of the audience house as though it were perfectly normal for them to be there, which it wasn't.

Things were tense onstage. First, Philippa Larson hadn't shown up. She had been helping throughout rehearsals whenever questions about Shakespeare's language arose, and now in the final days before the opening she had been acting as the prompter, helping those actors who weren't totally secure with all their lines. The older actors, especially, needed her, and she wasn't there. Then there were the usual problems that crop up during technical rehearsals: light cues mistimed, costumes that were too big to fit through doors and so on. Emma

Decker, who was directing, was clearly trying to keep her temper.

"Stop, stop, stop!" she cried when a sound cue failed to play. "Is there a problem?"

A muffled voice came over the loudspeakers. "Sorry, we weren't cued up."

Emma reached for a licorice stick from a jar on the table and chewed fiercely.

For a while, Phoebe and Rob sat in the back row and took it all in, their eyes wandering over the house, wondering where in the huge old building the Gorgon might be hiding.

The actor who was playing the monster in the play, Caliban, was Winston Lawrence, who taught theater history at a college in the Valley. Caliban is a violent, misshapen creature, but Winston didn't walk with a huge limp or contort himself all over the place to play the part. He just gave you a *feeling* of deformity, that things were not as they should be, and that the actual deformity lay within his soul. Caliban was bitterly confronting his master, Prospero, and Prospero (played by Emma's husband, Sam) was confronting Caliban right back, when the weird stuff started.

When thou camest first,
Thou strokedst me and madest much of me, wouldst
   give me
Water with berries in't, and teach me how
To name the bigger light, and how the less . . .

As Winston's Caliban spoke, a smooth, musical voice from somewhere above the stage began speaking the lines along with him, very softly. *"Teach me how to name the bigger light, and how the less . . ."*

Phoebe and Rob were instantly on their feet.

196

Winston stopped speaking, but the mysterious voice continued, *"That burn by day and night: and then I loved thee.
Cursed be I that did so!"*

Winston looked out into the house. "Is anybody else hearing
this?" he said.

Denise, the stage manager, spoke over the PA system. "Quiet
in the wings, please!"

"Let's go back to the top of Caliban's speech, okay, guys?" said
Emma.

Winston cleared his throat and began again.

★ ★ ★

Rob sped up the stairs, followed by Phoebe. They pushed
open the doors to the first balcony and looked in, dreading
what they might find. But the red plush seats were empty. From
below they heard the actors continuing the scene between
Caliban and Prospero. The kids ducked out and headed up the
steps to the second balcony. As they ran, Phoebe and Rob could
hear Sam's character, Prospero, the magician, speaking his lines.

> I pitied thee,
> Took pains to make thee speak, taught thee each hour
> One thing or other: when thou didst not, savage,
> Know thine own meaning, but wouldst gabble like
> A thing most brutish, I endow'd thy purposes
> With words that made them known.

To which Caliban replied like a whiplash:

> You taught me language; and my profit on't
> Is, I know how to curse.

197

The alien voice rumbled on over Winston's, and this time it was unmistakable—everybody in the theater heard it. *"You taught me language; and my profit on't is, I know how to curse!"*

The actors stopped, looking up into the fly loft and the lighting grid, and the stage manager came on over the PA.

"Okay, whoever's up there, come on out—we don't have time for this."

★ ★ ★

Phoebe and Rob cautiously pushed through the doors leading to the top balcony. The rows were dark and empty.

Onstage the big work lights came on with a thump, and the house lights rose, and suddenly Rob and Phoebe were revealed in the top balcony. In a flash they ducked down behind a row of seats.

"Up there!" someone onstage shouted. "There's someone in the third balcony!"

"Hey!" shouted Denise, the stage manager. "Who is that up there! What do you think you're doing?"

Denise came striding up the orchestra aisle with a flashlight in one hand and a good-sized wrench in the other. A couple of stagehands joined her, and the three of them headed for the balcony stairs at a run.

Emma was squinting with Sam up into the top tier.

"Come out and show yourself, or I'll call the police!" she shouted toward the heights above her.

Sam whispered to his wife, "Do you suppose it's Mickie Pine?"

"Since when did Mickie start memorizing the classics?" she said.

By the time Denise and the others reached the third balcony,

Phoebe and Rob had burst out of the loading dock doors on the ground floor. They didn't stop running for blocks.

It was a quiet night in Faith, and their running footfalls on the cracked, uneven sidewalk sounded loud in their own ears. A fog was drifting down off the mountain, flowing silently in and out of the circles of light cast by the street lamps. Finally, Rob and Phoebe slowed to a walk, breathing heavily.

"How can something that smells that bad love Shakespeare that much?" said Phoebe,

"I always said Shakespeare stinks," said Rob, and Phoebe slugged his shoulder. "Ow!"

"How are we supposed to talk him into going back to his own time?" said Phoebe. "What possible influence could you or I have over him?"

"And if it turns out we've got to take him back to Sid and the Gorgon's era?" Rob said. "How do we ever get back *here*? Sid can't bring us back, can he?"

"I've been trying *not* to think about that for weeks," said. Phoebe. "Ever since we saw that picture of the fossilized footprints. Rob, I don't want to die two hundred and fifty million years ago, I want to live my life!"

"Well, good luck with that," said Rob, not very helpfully.

"There's so much more we need to know—there's so much we should have been asking Sid all this time. Where is he?"

"I don't know," said Rob. "He was gone when I got home from school."

Suddenly a form stepped out of the shadows, right in front of them, and they both jumped.

"Hi, guys," said Billy. "Where've you been? I was looking for you."

"Don't ever do that again!" said Phoebe.

"Idiot!" said Rob.

"What did *I* do?"

The three of them walked on together in the dark spring night. Rob and Phoebe told Billy about the rehearsal and the voice that came from above the stage, but Billy interrupted them to say that he needed to drop out of the Gang of Six (minus one). He was really sorry about it, but he'd walked Angela home after school and she just wanted no part of Sid or the rest of it because it scared her half to death and it made the world make no sense, according to her. Things like houses and pot roasts and birthday parties didn't seem to fit in with gorgonopsids and glaciers, and Billy sort of understood what she meant. So he was sorry and he wished them good luck and everything, but he really liked Angela and couldn't do any more traveling with them.

"Thanks a lot, Billy," said Rob. "I always knew the human race could count on you."

"Come on, Rob," he pleaded. "I think she actually *likes* me— I mean, realistically, you think that's ever going to happen for me again? I can't give up Angela just to go traveling in time."

A cat suddenly yowled and raced across their path like a shot, disappearing under a car. Something about it made the kids stop dead still. From behind the hedge beside them they heard a dog's low warning growl. An owl hooted somewhere from the branches above them, and they heard the sound of wings. The air grew suddenly humid and warmer, and the lamplights started to waver. They heard claws on the sidewalk just behind them, and they whirled around.

"Sid?" said Phoebe to the darkness apprehensively.

"Close, darling, but you won't be getting the cigar," said the gorgonopsid. He reared up on his hind legs and roared, and they were engulfed in a cloud of stink and a blur of flashing, spinning light.

"No . . . traveling!" Billy's voice was lost in a great wind.

★ ★ ★

Sid returned from his travels with Philippa Larson in the early evening, just after Rob and Phoebe had gone off to the theater. Yellow Lab greeted him effusively, and Sid let the dog pummel him for a minute, leaping and licking and making urgent high-pitched whining noises. Then Sid said a calm word of command, and YL ducked into the crawl space under the house and Sid followed.

Sid noticed that Yellow Lab's food bowl was empty, and YL told him, in dog, that Rob hadn't fed him, but you couldn't believe YL, or any dog, when they told you something like that. Still, the lab did seem genuinely distressed.

"Where *is* Rob, boy?" said Sid, in dog. "Where did he go?" YL shook his yellow head; he didn't know. His dog grief overcame him instantly—Rob gone, food bowl empty—and he let out a mournful yowl. Sid gently tapped his snout with a paw and the dog stopped.

"Stay!" said Sid, and, with a tremendous show of resentment, Yellow Lab stayed while Sid slipped outside again.

In just a matter of minutes Sid returned, carrying between his jaws a good-sized ham bone that he'd found lying next to the Dumpster behind the town's small supermarket.

YL was enormously grateful and set to work on the bone immediately, gnawing and cracking and crunching, but Sid was uneasy. He delicately wiped the traces of ham from his mouth, spat with distaste into a corner beneath the house, and settled down to wait for his friend Rob.

He must have slept without meaning to. He dreamt of his spouse, growing weaker by the hour. He dreamt of Rob, sobbing on a mountain slope in mortal danger, and woke with a shout.

"Rob! Phoebe! We're coming!" he cried, and Yellow Lab woke with a start, his body already beginning to vibrate.

★ ★ ★

Everything was coated in a thick layer of dust. A pale light seemed to be coming from high above, and motes of dust, stirred by their arrival, swirled in the vertical shaft.

"Where is he?" Rob was the first to speak, looking around for the Gorgon.

"Where are *we*?" said Billy anxiously.

A smooth, dramatic voice made the three of them jump. *"To be, or not to be, that is* literally *the question."* The Gorgon emerged from the shadows, walking in an arc around the kids, seeming to ignore them. *"Whether 'tis nobler to suffer the slings and arrows of outrageous fortune . . ."*

"It's the theater!" exclaimed Phoebe, and as soon as she said that, Rob and Billy could make out the dim shapes of empty seats, row after row, stretching back into a void.

The Gorgon glanced at her. "It *was* the theater."

"What happened to it?"

Rob jabbed Phoebe with an elbow. "You're making *conversation* with it?" he whispered. "Let's go!"

"You mustn't think of running, Robert," said the beast, turning toward him suddenly. "Half the stage floor has rotted away, and the trap cellar beneath the stage flooded some years ago." He dropped his voice to a confidential whisper and said, "It's nasty down there."

"Some *years* ago?" said Phoebe. "When is it? *When are we?*"

The Gorgon walked in a circle again, moving with a stagey sort of grandeur. *"Tomorrow, and tomorrow, and tomorrow, creeps in this petty pace from day to day, to the last syllable of recorded time.*"

"That's from *Macbeth*," said Phoebe, fascinated in spite of herself.

The Gorgon lifted one long-clawed paw and put it to his snout. "Hush—bad luck to say the name of the Scottish play aloud!"

"I want to go home," said Billy quietly.

"You *are* home, you stupid little whiner!" The creature's voice was suddenly like a slap, and Billy and the others took a frightened step backward.

"Careful," said the Gorgon, smooth and theatrical again. "You'll go through the floorboards in a moment. But if you follow me, I'll show you the way home."

"Forget *you*!" shouted Rob.

"Don't you just wish you could, Robert Gates. But no, the critics all agree: my performance is *unforgettable*. Come. Follow. You really have no choice."

Rob and Phoebe and Billy found themselves moving just behind the great black beast, sleepwalkers in a waking nightmare. The shapes around them were vague and dreamlike. Were they actually walking, voluntarily cooperating with this monster? It was hard to tell. They moved from the stage down into the audience house and up the center aisle, following the gorgonopsid out into the lobby. The posters on the wall there were peeling and hanging limply from their frames, and the glass in the doors was broken and the doors boarded up. Then they were out on Main Street.

"Run!" cried Rob, but his jaw dropped and he stood rooted to the spot.

The rusted bodies of abandoned cars were strewn motionless

up and down the street. Windows were broken in nearly every building. The roof of the post office was caved in, a light pole had fallen onto the bank, and a cloud of flies buzzed around the rotting carcass of what might have been a goat, right in front of the hardware store. In the air was a hanging brownish haze so thick that the very mountains above were barely visible.

"Be it ever so humble, there's no place like . . . well, you get the picture." The Gorgon was looking around like a sightseer.

"What happened here?" said Phoebe, tears standing in her eyes.

"Where to begin? There were the oil wars, of course—they started during your lifetime—and let's not forget the religious wars, shudder, shudder. But you could take it back much further. Humans have been working at their own destruction for *such* a long time."

"Our lifetimes?" said Rob. "You mean, this is sometime in the future and we're not alive anymore?"

"Oh, it's the future all right, but I have a feeling you may turn up any minute now."

As the Gorgon was speaking, a painfully thin white-haired man came out of the only building on Main Street that was even halfway kept up. The kids heard music as the door swung open, and smoke drifted out with the music. The white-haired man had once been tall, they could see, but now his back was stooped, and his head seemed to shake on his neck, like one of those dolls in the back windows of cars.

"That looks like my uncle Fred," whispered Billy.

"Wrong again, chum," said the Gorgon cheerfully.

"Oh, my God," breathed Phoebe, realizing who it was. "Billy . . ."

"What?" said Billy. He looked again at the white-haired man with the thin face and the milky bluish eyes. "No, uh-uh, no way . . ."

A second man pushed out of the saloon (which is what the place obviously was) with another burst of music. He, too, was skinny. He was dressed in dirty jeans and a stained white T-shirt. His hair was dark brown with flecks of gray. His face was haggard. He had a close-cropped stubble of graying beard.

"Oh, man," said Rob under his breath.

The jeans-clad man squinted up at the sky and reached with his right hand for a pack of cigarettes in his T-shirt pocket. He shook one up, stuck it between his lips, and put the pack back in the pocket. Then, also with his right hand, he reached into his jeans pocket and pulled out a book of matches, opened it, and bent a match back over the scratcher and lit it. He drew deeply on the cigarette and exhaled a cloud of smoke into the already smoky sky.

But what the three kids were staring at was the man's left arm, which hung lifelessly at his side, the hand a mangled mess.

"What happened to my hand?" said Rob finally, with a voice like lead. Then his volume rose. "I'm left-handed. What happened to my left hand?"

The Gorgon sort of shrugged. "Search me," he said with a kind of giggle, and Rob suddenly turned on him and brought his two clenched fists down hard on the Gorgon's head, just above his yellow eyes. Fast as a snake the gorgonopsid's massive tail swung round from behind, caught Rob at the ankles, and pulled him to the ground, the back of his head hitting the pavement with a nasty thump. "Manners, Master Gates," said the beast, his yellow eyes flashing. *"Manners."*

Phoebe knelt beside Rob protectively. "Don't you touch him!" she said with a fire of her own in her eyes.

"Believe me, I'd rather not," said the Gorgon. And then his voice became singsong. "Don'tcha wanna see how *you* end up, princess?"

"No," she said uncertainly.

"*Sure* you do!"

There was no doubting it now—they weren't walking, they were being levitated or something. Now Faith was down in the brown haze below them and they were on a mountain plateau on the other side of town from Stair-Master. The old mansion there had·belonged to a wealthy Dallas oilman, Mr. Roses, and although he and his family only used it two weeks a year, it was always kept trim and freshly painted and the lawn crisply mowed by caretakers. Now, though, the front was overgrown, the paint was peeling and faded, and a portion of the broad front porch had halfway collapsed. Dozens of cats lounged on the porch or sat on windowsills grooming themselves, and there were bowls of cat food scattered everywhere.

"You're the richest woman in Faith, princess. You call this place your castle, which is kind of cute, I guess, if you can stomach that sort of thing. You used to keep a couple of bodyguards, but you're all alone now—except, of course, for your cats."

A thickset, hard-faced blond woman stepped out onto the porch holding a shotgun, squinting suspiciously at the visitors on her property. Cats swarmed around her ankles, and her braid hung down her back, all the way down to the cats.

The Gorgon dropped his voice to a concerned murmur. "You turned out a little *strange,* Phoeb."

"Shut up!" screamed Rob suddenly. "Shut up!"

The figure on the front porch, startled, quickly pulled her head and her shotgun back inside the house and slammed the door. They could hear the sound of locks and bolts being thrown. Phoebe stared at the door, a numbness coming over her.

"Let me see," said the Gorgon, "what else? The Mitchelsons' stables did good business for a time, when cars became too costly for anyone but the richest to maintain. But then the depression worsened and their horses began to be more valuable as food than transportation, if you get my meaning."

"Shut your stinking mouth!" cried Rob, sobbing in spite of himself. "Just shut up!"

"I don't really know what became of Donna after her first bite of horse," said the beast, ignoring him. "You have to understand, she'd lost a lot of weight. Young Aran McBell enlisted in the army for . . . which war was it? Petroleum? Religion? The War of the Flags, I think it was. He lost his comical head somewhere over the China Sea, poor boy."

"Shut up, I said!"

"Oh, and then there's Angela," said the beast. Billy looked at the Gorgon with pleading eyes, but there was no mercy there.

"Funny story. Her father got Forest Service work in southern Florida, down in the Everglades, and he moved the whole family down there. Well, the Everglades flooded in no time, and Mr. Cruz was out of work. The ice caps had been melting for decades, of course, but the melt accelerated, faster than anyone could have predicted, Arctic and Antarctic, and in just a few years they were pretty much history. These days Miami is a row of deserted high-rises standing like a bunch of old ladies, wading up to their knees at the seashore—you can really get a bargain if you're willing to live with rats and swim to work. Anyway, Angela was, alas, carried off by one of the first new outbreaks of typhus."

The kids actually seemed to *see* these things as the creature spoke. Images of death and decay moved like a horrific slide show, in and out of their vision. They realized gradually that the town cemetery was beneath their feet, that it covered the hillside they were standing on. There was Jane Traylor's broken gravestone, and here was Lucy Gates' marker, overgrown with prickly creepers, and Keith and Julie Springer's. The kids had tears streaming down their faces, and Rob's body shook with sobs. The total lack of hope felt like a lack of oxygen—or maybe it was a literal scarcity of oxygen in the foul atmosphere of Faith. One by one they sat on the ground and hid their heads in their arms.

"And all this is what you get if you and the diictodon *succeed.* This is what you get if you *save* the races of mammals! Human beings get to destroy creation! I mean to say, *what is the point?*"

Rob felt a paw on his shoulder and he threw it off blindly, scrambling backward and shielding his face.

"Rob," said a gentle, gravelly voice, "it's a lie. It's an illusion. Listen to me. He's a liar, children."

Phoebe lifted her head and gasped, and Billy looked up, and finally Rob brushed the tears from his eyes and blearily saw Sid standing there, facing the Gorgon. Yellow Lab stood at his side, growling low, his hackles up.

"*Who's* the liar?" said the Gorgon steadily, staring at Sid. "Aren't *you* now lying to these children? Desperate for their approval, their cooperation, their affection?"

There was a tense silence between them.

"Do you dare tell them the truth, old fool?" said the Gorgon.

"He's showing you a possible future," said the diictodon after a moment. "It all *could* turn out this way. But it doesn't have to. You have something to say about whether life ends this way or not—you and others like you."

The brown haze began to dissipate as he spoke.

"Well said!" said the Gorgon sarcastically. "Hear, hear! Rooty-toot-*toot,* old boy!"

As the kids watched, the old mansion on the mountain became a brick wall extending high above them.

"Ah, well," sighed the gorgonopsid. "I thought I was rather good, I must say. I especially liked the cats and the dead goat on Main Street, but then, detail is everything. Anyway, I simply *love* goat—they don't have goat back where I come from, so it's as good a reason as any to stick around."

For the kids, everything that had seemed so devastatingly real a moment earlier began to dissolve. The mountain itself shrank to become the wooden floor beneath them, and the cemetery crumbled to a scattering of sawdust on the floor. Main Street turned itself into the setting for Faith Rep's production of *The Tempest,* and as the two creatures from the Permian era continued their face-off, Rob, Phoebe, and Billy found themselves back in their own era, on the theater's deserted stage.

"Our revels now are ended," recited the gorgonopsid, highly pleased with himself. *"These our actors, as I foretold you, were all spirits and are melted into air, into thin air."* Someone was approaching the stage; footsteps were growing louder. The Gorgon lowered his massive head in a mock bow.

"And so, to thunderous applause, he exits!" The Gorgon sprang into the darkness of the wings and was gone.

The three kids slowly stood. Rob kept gripping his left hand with his right, as if to assure himself that it was really there.

"Home now," said the diictodon. "Quickly—people are coming!"

Sid leapt from the stage and darted out a side exit, and Yellow Lab and the kids ran after him just as Denise, the stage manager, walked onto the set, wearing a headset and talking into it. She wrinkled her nose.

"Leslie," she said into her headset, "bring a mop. The rotten egg smell is still with us."

Outside, as they made their cautious way home for the

second time that night, Sid was shaking his head. "That man Jenkins has been feeding him."

"What do you mean?" said Rob.

"I mean it may not have been the Gorgon that killed all those pets," said the synapsid darkly. He glanced at the yellow lab, trotting along at his side. "It may have been Jenkins who attacked the horses, too. I think he's been training the gorgonopsid, in a way—as one would train a dog, with . . . treats."

It was a horrific thought.

"We've got to get this over with," said Rob, his brow furrowed into a dark knot.

"I know," said the diictodon. "There's been murder done by this man Jenkins, and he has to be stopped."

"Murder?" said Phoebe.

"Jenkins and one of his colleagues happened upon the Gorgon during that same trip when my mate and I first saw you two. The colleague saw a scientific miracle. Jenkins saw only the potential for financial gain, and murdered his friend for the chance to use the Gorgon for time traveling."

"How do you know all this, Sid?" Phoebe asked.

"Your friend Philippa Larson told me. Jenkins told her the whole story moments before he threw her off the mountain."

"He did *what*?" said Rob.

"Is Ms. Larson okay?" said Phoebe.

"For now," said Sid.

He glanced at the kids with concern. All three looked confused and exhausted.

"Try not to worry too much," said Sid, "or think any more about it tonight." But Sid's own face was a little map of worry all the way home.

20
ANOTHER OPENING

While it's not a completely unusual thing for people in Faith to go missing, for Philippa Larson to disappear days before the end of the school term raised genuine alarm.

Green-haired Jimmy was on duty at the hotel when Sheriff Pete came calling. He took the sheriff up to Ms. Larson's room, rapped on the door, and called her name. Finally he used a passkey to let the sheriff in. The two little rooms she'd occupied for at least the past twenty years were crowded to overflowing with books, periodicals, and old photos. There were images of Faith as it had been when Philippa was a girl, and photos of Faith going back to the earliest days of the old mining camp. There, in a picture on the wall, was Main Street as it had looked in the early 1900s, when there were ten thousand people living in town instead of five hundred. Saloons predominated, the town was wild, and the era was referred to as "the Roaring Naughts" (like the Roaring Twenties, only with zeros).

There was a photo from the 1950s of Philippa Larson herself at age nine or ten, standing in an old miner's wagon—it was called a mucker's bucket—while a twelve-year-old boy on crutches stood beside it. Philippa seemed to be wearing bifocals even then, and her prominent teeth were encased in a desperately complicated cage of braces. But she was smiling through all that hardware. The boy on crutches—Philippa's brother—looked like he could have been Rob's twin.

On a crowded desk in her bedroom was a short stack of manila folders with Phoebe and Rob's names on the covers, and in the folders the sheriff found a whole dossier of their researches into the creatures of the Permian era, which Pete leafed through without pausing. He came to a couple of articles about the paleontologist Dr. Richard Jenkins and he slowed down. The last clipping he came to, the one with the most recent date in the folder, was a news article from El Paso, reporting the discovery of a decomposed body in a riverbed on a rural ranch. The corpse hadn't yet been identified.

The sheriff looked grim. "Isn't that fella Jenkins staying here in the hotel?"

"Yes, sir," said Jimmy. "I mean, no, sir," he said immediately, self-conciously stuffing his green-painted fingernails into his pockets.

Sheriff Pete raised his massive eyebrows.

"I mean, he was staying here for weeks and weeks, and then he checked out," Jimmy said.

"When?" said Pete.

"Just this morning, sir. Checked him out myself."

The sheriff said a four-letter word and pressed the talk button on his radio. "Keith, step on over to the hotel, will you? I don't like what I'm finding."

Jimmy had never felt comfortable in the presence of the sheriff, and especially not now. Pete shifted a big wad of chewing tobacco from his left cheek to his right with his tongue, and Jimmy said, "I'll just be at the front desk if you need me."

"Be much obliged if you stay right where you are, son. I need you to let me into another room—one recently vacated by a rapscallion named Jenkins."

★ ★ ★

At the same time, down in the bank, a scene was playing out that would be remembered locally, if not understood, for years.

Dr. Richard Jenkins had just turned away from the teller's window with a gleam in his eyes, tucking a cashier's check into an envelope and folding the envelope into the breast pocket of his sport coat. Old Nancy Sweet, the postmistress, was next in line, and she nodded at Jenkins but didn't smile. She was one of the few who *hadn't* believed in his new mining venture.

The man didn't even see her as he strode toward the door, but he did see Adelaide Parsons when she moved to intercept him.

"Excuse me, ma'am," he said with a distant smile.

"No, Patrick, I'm afraid I can't excuse you," said Adelaide, also smiling, in a warm and loony way.

Jenkins tilted his head sympathetically. "Perhaps someone here can help you, ma'am, but I'm in something of a hurry, and you seem to have mistaken me for someone else."

He started to move around old Adelaide, but Wynola suddenly appeared, flanking him.

"Mr. FitzHugh," said Wynola, "you need to listen to my sister. She's not quite as crazy as she looks. Very nearly, but not quite."

"The first time you lived in Faith," said Adelaide, "you called yourself Patrick Mulcahy FitzHugh. That was your pen name. Remember?"

Jenkins glanced around at the other people in the bank, as if to say, *Are you seeing this?*

Adelaide noticed his glance and answered it. "Patrick, everyone in town knows how long I've been waiting to have a word with you—*everyone!*"

He tried to pass between the two women, but Adelaide interposed her umbrella.

"What we're wondering, dear, is how you sleep at night," she said.

"Excuse me," said Jenkins with no good humor in his voice now. "Let me pass."

Everyone in the bank was watching the unfolding scene.

"Daddy told us about you," said Wynola, "and how you scammed this whole town out of the silver in our mines. Daddy told us about Serenity, too—*surely* you haven't forgotten Serenity."

Jenkins' eyes darted above their heads as he considered his options.

"She had a child by you, you know, poor misguided girl," said Adelaide. "You quite won her heart in 1890, when she was only seventeen, but then you disappeared from Faith. Well, she couldn't wait for you forever. She married Jeb Larson eventually, Philippa Larson's great-uncle, but he died in the mines within a year, and Serenity was alone and childless and thought she'd be so for the rest of her life. And then, fourteen years later, in the year of the Great Fire, you came back."

"Please let me pass, ladies," said Jenkins. "I don't know what you're talking about, or who you're talking about, but you need to let me pass."

"Great-granddaddy Lemuel let Serenity raise the baby as a Parsons, bless his normally stone-cold heart," Wynola said.

"She named the boy after you. I wonder if you realized that," said Adelaide. "She named him Patrick Mulcahy Fitzhugh Parsons. That was our father."

Townspeople in the bank were murmuring, adding up the names and dates and searching their memories. In a town as small as Faith, with a history everyone shared, this was the local sport—it's what you did on rainy Sunday afternoons, you figured out how everyone was related to everyone else.

"My sister said you'd be long dead by now," said Adelaide, "and so did everybody else. But I was right, wasn't I? When you disappeared from Faith, our daddy, Patrick, was just a baby, but from his mama, Serenity, he had a photo. Just one, taken of you a day or two before the Great Fire."

Adelaide took a framed sepia portrait from her handbag. Jenkins glanced down at it briefly and looked up with a wild, hunted face.

"Don't you want to give your granddaughter a kiss?"

Eighty-one-year-old Adelaide smiled up at the man sweetly, and actually raised her arms, as if to embrace him around his neck, but before he knew what was happening, she had snipped a lock of his black hair with a tiny pair of scissors.

Jenkins thrust Adelaide aside roughly and pushed his way out of the bank.

"You owe us, Grandpa!" Wynola cried after him. *"You owe us all!"*

Jenkins walked briskly up Main toward the municipal lot, where his black SUV was parked.

Just minutes later, Deputy Keith Springer ran out of the Faith

Hotel in time to see Jenkins' SUV disappear, driving fast on the road that led south, past the Conoco and out of town, down into the Valley. Keith and everyone else assumed Jenkins was in it, and the sheriff put out a call to the Valley police. But Dr. Richard Jenkins had been planning this moment for a long time, and he wasn't about to make any mistakes.

★ ★ ★

At Faith Middle School, meanwhile, another drama was being played out in the cafeteria. Angela had rejoined the Gang at their table, sitting close to Billy Springer. Blatant romance like this didn't happen every day, so everyone paid attention.

"I thought you weren't going to do any more traveling," said Angela.

"The Gorgon just grabbed us," said Billy, "it wasn't a choice. He showed us stuff about our future, and it was all so scary that I *can't* promise not to do any more traveling, Angela. I'm really sorry, but all this is important—we have to help Sid do what he has to do, and we have to help ourselves, and . . ." Billy seemed to lose steam at this point, but then he rallied boldly. "And there are just some things a man has to do!"

Rob made a show of stuffing a paper napkin into his mouth to stop from laughing, and Phoebe jabbed him under the table. Everyone waited, the way you'd wait if you were watching a soap opera—what would she say?

What Angela said was, "Okay, Billy. I'm in. What do we do?"

Billy positively beamed. He glanced questioningly at Rob and Phoebe.

"Here's the deal," said Phoebe. "We know that the Gorgon hides out in the theater. Sid thinks if we get him alone, without his evil master around—"

216

"Feeding him treats," interjected Rob grimly.

"—we stand a chance of talking the Gorgon into going back where he belongs."

The kids were silent for a moment. Then Aran said, "That's the craziest thing I ever heard in my life."

"Sure is," said Donna.

"Totally," said Angela.

"Yeah," said Rob. "We know."

"We know," echoed Phoebe.

"You're saying you saw our future?" said Aran.

The three kids who'd traveled with the Gorgon didn't say anything.

"I think that's what you said, Billy," said Angela.

Billy shifted his gaze from Angela to his sneakers. "Well, yeah, but it was just a possible future. It might not come true."

"So?" Aran was indignant. "What happens to me?"

"Were we adults or something?" Donna asked. "Were we gross?" Another silence.

"Why aren't you saying anything?" Aran persisted.

"What happens to *me*?" asked Angela.

"I'm not going to let anything happen to you," said Billy. And then, to everyone's astonishment, the young fool kissed her on the lips, right there in the school cafeteria in front of everybody.

"Eww!" said Rob.

"Hubba hubba!" said Aran.

Donna looked away and Phoebe tried not to laugh, but Angela had the last word.

"You've got a piece of lettuce between your front teeth, Billy," she said not unkindly, looking away and blushing.

And Billy's face went from white to crimson in an instant, but you could see the pride in his eyes, even as he got a fingernail in there to get the lettuce out.

217

It was opening night in Faith.

Jane Traylor had invited Lucy and Rob Gates for a supper of vegetarian lasagna before the show. Lucy was still feeling a little shaky. First there had been the terrifying moments in the dark with an evil-smelling madman who told her he hated her son. Then her new boss had skipped town, and everyone knew by now that he was wanted for questioning concerning the disappearance of Philippa Larson. The mystery had deepened when police found Jenkins' black SUV down in the Valley with Mickie Pine passed out behind the wheel, a dozen empty beer cans in the front seat. He claimed Jenkins had given him the keys to the SUV and told him to take it for a spin. Where Jenkins was, no one knew.

Rob and Phoebe were quiet during the meal, too nervous to eat much. They asked to be excused after only a token bite of Jane's carob mousse.

Back in Phoebe's room, they found YL standing above Sid, who seemed to be sound asleep on the closet floor. The dog looked up at the kids and whined.

"Sid?" said Phoebe. "Sid!"

The diictodon's eyes fluttered open. He lifted his head. "What? Oh, sorry! I must have shut my eyes there for a moment."

He gave his head a shake and stood up, a little shakily.

"Do you feel okay, Sid?" said Rob.

"Absolutely!" He gave his head another shake. "I have a good feeling about tonight, I really do. Jenkins is gone, and we'll have the Gorgon all to ourselves. Without that awful man to confuse him, I really think he'll listen to reason." Rob and Phoebe glanced at each other doubtfully.

"What are these for?" said the diictodon, pointing to two bulging backpacks on Phoebe's bed.

"Our backpacks?" said Phoebe. "Supplies for the trip." She unzipped hers. "Water, cheese, trail mix, that sort of thing."

Sid cocked his head, looking confused, while Phoebe unzipped Rob's backpack. "Hey, that's mine!" said Rob.

"A comic book?" said Phoebe. "You thought you might need something *to read*?"

"When do I get to judge what *you* packed in *your* backpack?" Rob said.

She continued looking through the pack. "*Bubble* gum?"

"Leave it!" said Rob.

"Okay, okay." Phoebe lifted out a big plastic sack of grapes.

"They're for Sid. Put them back!" said Rob.

"Sorry!"

Sid cleared his throat. "Excuse me," he said, "but what is all this for?"

Rob snorted with impatience. "If we have to go all the way back to the Permian era with you and the Gorgon, we figured we just might need a little something to snack on!"

"See, we don't know how long it'll take, Sid," said Phoebe. "And we don't really know how Rob and I will get back home. Do you have any ideas on that?"

"Oh, dear me," said Sid. He dropped his head and drew a deep, rasping breath. Then he looked up at them again. "You were willing to go all that way?"

"Isn't that what we're *supposed* to do?" asked Phoebe.

"My spouse was right about you. You two are very special. Courageous. If I could cry, I would."

YL whined and clattered a bit with his big feet on the bedroom floor between them.

"You too, YL," said Sid. "Very special indeed." Sid turned back to Rob and Phoebe. "You will help me—and all mammals, and the whole wide world—if you help me get the Gorgon back to 1904 with me. I'm not asking you to do anything more."

"But what about the picture of the fossilized footprints, yours and ours?" said Rob.

"What picture?"

"We saw it online," said Phoebe.

"I don't know anything about that, but I am deeply moved by your selflessness, believe me. I think this is what will sway the Gorgon to our way of thinking. To see the *good* in humankind, instead of what he's used to seeing. As far as I know, the only human who ever actually communicated with him was Dr. Richard Jenkins—not the best your species has to offer."

"If we do get to talk to the Gorgon, what do we say?" said Phoebe.

"Just follow your instincts. Your heart. I'm not worried about you. Although I would advise keeping back from those fangs of his."

"Thanks," said Rob. "Note to self: keep away from the fangs."

"Okay, Sid," said Phoebe, "time to put on the muzzle."

Phoebe had borrowed a leather dog muzzle from Janet Bright. It would cover up the tusks so he'd be able to pose as a dog and go with them around town without attracting too much attention. Sid wasn't thrilled with the idea.

"What if I need my tusks?" he said as Rob fitted the muzzle over his head. "How do I get this thing off?"

"There's a snap right here," said Rob, guiding Sid's fingerlike digits to the bottom of the muzzle. "There—you look like a real dog, Sid old boy!"

"It's all very degrading, I must say," muttered Sid. "No offense, YL."

"Phoebe!" Jane Traylor called from the kitchen. "Rob! Let's get going. It's almost curtain time!"

"We're gonna walk, Mom," Phoebe shouted. "We'll see you after!"

★ ★ ★

Rob and Phoebe decided to bring their backpacks anyway—Shakespeare could be longish, and some trail mix might come in handy. As they made their way through town, they were joined by the Gang of Six (minus *none*). Rob held the aluminum walking stick in one hand and Yellow Lab on a leash with the other. Since YL eagerly thrust his nose into every passing crotch, people tended to focus on him rather than Sid, whom Phoebe led, muzzled, without attracting any particular attention. They tied YL by his leash outside, behind the theater, with bowls of water and food, and they sneaked Sid in through a side door and up the complicated series of stairs to the top balcony, high above the stage. Nobody ever sat up there, generally, because the view was almost straight down to the tops of the heads of the actors. The kids thought it would give them the best vantage of the entire theater, and besides, they *liked* to watch plays from up here. They were all veteran theater-goers. They settled into the first row, Sid hidden down at their feet.

Rob unscrewed the top of the walking stick, turned it around, and screwed it back together, revealing the electronic equipment.

"What is *that*?" whispered Aran.

Rob threw the switch and pointed it out over the audience. A moment later it emitted a low, slow beeping sound.

"That's what humans sound like," said Rob. The three boys

saw two words scroll across the LCD: HOMO SAPIENS . . . HOMO SAPIENS . . .

Rob pointed it down where Sid crouched, and the tone became musical and the scroll changed to DIICTODON . . . DIICTODON . . .

"Hey, watch it with that thing," said Sid, his voice muffled by the muzzle.

Donna hunkered down in her seat and turned to Phoebe. "This whole thing is freaking me out, actually," she whispered.

"I know. It's beyond weird."

"I can't tell you how scared I am."

Phoebe smiled at Donna. "You just did," she said. "It's good to talk about it when you're afraid." Phoebe realized she was quoting Sven, and she thought wistfully about therapy, missing it.

Donna smiled back. "I'll get us a lemonade before the play starts." As she stood up to go down to the lobby, a muffled voice from beneath their seats said, "A bag of nuts would be nice."

"Right," said Donna, glancing down at Sid and shaking her head. "A bag of nuts."

★ ★ ★

The play cast its spell from the first moment. Up in the front row of the top balcony sat six kids and one diictodon, all of them so caught up in the world of Shakespeare's *Tempest* they almost forgot what they were there for. Under the cover of darkness, even Sid dared to peek down at the stage over the balcony rail. He'd undone his muzzle and was quietly munching peanuts and cashews, one at a time, watching and listening intently.

Onstage, the young shipwrecked prince, Ferdinand, wandered on, grief-stricken, believing that his father had drowned in the tempest that he just barely survived. He was played by Tom Dushane, a seventeen-year-old who was the lead singer in the band that Jimmy with the green fingernails played in. At least half the girls in town had a crush on him.

"Nice tights," whispered Donna, and Phoebe bit her lip and nodded.

> Sitting on a bank,
> Weeping again the king my father's wreck,
> This music crept by me upon the waters . . .

It was a magical world, and the audience was caught in its spell. The only critters the critter detector detected were the human kind. After the first hour, Sid grew increasingly anxious.

"Where can he be?" he muttered.

Phoebe leaned down to whisper to him. "Maybe the gorgonopsid left town with Jenkins?"

"Let's hope not."

A moment later, in the darkness, Sid suddenly cocked his head, listening. He set his bag of nuts on the floor by Phoebe's ankles and quietly moved to the exit. The kids didn't notice.

Onstage, the monstrous character, Caliban, was drunk and loud, swearing that he was going to quit being Prospero's slave, pledging allegiance to his new master. Suddenly a second voice joined his, speaking his lines along with him:

> No more dams I'll make for fish
> Nor fetch in firing
> At requiring;
> Nor scrape trencher, nor wash dish—
> 'Ban, 'Ban, Ca-caliban
> Has a new master: get a new man!

The actor sped up, and the alien voice sped up; he slowed down, and the strange voice spoke louder, repeating the lines:

'Ban, 'Ban, Ca-caliban
Has a new master: get a new man!

People in the audience looked at each other questioningly. *"Freedom, hey-day!"* cried the voice, *"Hey-day, freedom! Freedom, hey-day, freedom!"*

★ ★ ★

Up in the top balcony, Rob was out of his seat, dashing for the side exit, Aran and Billy running after him.

"Wait!" said Phoebe in an urgent whisper. "We're not supposed to get separated from Sid!" But the boys were gone. That was the moment Phoebe realized that Sid was no longer with them.

"Where is he? Where's Sid?" she said in a panicky voice, and someone in the balcony below said, "Hush!"

Cashews and peanuts went skittering beneath the seats as Phoebe moved to the exit that led down to the street.

"Phoebe!" hissed Donna. "Where are you going? Don't leave us!" But Phoebe didn't even look back before she was gone.

Donna and Angela sat stiffly in their seats, the play carrying on far below them, and the first wisp of a nasty odor drifting down behind them.

★ ★ ★

Rob moved briskly along the corridor, leading with the critter detector, while Aran and Billy came after. They heard running steps coming toward them from around a corner, and they braced themselves, Rob holding the walking stick like a spear before him.

It was Denise, the stage manager. "What the hell? You kids get back to your seats!" she said. "There's some crazy guy loose in the theater—now go on!"

"Okay," said Rob. "Sorry." Denise ran on to the end of the corridor and down a flight of steps.

Rob pushed through a door that led into the audience house at the mezzanine level and stood there for a moment, pointing the walking stick over the audience, down to the stage, and up to the lighting grid above. Billy and Aran stood just behind him in the dark, scanning the area with their eyes.

"Turn off that *pager*!" whispered someone in the audience, and Rob quickly pulled the walking stick back. He was trying to turn down the volume when the low and steady beep changed to a throbbing musical tone. Rob froze. The device was pointed up at the top balcony, directly at the Gang's own row, his friends' row. The LCD flashed GORGONOPSID . . . GORGONOPSID . . . GORGONOPSID . . .

★ ★ ★

Behind the theater, Yellow Lab strained at his leash, peering off across the flume. Someone over there was moving in the dark. YL whined, his ears cocked, scenting the air, his body tense and trembling.

Dr. Richard Jenkins evidently hadn't left town. There he was, silently crossing Angela Cruz's yard to the pen where Whiskers, the white goat, was tethered. He took an ugly-looking folding knife from a pocket and opened it. He stooped over the goat.

"Bark! Bark! Bark! Bark!" YL went absolutely nuts. The streets of Faith echoed with it.

Jenkins straightened up and cursed, the goat bleating frantically and stumbling. The man glanced nervously back at the Cruz house and then strode from the lawn to the wooden bridge over the flume and across it, bloodied knife in hand.

"Bark! Bark! Bark! Bark!" Yellow Lab bared his teeth, his hackles up, leaping furiously, each time yanked back again by his leash.

"Shut up, you damn dog," hissed Jenkins, heading for YL.

At that moment, YL snapped the leash. The dog rushed at the man, snarling. Jenkins froze for a second, then turned and ran, ducking into a door near the theater's loading dock and slamming it behind him.

"Bark! Bark! Bark! Bark!"

"YL!" said Sid, pushing his way out of the theater's rear exit.

"Bark! Bark! Bark! Bark!"

"Be still!" Sid commanded, and the dog whined a high-pitched whine, running to Sid and back to the door and back to Sid again. "Good dog, good dog," Sid was peering across the flume.

"Oh, no," he breathed to himself. "Oh, no." Sid took off across the wooden bridge, and YL followed.

Whiskers, lying on the ground, raised her head and bleated when Sid approached. Her snow-white fleece was stained scarlet.

Sid ran a paw gently over her body. She vibrated for a moment, bleated again, and then struggled to her feet. Sid exhaled with relief, and YL capered around the goat in dog ecstasy.

Whiskers bleated.

"That's right, dear," said Sid. "I couldn't agree more."

Just then, Phoebe rushed out of the theater's rear exit.

At the same time, bright yard lights outside Angela's house

switched on, and Angela's father, Vidal, came out of the house with a rifle.

Vidal Cruz saw his daughter's pet goat standing in the yard, illuminated by harsh lights, a bloody stain near her throat and running down her side. He saw a bizarre tusked beast beside her. Vidal raised his rifle. Sid turned and leapt into the flume, and YL followed. Vidal fired.

Running to the edge of the water, he fired again. And again. And again.

The water, black and barely visible in the darkness, ran foaming along the watercourse, flowing down through town toward the flats and the valley and the Rio Grande beyond.

Sid was gone. Yellow Lab was gone.

Phoebe stared in numb disbelief.

A police car roared up and screeched to a halt, its siren blaring, its colored lights spinning.

★ ★ ★

Donna and Angela couldn't move. They sat in their seats, enveloped in air so bad it was like a kind of malice, and the Gorgon, behind them, whispered in their ear.

"Don't you just hate it when this happens? You're enjoying an evening at the theater, and then some perfect *beast* goes and spoils it all."

The gorgonopsid was draped over the empty row of seats behind the girls, with his massive head swaying just above them and his razorlike claws dangling behind their seats.

"So . . . what? You girls couldn't get a date?"

Angela and Donna stared rigidly ahead, barely able to breathe.

Rob, Aran, and Billy pushed through the doors into the top balcony at a run, and stopped dead.

"Ladies and gentlemen," said the Gorgon, "Wynken, Blynken, and Nod!"

"Where's Phoebe?" Rob asked the others. "Where's Sid?"

Donna shook her head, petrified.

"*Sid?* That's what you call the old fool, is it?" said the gorgonopsid. "Cute."

"Listen," said Rob to the gorgonopsid, "you've got to go back to your own time. Sid says he'll meet you in 1904, and then you guys can go back together."

"Oh, really?"

"Sid said you might listen to us kids."

"Fascinating! Why ever would I do that?"

"I . . . I don't know," Rob muttered. "I wish Phoebe was here, she's the one who can talk."

"You wish Phoebe *were* here," smirked the Gorgon.

Rob saw the eyes of his friends all on him, everybody counting on him. "I guess Sid thought if you got to know some kids, like Phoebe and me and our friends, you wouldn't think the human race was such a total waste."

"Remarkable!" said the Gorgon.

"You know, it's really easy to be sarcastic," said Rob, his voice starting to tremble with anger. "That way, you don't have to listen. I do it all the time myself, and I wish I didn't. 'Cause there's probably some stuff worth listening to."

The Gorgon belched.

"Great. Very clever. Much better than anything the human race could come up with!"

Someone from the balcony below said, "Will you kids up there be quiet!"

Rob lowered his voice to a fierce whisper. "Because of you, Mister Gorgon, there'll be no Leonardo da Vinci, no Raphael, no Rembrandt! They were all left-handed, by the way—like me."

228

They're my heroes, but because of you, they'll never exist, none of those paintings will ever be! No one will get in a boat and sail around the world for the first time like Magellan. There won't be any boats! There won't be medicine or science or inventions, or the Golden Gate Bridge or pancakes or anything!"

"Are you going somewhere with this?" said the Gorgon in a bored tone, but his yellow eyes were locked on Rob, as though he was listening intently.

"Because of you, no Shakespeare! All those words, unwritten. Thanks a lot!"

"You dare talk to *me* of Shakespeare?" said the gorgonopsid, peering at the stage far below. "In the old days they truly knew how to *do* Shakespeare. There was none of this timid, minimal stuff. Back then, there was some *meat* on the bones, you could really sink your *teeth* into it!"

Something was happening. The air was quivering and humid and filling up with cigarette and cigar smoke. The floor beneath their feet was suddenly slimy from chewing-tobacco spit.

"Oh, my God," said Donna, glancing down at the stage below.

The production's simple bare scenery was dissolving, transforming to a massive, heavily painted panorama, with golden clouds floating above a storm-tossed sea, and a painted rocky cave. Instead of Sam Stone in the role of Prospero, there was a majestic figure in elaborate costume, wearing furs and gold braid, advancing down toward a row of footlights that hadn't been there a moment before.

"The great Loomis acted the role of Prospero right down there," whispered the Gorgon, "and I was here to see him."

"Come on, Stinky, let's go," said a voice from the back.

Jenkins stood in the door at the top of the balcony, wiping his hands with a blood-red handkerchief. "I got some business to take care of back in old Faith."

229

"Where's Phoebe? Where's Sid?" said Rob, almost vibrating with hatred. *"What did you do to Ms. Larson?"*

In answer, Jenkins strode down the steps and in one swift motion wrenched the critter detector from Rob's hands. "I'll take that!" Jenkins turned to the Gorgon.

"Okay, Body Odor," he said to the creature, recapping the aluminum walking stick, "let's get crackin'. I was hoping to have a little fresh goat for you, but I ran into a snag, so to speak."

The Gorgon's yellow eyes flashed up at the man dangerously for a moment.

Rob turned to the gorgonopsid. "You let him treat you like that? Just for a piece of *goat*?"

"I don't need his help catching dinner, and never did," said the Gorgon. "I let him *think* he was taming me with his treats. I wanted to see how low a man would go." The beast turned back to the play.

Onstage, the man in the braid and furs, holding an ornate staff, addressed the audience in a huge voice, with heavy vibrato.

> Our revels now are ended. These our actors,
> As I foretold you, were all spirits and
> Are melted into air, into thin air,
> And, like the baseless fabric of this vision,
> The cloud-capp'd towers, the gorgeous palaces,
> The solemn temples, the great globe itself,
> Ye all which it inherit, shall dissolve
> And, like this insubstantial pageant faded,
> Leave not a rack behind.

"Okay, okay," said Jenkins, "enough culture!"

Prospero raised his staff and brought it down over one knee, breaking it in two. And then he was gone. The footlights and the lurid painted scenery were gone, and the Gorgon and Jenkins were gone. There was just Sam standing on the stage in Prospero's simple robe, addressing the audience at the end of the play.

Sid's plan had failed utterly. Rob sank into a seat and held his head in his hands.

At that moment, from outside the theater, there came the muffled sound of a rifle shot.

> "We are such stuff (*said Sam as murmurs grew throughout the audience*)
> As dreams are made on, (*another shot*) and our little life (*another shot*)
> Is rounded (*another*) with a sleep.

A police siren wailed outside. The kids looked at each other, and then without a word they pounded down the stairs.

21
LOST

Yellow police tape was stretched across the bridge, so the theatergoers were milling around on that side of the flume, trying to see what was going on in the Cruzes' yard.

Angela had her arms around Whiskers' neck, and the other kids stood in a tight circle around Phoebe, who was crying and whispering to them and pointing down the flume, explaining what she'd seen.

Meanwhile, Mr. and Mrs. Cruz were talking to Sheriff Pete and Deputy Keith.

"Tusks, you say?" said Pete.

At this, all the kids looked up at the adults and listened.

"Tusks, I swear," said Vidal Cruz.

"Just like Mickie Pine said, remember, Pete?" said Keith.

"But the strange thing, Pete—this creature, it had a muzzle hanging around its neck," said Vidal.

"What do you mean?" said Deputy Keith.

"I mean, a dog's muzzle—like it was somebody's pet or something!"

Sheriff Pete slowly turned to Deputy Keith. After a moment, Keith slowly turned to the row of kids looking up at them, including his own son, Billy. Mr. and Mrs. Cruz turned and looked at the kids, too.

"Billy?" said Deputy Keith.

"Angela," said Mrs. Cruz, "do you know anything about this?"

★ ★ ★

The kids sat nervously on folding chairs in a sort of conference room in Faith's small police station, waiting for Sheriff Pete to come in and question them.

Whole nests of butterflies fluttered in their stomachs. Phoebe kept pulling out a damp handkerchief and blowing her nose, and her eyes were red. There was a smell of burned coffee in the air, and a stale mop odor.

"Do you think your dad hit them?" said Rob to Angela in a low voice. "Sid and YL?"

Angela brushed tears from her eyes.

"Is your dad, like, a good shot?"

Angela took a deep breath and nodded. The room was silent except for the tick of an old-fashioned wall clock.

At that point Sheriff Pete walked into the room, followed by Deputy Keith, who quietly shut the door after him. Pete slowly crossed the room and sat on top of a desk at one end, crossing his weathered old cowboy boots. Keith took up a position just inside the door, leaning against the wall. Billy's eyes darted to his dad and then sank to his sneakers.

"So, kids," said Sheriff Pete, "what's goin' on?"

Silence.

"You lost a horse, Donna, not too long ago," said Keith. "The other one, she's gonna make it, thank God, but it was close."

Silence.

"The Cruzes have little kids, remember," said the sheriff, switching tactics. "There's a toddler living in that house. What if it was your little sister, Angela? What if it was little Lily who wandered out into the yard for some big-tusked beast to find? Ask yourselves."

"Wild animals are just that, guys," said Keith. "They're wild. Maybe you think you're in control, but you're not."

Silence. Keith glanced over at Pete, who lifted his Stetson, smoothed back his grizzled gray hair, and replaced the hat.

"Vidal Cruz says this thing that attacked that goat was wearin' a dog muzzle. It was undone, just hanging loose around its neck, but it kind of makes me think somebody here thought they could make a Fido outta this thing."

The kids all looked down at the floor again.

"Billy?" said his dad. "You gonna tell us what all this is about?"

Billy gave a little shrug and said nothing.

"What about you, Rob Gates?" said Pete. "Your ma's waitin' in the lobby. So's yours, Phoebe. They're just down the hall, and they're lookin' pretty scared. They been cryin'. Now, you all gonna tell us anything to help matters here?"

Finally Rob cleared his throat.

"I'm pretty sure I know what attacked Angela's goat, Sheriff," he said, and the others looked at him in surprise.

"It wasn't the animal Angela's dad shot at. That was a di-ictodon from the Permian era, two hundred and fifty million years ago, and he's a total vegetarian. He came out of the mountain in—March, wasn't it, Phoeb?"

It suddenly dawned on Phoebe what Rob was doing, and her look of amazement turned into a smile.

"Middle of March," she said.

The last time they had told the truth to grown-ups about what was happening, nothing worse had come of it than a few weeks of psychotherapy.

"The diictodon was following a two-hundred-and-fifty-million-year-old gorgonopsid," Rob continued. "Definitely *not* a vegetarian, a real bloodthirsty type, but we know he didn't hurt Angela's goat 'cause the Gorgon was at the theater tonight, watching Shakespeare."

Pete and Keith exchanged glances.

"They need to get back to the Permian-Triassic boundary before they all die out," said Phoebe, "and we're trying to help them."

"Honest, Sheriff," said Rob, "I'm pretty sure the guy you want is a human being named Dr. Richard Jenkins. He's been killing pets to feed the Gorgon so he can travel back in time and buy up all the silver in the mines before it's discovered."

Sheriff Pete stood up, his leathery face creased into a frown. "I see," he said. "And you others go along with all that?"

Donna was the first to nod, then Aran grunted and nodded, and finally Billy did, too.

"You sure about that, Bill?" said Deputy Keith, and Billy nodded again, without looking at his father.

"Well," said Pete. "I must say, I'm real disappointed here."

"*Real* disappointed," added Keith with an edge to his voice, looking at his boy.

The sheriff tilted his Stetson back on his head. "You children get along home now. I'll be speaking with your parents, don't you think I won't."

The kids stood and shuffled past Keith out the door.

"You, Rob Gates," the sheriff said abruptly. Rob didn't turn, but he could feel the sheriff scowling at him anyway.

"You need to watch yourself around me from now on, boy. I can see you're turnin' out no better'n your no-good daddy."

The blood drained from Rob's face, but he just kept walking.

★ ★ ★

By the next day, word of the attack in the Cruzes' backyard and the strange creature that seemed to have been responsible had spread throughout town. The fear rose again that the original horse-killer had been not the mountain lion but something more exotic and frightening. And now, whatever it was, it had been shot dead or drowned—or else it was still on the loose among them.

Before school that morning, Rob had set out to search for Sid and Yellow Lab, to follow the course of the flume to where it ended in the flats below town, where the water flowed through a waste treatment plant, and then way down across the valley to the Rio Grande. But almost before he'd started, he'd seen Sheriff Pete and Keith Springer sitting in their squad car by the side of the road, watching him with unfriendly eyes. Rob had turned around and walked to school instead.

Phoebe, heading to school that morning past the church, had seen Pastor Mosely outside, spelling out the title of next Sunday's sermon in white letters on the bulletin board: "How

Old Is Earth? The Multimillion-Year Lie." Pastor noticed Phoebe, and for once he didn't smile or say hi, but followed her with his eyes, looking grim.

People once again locked up pets and kept an eye on their livestock. Up at the Mitchelsons' stables, Brad, Thelma, Nick, and Janet took turns monitoring the corrals and fields when the horses were out, riding among them with rifles slung across their saddles, and double-locking the stables when the horses were shut in at night.

Rob and Phoebe and the other members of the Gang of Six hadn't been *un*popular before any of this arose, but theirs had never been the cool table in the cafeteria. Now they were regarded as much more odd and uncool than before.

Teachers also looked at the six of them differently: some were watchful and suspicious, while others mocked them for coming up with such a bizarre story. Principal Dunne even brought up the subject at a faculty meeting: Were these kids on Drugs? Had they fallen into the hands of a Strange Cult? Or was this just a symptom of end-of-term Silliness?

But Rob and Phoebe barely noticed any of this. Where was Sid? Where was YL? Even as the Gang's table in the lunchroom was turning into an isolated island, that was the biggest question on their minds. Had Sid and YL been shot? Were they lying somewhere downstream even now, injured or worse? Every hour without Sid and the yellow lab chipped away at the hope they would ever see them again.

"I can't hear him," Phoebe kept saying, and Rob explained to the group that Phoebe sometimes seemed to be able to hear the diictodon from afar. But not now.

Rob and Phoebe kept checking the crawl spaces beneath their homes and finding them empty. Before she went to bed at night, Phoebe tried to empty her mind of distractions and listened as hard as she could. But no.

"I can't hear him, Rob," she said sadly into her walkie-talkie as she lay in bed, moments before falling asleep. "I can't hear him anymore."

Another day passed, and another, with no sign of their friend. As their moms watched with concern, Rob and Phoebe moved from shock and disbelief to despair.

22
THE SUMMONS

Kevin Scudder, Chad's older brother, worked in the sewage treatment facility just south of town. Almost all the Scudders worked in sewage treatment at some point in their lives—when they worked, which wasn't always.

Kevin was seriously freaked. It was a dark day, with heavy black clouds rolling across the valley floor and ganging up on the slopes above town, just spoiling for a fight. By noon you'd swear a sick version of night was falling fast. Distant thunder rumbled from mountain to mountain, once in a while punctuated by a flash and a bone-shivering thunderclap. Kevin was just about jumping out of his skin. He popped open another can of diet soda and cranked the heavy metal on his boom box as high as it would go, trying to drown out his fear. He sat and smoked and stared with frightened, bloodshot eyes out the grimy window. It wasn't the storm about to break that scared him witless.

It wasn't the thunder. It was the fact that he was supposed to be all alone at the facility, and he knew he wasn't.

The boom box voices were screaming loud nothings about death, mega-death, and giga-death, and it wasn't soothing Kevin's mind the way he'd hoped it would, so he finally turned the volume back down to zero.

"Who's there?" he croaked, for maybe the twentieth time, and listened with all his might.

There it was. A long low moan, and the voice of an old man saying, "Help me." It wouldn't occur to Kevin that the voice had a British accent, not in so many words. But it jarred a memory he had of a grade school visit to the Faith Rep, his class seeing a holiday show, and an old guy in a nightcap saying "Bah, humbug"—the voice sounded something like that.

Kevin picked up the cordless phone from the desk and moved to the building's back door. He squinted through the dirty, cracked pane of glass, then cautiously pushed the door open and stepped out.

"Help me." The voice was wheezing and faint but unmistakable.

Kevin resisted the impulse to duck back inside. He took a deep breath and walked hesitantly out onto the iron platform that surrounded the circular building, peering over the rail. On the downhill, or valley, side, treated water emerged from beneath the facility, with chutes fanning it into three large circular cement pools, to be further purified by chemicals and the sun's cleansing ultraviolet rays. The sky above was a sickly shade of green.

Kevin crept along the rail to the opposite side of the building, where rushing clear water from the flume passed through a sluice into the plant. A warm stinging wind whipped up from the valley, the light grew dimmer, and the rumblings of thunder became a continuous growl.

Wait a minute, Kevin thought. *That ain't no thunder growling.*

It was coming from below. He peered down into the gloom, and then he saw it. He tried to scream, but nothing came out except a hoarse sort of squeak. There below him, pressed against the sluice with a lot of trash and plastic grocery bags and somebody's old skateboard and a dead squirrel, was what Kevin took at first to be an elderly naked man with a hideously ugly face. And then he saw the deep dark eyes, and the eyes saw him, and the face suddenly wasn't so much ugly to him as troubling, but it for sure wasn't human.

A skinny, filthy yellow labrador was down there with it, like it was standing guard over it, looking up at Kevin, baring its teeth, and growling.

"Help me," the thing said in a weak, wheezing voice.

Oh, God, it talks.

Kevin's fingers were trembling so much he could hardly dial the phone in his hands. By the time Kevin punched in all the numbers, the storm had broken over Faith.

★ ★ ★

Mrs. Peabody was talking to her seventh-grade English class about how they had done on their final exam when Phoebe stood up from her desk abruptly and said, "Help me."

"That's what I'm *trying* to do, dear," said Mrs. Peabody, but Phoebe ignored her and ran to the window. A searing flash of white light streaked across the dark sky, followed almost immediately by a deafening clap of thunder. The entire class jumped, car alarms went off in the faculty parking lot outside, and the rain finally came lashing down.

"Get away from the windows, Phoebe," Mrs. Peabody said

241

above the racket of the rain, the wind, and the car alarms. "Phoebe?"

"She's so mental," said Arabella Giddens, and several kids laughed.

"You know, Arabella," whispered Angela, who was sitting just across the aisle from her, "you're actually a total bore."

"Shut up, Cruz!"

Phoebe unclipped the walkie-talkie from her belt and switched it on.

"You are not allowed to use that thing in here, Phoebe, you know that," said the teacher, her jewelry positively jingling with irritation.

Phoebe never took her eyes from the window. She pushed the talk button and spoke.

"Rob, I'm hearing him," she said. "He's in terrible trouble and he's telling me where he is. Meet me outside, and don't forget your backpack."

As Phoebe ran past the astonished Mrs. Peabody and out the door, Arabella shouted after her, "Beam me up, Scotty!" and everybody laughed.

"So lame," said Angela. She stood up and followed Phoebe out.

★ ★ ★

Rob, hanging on to his backpack with one hand, pelted along the corridor, accelerated round a corner, and ran full tilt into Principal Dunne, knocking him down flat. Rob was down there with him on the floor, a complicated mass of grunts and flailing legs and arms. *It couldn't have been the student hall monitor,* Rob was thinking, *or the custodian, or even the guidance counselor. No, it had to be the freaking principal.*

Rob said, "Sorry, sir," extricated himself, looped his backpack over his shoulders, and kept on running. Principal Dunne's breath was knocked clean out of him, and it was a full minute before he could start Yelling in Capital Letters.

Rob ran into Billy Springer's math class, grabbed him by his shirt collar, and dragged him into the corridor just as a gigantic thunderclap hammered the town. All the lights in Faith Middle School (and all the rest of Faith) flickered and went out. Billy said it felt like the end of the world, and Rob said, "I sure hope it doesn't turn out to be."

Students and faculty were stumbling into the corridors in the almost total darkness, and every car alarm in Faith was ringing its head off. Rob and Billy pushed through the milling crowd and out the front door. They found Phoebe there, dancing with impatience, and Angela with her, both of them sheltered under the concrete portico.

"Come on!" Phoebe cried, and they all took off running through the pouring rain. But they were way too late.

★ ★ ★

They had Sid in a cage big enough to hold a large dog, locked with a police padlock. Deputy Keith had responded to Kevin Scudder's call, and he'd enlisted Janet and Nick Bright's help. In the midst of the downpour, the three of them had managed to gently lift the diictodon off the sluice, hoist it with a harness up onto the back of Nick's pickup truck, and lay him down in this big cage. Sheriff Pete had watched the whole procedure with something less than approval.

Phoebe, Rob, Billy, and Angela were halfway down to the sewage treatment facility when they encountered the slow-moving procession coming up the road beneath Shotgun Hill: Sheriff Pete in his squad car was in the lead, with Kevin

Scudder sitting in the backseat, jabbering and gesturing and flicking the ashes from his cigarette out the window. He was followed by Nick Bright, driving the pickup slowly, with Janet crouched in back, in the rain, gripping the cage and staring into it in confusion and concern. Yellow Lab trotted alongside the truck, drenched and dirty, looking up at the cage with a worried dog look. At the rear of the procession was Deputy Sheriff Keith Springer, driving the town's other squad car.

Rob ran alongside the pickup and vaulted into the back. He was reaching through the bars of the cage when Janet grabbed him from behind.

"Rob, no!" she grunted, pinning Rob's arms, and Nick braked gently and stopped the truck, along with the whole procession. Phoebe climbed into the back of the pickup, signing again and again to Janet the word *friend.* Deputy Keith got out of his car.

Sid lay on his belly, his eyes half closed. His hide was shriveled, and it had turned a dead-looking shade of gray. His breathing was labored, and he kept licking his jaws with his long tongue. The leather muzzle was hanging loosely around his neck.

"You're killing him!" Rob yelled, pulling free from Janet's grip.

"Rob, now, just a second here," said Keith, in a calm-down sort of voice.

"He's dying, can't you see that?" cried Rob.

"Okay, okay, let's just everybody not get crazy here, okay?" said Keith.

Yellow Lab leapt up into the back of the truck. It was getting pretty chaotic back there, but Sid barely moved, and if he recognized Rob and Phoebe, he didn't show it. There was an ugly tear in his back on the right side, jagged and crusty, which must have been where the bullet had entered.

Billy and Angela stood in the road next to the truck, both of them soaked to the skin. "Dad," Billy said, "you've gotta believe us, he's not dangerous."

Sheriff Pete got out of his car and came ducking back to the truck, tilting his Stetson to ward off the rain and looking disgusted.

"Now what is all this, for crying out loud?" he said.

"You kids," said Keith, "you climb into my car and come along with us. We'll get this sorted out."

Nick had gotten out of the truck's cab, and he and Janet were signing the same thing over and over to Phoebe: "What is it? Is it a lizard? What kind of thing is it?"

Other townspeople were gathering now despite the downpour, holding umbrellas or folded-up newspapers over their heads, staring in shock and revulsion at the creature in the cage. The power was still blacked out, and car alarms were still going off all over the place.

"Let's get this show on the road, Keith," said the sheriff.

"You don't understand!" cried Rob, almost sobbing with frustration. "You don't understand what's at stake here!"

"No, son," said Keith, "I surely do not understand. So you just climb into the car and we'll talk it all out at the station and maybe you can help us understand."

Suddenly Phoebe saw her mother approaching on the street, dripping with rain, staring at the cage that her daughter was clinging to, and the creature inside it.

"Phoebe!" cried Jane Traylor, running to the truck, and Phoebe looked down at her mother desperately, her face streaming with tears.

"Mom, this is him," she said. "This is him, Mom. *Now* do you believe me?"

Jane put one hand to her mouth. "Oh, my God," she whispered.

Sheriff Pete put an end to the scene on the street by telling them all to shut up or else he'd shoot the damn thing then and there and be done with it. They were to follow him to the police station, where they would all continue to shut up and cooperate fully, or he'd lock 'em all up.

Well, there was no arguing with the law, at least not just then. Rob and Phoebe flat out refused to ride in the back of Pete's car or Keith's—they put up such a protest that Keith agreed to let them ride the rest of the way in the back of the pickup with the cage, as long as they promised to keep their fingers and hands safely away from the beast. Billy boldly told his dad that he and Angela meant to walk behind the truck, and Jane Traylor said that's what she would do, too, and Keith finally said, "Sure, fine, whatever," and walked back to his car. The rain had tapered to a drizzle by this point, and the procession continued slowly toward the top of town and the police station.

Phoebe put her face to the cage. "Sid," she said. "Can you hear me?"

Rob leaned into the bars and said, "How are you doing, buddy?"

The long tongue came out again and made a circuit of Sid's jaws, as though it were searching for an answer, but he made no other sign of having heard Rob or even being aware of his presence.

Janet tapped Phoebe's shoulder and started signing ASL.

"She says the sheriff was going to shoot him right there at the sewage plant," Phoebe translated, "but she and Nick stopped him. She says Pete finally agreed to keep the creature alive long enough for a team from the university down in Arenoso to examine it. Janet thinks she could get the slug out of his back if she just had her equipment and a little time, but she and Nick are afraid the sheriff won't keep his promise—they think he's

246

planning to put him down as soon as they get to the police station."

"Ask Janet how they got him into this cage," said Rob suddenly.

Phoebe signed the question, and Janet signed back.

"They just lifted him off the sluice at the water plant," Phoebe translated, "into a harness thing, and laid him in the cage."

"They *touched* him? And nothing happened?"

Phoebe signed again, and Janet signed back with a puzzled look on her face. "Yes, they touched him," Phoebe translated, "and no, nothing happened."

The implications were obvious.

"He's not doing so well, is he," said Phoebe softly, and Rob shook his head. Yellow Lab put his nose in Rob's lap and whined.

"We've got to get him away," Rob said. "We can't trust the grown-ups with this. They're not ever going to believe the truth about Sid."

"Maybe my mom will," said Phoebe, "now that she's seen him."

"Yeah, but what good'll that do us? Everybody already thinks your mom is crazy."

"Yeah, you're right, I was forgetting," said Phoebe, mopping the rain from her face with a handkerchief.

"Sid, you gotta listen to me," Rob said through the bars of the cage. "You really need to live. Just live, okay?"

As they watched, Sid exhaled with a raspy sound, and his body shuddered slightly. Long, frightening moments passed, and then he slowly drew breath in again.

Janet Bright stared at the strange creature in the cage, mesmerized. She was, after all, a veterinarian, a scientist, and she already realized that this was probably the most exciting thing that would ever happen in her professional life.

They were all just passing the bank when an idea crossed Rob's face. He dug in his jeans pockets and pulled out a set of keys triumphantly.

"Adelaide Parsons' car keys!" he whispered excitedly.

"You can't be serious," said Phoebe. "Rob, you got those keys *weeks* ago. Do you mean to say you haven't changed your jeans since then?"

"I change 'em all the time," he replied defensively. "I *rotate,* okay? Geez!"

Rob leaned over the back of the pickup.

"Billy," he said, "do you have your master key with you?"

Billy, walking behind and brushing the drizzle from his eyes, shook his head. "I can't find it, I've been looking all over."

Angela reached under the top of her soggy blouse and pulled Billy's lanyard from around her neck.

"Remember?" she said. "On the glacier? You saved me with it."

"Oh, yeah," said Billy, blushing.

Rob reached down and took it from Angela.

"You need to handle everybody on this end," he said to Phoebe, giving her the lanyard with the police master key attached.

At that moment Aran came sprinting up the street, with Donna running just behind.

"Oh, my God," said Donna, seeing the cage.

"Okay," said Rob. "All of us have to be cooler and smarter than we've ever been in our lives. I'll just be a minute—make sure Sid's ready to move when I come back."

Rob leapt off the back of the truck, and Yellow Lab leapt after him.

"Rob?" said Jane Traylor, but both boy and dog knew how to run. In an instant they had vanished. Jane looked questioningly at her daughter, and Phoebe said, "Mom, you're gonna have to go along with some pretty major stuff here," and then she turned and put the police master key into the lock on Sid's cage, staring Janet Bright in the face the whole time.

★ ★ ★

The old Oldsmobile had been sitting out on Main, taking up space in front of the bank for weeks. It was inconvenient, but everybody knew whose it was and nobody cared very much. It wasn't even locked—Faith was that kind of town.

The plastic seat covers crinkled as Yellow Lab jumped into the front. Rob pushed him to the passenger side and slid himself into the driver's seat. He could barely see over the steering wheel.

"Thanks for not teaching me how to drive, Dad," he muttered bitterly.

It started on the second try. He moved the gearshift on the steering column to drive and the car lurched forward into the car ahead of it with an ugly crunch. Rob's left foot pounded the brake, fast.

Okay, no damage done, he said to himself, *or not much, anyway.*

Rob craned his head around to inspect the rear of the car. Big plastic water bottles remained back there—water from the well that opened your eyes to the mysteries of life, according to Adelaide, and kept your bowels regular.

Fortunately, there was no one parked behind. He shifted into reverse and slowly backed into Main Street in a big arc, reversing 180 degrees until the rear of the station wagon faced uptown, toward the police station. And then he just kept on backing, one hand on the wheel, his torso twisted around, his eyes focused out the back window. The rain started up again, and Rob just kept going, reversing all the way up Main, sometimes faster, sometimes slower. The one car he encountered, which was heading down Main, was Pastor Mosely's van. It couldn't have been anybody else's, thought Rob; it just had to be *Pastor's*. Reverend Mosely turned sharply, giving Rob a wide berth and a hard look as he passed him.

Rob breathed with relief. His backward driving wasn't perfect, or even good, but so far he hadn't crashed or hurt anybody. He kept on going.

★ ★ ★

Sheriff Pete pulled his car into the municipal parking lot behind the police station, with Kevin Scudder still jabbering and gesticulating from the backseat.

Nick brought the pickup truck to a slow, gentle stop in front of the station. Keith pulled his car out around it, to Phoebe's great relief, and turned into the police area of the parking lot behind the station just as Pete had done. *Thank God for routine!* Phoebe thought. They would be out of sight of both the sheriff and the deputy for at least a few seconds.

Nick was getting out of the truck's cab, and Jane was starting to ask Phoebe questions that it was way too late to ask, when Phoebe said, gently but firmly, "Mom, stop talking. You guys? You need to get out of the way, right this minute."

Phoebe was staring back over their heads, down Main Street. Almost in unison the others turned round and looked.

An old station wagon was backing its way up the road, veering first one way and then the other, slowing down and then speeding up in an alarming fashion. It was headed directly for them.

"Children," said Jane Traylor, "avoid that car." They all scattered as the back end of the station wagon butted up against the back end of the pickup with a clunk, Rob's anxious face visible through the back window.

Rob shifted and drove forward a couple of feet, then stopped.

"Billy, open the back of the wagon," said Phoebe. "Aran, Donna—get up here and help me, please. Mom? Go intercept Pete and Keith. Make something up—talk to them about the vegan life or something. Tell them you'll have the SPCA on them for cruelty to prehistoric creatures. Will you do that? For me?"

Jane hesitated for just a moment, glancing doubtfully at Rob behind the wheel of the Oldsmobile and then at the strange animal lying motionless in the cage.

"Take it straight home," Jane whispered, "and stay there. I'll do my best. Be careful, honey." Then she strode off around the building to speak with the authorities.

Nick Bright looked a little alarmed at what was going on, but Janet started signing fast, and Nick seemed to nod in agreement, although a bit apprehensively. The kids lifted Sid from the cage and laid him gently in the back of the station wagon. No one vibrated; no one went anywhere in time. They looked and felt more like pallbearers than time travelers.

Phoebe got in the back, kneeling on one side of Sid, with Angela on the other. Donna and the boys piled into the backseat, and Yellow Lab scrambled awkwardly from the front seat, climbing over the seats and over the kids to get into the back, making the car and everyone in it even wetter and dirtier than they already were. Yellow Lab flopped down beside the synapsid and heaved a great sigh. Sid's big black eyes fluttered and seemed to look up at the dog as Rob put the car into drive and drove. For a second there, Phoebe thought Sid's lips moved and YL's ears pricked up.

★ ★ ★

"What's she saying? Will someone just please tell me what this woman is saying?" Sheriff Pete was furious, and Janet Bright, explaining in sign language why the creature wasn't in the cage anymore, was just making him angrier. He turned his glare on Jane Traylor.

"I was with *you,* I didn't see a thing," she said, almost honestly.

"This cage was locked, was it not, Keith?" said Pete, ignoring Jane.

"I'm pretty sure I locked it, Pete."

"So how'd it get unlocked? What are these kids doing? Where'd they go with that little monster, dammit?"

"She's deaf, Sheriff," said Jane. "No matter how loud you talk, she's not going to hear you."

Pete turned his back on her, muttering.

"What's that you said, Officer?" said Jane.

"Nothin'."

"Oh, I think you said *something,*" Jane said. Janet, reading everybody's lips, stifled a laugh and signed to Jane, "He called you a lady dog."

"Listen, Pete," said Keith, "it's just a few kids on foot, and that thing they're carrying is half dead. We'll find them." He turned to Nick and Janet and said, "They *were* on foot, right?"

Nick and Janet both signed back, and Keith looked helplessly to Jane. "Do you know what they just said?"

"Yes," said Jane. "They said they can't hear you—they're deaf."

★ ★ ★

"Mom said we can hide him at our place," Phoebe said as Rob drove them all down Main. The rain had stopped completely, and the clouds were giving way to big patches of late afternoon blue.

"And how long before they come for him there?" said Rob.

"It's no good, Phoebe. We've got to get him home—*all* the way home."

"He's too sick to travel, Rob."

"Probably. But he's got to do it anyway." Rob suddenly turned right off Main and headed up the road that passed Shotgun Hill, toward the mountainside meadow, high above town.

"Hey, Rob," said Aran. "Grand Theft Auto! We're living it!"

Rob and Billy nodded with a grim sort of satisfaction, and each of the girls in the car shook their heads, with pity for the male of the species.

Phoebe carefully undid the tattered leather muzzle that still hung round Sid's neck and removed it.

"Angela?" said Phoebe. "Grab one of those water bottles from the back."

Angela opened one of the plastic bottles and poured a little water into Phoebe's cupped hands. Phoebe held them before Sid's snout, but he didn't move. She let the water drop through her fingers onto Sid's head. A moment later his eyes fluttered.

"More," said Phoebe. Angela gave her a refill and Phoebe held it just beneath Sid's jaw. Nothing happened.

"More," Phoebe said again. This time she gently lifted Sid's upper jaw and let a few drops of water fall on his tongue. The diictodon's long pink tongue emerged tentatively, searching.

"More, please," said Phoebe, and Angela tipped the water bottle over Phoebe's cupped hands again.

Sid lapped that up as well, this time lifting his head a bit. Everybody was watching now, even Rob in the rearview mirror.

"More," said Phoebe. "Move *over*, YL. More water."

Whether the water was magic or just good plain well water, it was working some kind of magic on the diictodon. He coughed and rattled from somewhere deep inside him. Phoebe put her head to his.

"I think he's trying to say something," said Phoebe quietly.

Rob pulled off the road onto a path leading up into the high hillside meadow and brought the car to a stop. They all listened.

Sid *was* trying to speak. At first they couldn't make it out, his breathing was so labored. It sounded like . . .

"Fetch," Sid rasped, barely audible, turning his eyes to the yellow lab. YL sprang up eagerly.

"Fetch." The dog started squealing with anticipation.

"Fetch . . . them," whispered Sid.

Yellow Lab responded by scratching urgently at the back window.

"Should I let him out?" said Phoebe, confused, with one hand on the back window's handle.

"Sure, I guess," said Rob. The moment she swung it open, the dog leapt down into the meadow and raced like an arrow up into the dense woods above.

At the same time, Donna, looking out the back of the car, said, "Guys? I think we're busted."

Far below, two squad cars were snaking up the road toward them.

Rob started the car instantly and headed off the road, up the hill toward the meadow above.

★ ★ ★

The old Oldsmobile station wagon wasn't built for off-road driving, that was for certain. It was big and heavy and lumbering, and its front and rear bumpers were thudding into the sod with every little dip and rise in the terrain. The larger rocks made terrible noises as they scraped the car's underside. Rob drove the station wagon in zigzags up the mountain. When the slope was too steep, the car lost traction and the wheels dug into the turf, and he'd have to cut back until he could find a gentler angle. The kids were jolting all over the place. Phoebe and Angela did their best to cushion Sid with their arms, but it was a rough ride.

"I don't see the cops," said Aran, craning out a rear window. "Ouch!" He pulled his head back in, rubbing it where it had made contact with the window-frame. "Hey, Gates, who said you knew how to drive?"

"This is really not good for Sid, Rob," said Phoebe from the back.

"Yeah, Rob," said Billy, who had gone completely green, "it's not good for Sid."

"Okay, okay," Rob said, his eyes flashing in the rearview mirror. The car rolled to a stop on the grassy slope, and Rob switched off the ignition. Billy got out of the car fast, one hand cupped over his mouth. He hurried to a clump of bushes on the hill above them and disappeared. Sid's eyes were shut. His breathing was uneven and his lungs sounded full of liquid.

"Let's get him out onto the grass," said Phoebe. Donna got out of the car and opened the back for them, and the three girls carefully lifted Sid and laid him gently on the green cushion of mountain grasses.

The kids stretched. Everyone felt glad to get out of the car, glad to be in the air, glad that, for now at least, they seemed to have eluded the police.

"They must not have seen where we turned off the road," said Aran.

"Yeah, but the road dead-ends up there, around twelve thousand feet," said Rob. "When they come back down they'll know I went off-road, and they'll be looking for where."

In the lengthening shadows just before dusk, they saw a small herd of long-eared mule deer appear on the crest of a hill, lit by a golden light. A mother jackrabbit and her litter of bunnies hopped into sight on a slope to their left and stopped. A fox dashed out from the line of trees ahead and froze, staring at them.

Rob knelt beside Sid and stroked his head. The breeze sighed across the face of the mountain, and the car's engine block ticked as it cooled.

"He's not in any shape to travel, Rob," said Phoebe quietly.

"I know he's not." Rob drew his hand gently along the synapsid's back, feeling the texture of his hide. As Phoebe watched, Rob lay down in the grass beside Sid, put his mouth to the creature's ear, and whispered. "You're not going anywhere, are you, buddy. So we'll just stick together until it's all over . . . for all of us. Okay? Me and Phoebe will be right beside you."

Phoebe knelt on Sid's other side, stroking his head. "Phoebe and I," she said automatically, and the diictodon exhaled in a way that almost seemed like a little laugh. Then he coughed, and a line of pinkish spit came from his mouth.

"We're right here," said Rob. "Okay?"

Sid turned his eyes on Rob and drew in a long, noisy breath.

"I'm sorry I teased you so much, Sid. I didn't mean any of it." Sid blinked and drew another breath.

Phoebe went to the car and came back with Rob's backpack. "The grapes you packed," she said, pulling out a plastic bag. "It feels like a long time ago."

She knelt and put a grape by Sid's mouth. His big black eyes looked up at her for a moment and then fluttered shut. His sides rose and fell with a raspy sigh. Phoebe looked at Rob, and Rob looked away.

"What are those deer doing?" said Aran, looking off at the crest of the hill where they'd first appeared.

The deer hadn't run away; they just stood and watched, and now the lead deer, a buck, was stepping cautiously toward them. Two does behind him stepped forward, their long faces going up and down, scenting the air, their big eyes staring. They were moving closer, and more deer followed behind them.

"The jackrabbits . . ." Donna's voice trailed off. The rabbits were slowly approaching them also, taking a couple of hops forward, then pausing, their noses twitching, and hopping forward again. And where had all those *other* rabbits come from, and all those squirrels and chipmunks?

"Look at that fox!" said Phoebe, standing. It was running back and forth, staring at them, and then running toward them, zigzagging excitedly. And then there were two foxes. And then there were six.

"Guys." Billy's voice startled them, stepping out from behind the bushes, about a dozen yards above them on the slope, wiping his mouth with a handkerchief. "Something's happening," he said.

Behind Billy stood at least a dozen bighorn sheep. The bighorns began to advance, and soon Billy was surrounded by them, their massive curled horns brushing his elbows. The sheep were all staring at the Last Synapsid.

Rob's hand, lying on Sid's back, began to vibrate slightly. Rob quickly drew it back and stood up.

"Sid?" he said.

The kids suddenly ducked as a whole fleet of bats swooped above them with a rush of wings, and then another fleet, and another.

Yellow Lab raced down out of the dark line of trees above, flying like an arrow straight to Sid, stopping and panting and drooling above him for a moment. With great effort, Sid lifted his head to the dog and croaked, "Fetch."

YL said "Bark!" and raced back into the woods again. Phoebe and Rob, standing beside Sid, looked at him questioningly. His breathing was still noisy, but he seemed to be drawing more air in, and his hide was not quite the lifeless gray it had been earlier.

The air around them became more humid and began to smell like a barnyard or a stable, full of earthy life. And the animals kept coming.

The kids on the mountain turned in circles, awestruck, trying to see it all. There were posses of racoons, and a delegation of hedgehogs, and another of possums. Tiny shrews crawled up out of holes in the ground, wriggling across the turf, singly and in pairs. Voles and harvest mice crept out by the dozen, and then by the hundreds, until it felt like the whole earth was alive and moving.

Even when a large black bear ambled out of the woods, with a couple of cubs trailing her, no one seemed to be afraid. The smaller animals parted before the bears, giving them plenty of room, but all the creatures, big and little, were focused on Sid, not on each other or the humans.

Rob pointed. "Mountain lion, Phoebe," he said quietly, knowing that it was one of Phoebe's fondest dreams to see one. "Over there." The beast became visible, walking out of shadow with the sensuous, sinewy walk universal among cats. The smaller creatures opened a path for her. She moved slowly toward them and stopped, looking at Sid. Two more lions emerged from the shadows and approached, and then a Canadian lynx.

Phoebe gripped Rob's shoulder wordlessly and Rob nodded, staring at the ever-appearing beasts.

Billy pushed his way out of the bighorn herd, politely saying "Excuse me" to the sheep, and "Pardon me, I beg your pardon" the whole way. He made his way to Angela and they held hands, looking at it all.

"You smell like sheep," whispered Angela, smiling.

Aran caught Donna's eye and nodded. "You've got company."

She followed his gaze and realized there was a row of white-footed mice sitting on one of her shoulders, their tiny hands at their tiny faces, as though they were attending a play and about to applaud. Donna had been afraid of mice her whole life, but now she just beamed. Aran put a finger up to the mice, and one of them stepped daintily onto it.

"Water, please," said Sid, his voice cracking but stronger than it had been moments earlier. Phoebe was about to pour water into Rob's cupped hands, but Sid spoke again. "In the wound. Water in the wound."

So she tipped the plastic bottle of Adelaide Parsons' mystery-and-regularity water over the ugly, blood-crusted knot in Sid's back. Steam rose from the wound with a faint sizzling sound, and then a deep ruby-red glow emanated from it.

"Oh, dear," said Sid, closing his eyes, "that stings. The diictodon took a deep rasping breath, and the glow intensified. He took another deep breath, and a dark reddish orb appeared within the wound, just below the surface of Sid's hide.

"Pluck it out," he said hoarsely. Phoebe and Rob glanced at each other. "Phoebe! Please! Pluck it out."

Phoebe took a deep breath and with thumb and forefinger reached for the wound in Sid's back, thinking, *Veterinarians must do things like this every day.*

"Quickly!"

As gently as she could, she held open the edges of the wound with the fingers of one hand. Sid gasped and closed his eyes. With thumb and forefinger of her other hand, she gingerly plucked out the glowing slug and immediately dropped it on the grass. "It's burning hot!" she cried. There was a searing pain in her hand, which was already starting to blister in thumb, finger, and palm. The bullet sizzled in the moist grass, the reddish glow beginning to fade.

"Humankind's bitter seed," said Sid. "The only animal who hurls death from a distance into the bodies of others." Sid's voice was growing stronger, his breath coming more evenly.

"It hurts," said Phoebe simply, staring at her wounded palm.

"Yes," said Sid, "it does. Keep it, and remember."

Phoebe reached cautiously for the irregular slug, by now just a dull gunmetal-gray ball. It was already cool enough to touch, and she put it in her pocket. All the creatures on the mountain were watching closely.

The diictodon slowly stood. "Help me up onto that rock, Rob, if you'd be so kind."

Rob hoisted Sid up onto a large flat ledge, feeling a faint tingling vibration up and down his arms. "Let me go now," said the creature. "I can do this." His breathing was becoming quieter and steadier as he looked out over the mountain slope and the gathering creatures, and he stood up ever straighter. Yellow Lab zoomed into sight again in the fading light with a train of noisy coyotes at his heels. He led them running in circles round Sid and the kids, the coyotes yelping and crying in excitement. As the coyotes continued to circle, YL raced off once more into the woods. A few moments later he returned at a much slower pace, followed by martens and marmots, skunks, and a lone armadillo. It was dusk now on the mountain, soon to give way to dark.

Sid cleared his throat, and the coyotes went silent and stopped circling. All the other creatures on the mountain became suddenly still, except for four elk that were just loping over the crest of the hill. Then they stopped as well.

"My children," said the synapsid. As soon as he said it, the creatures on the mountain all spoke at once, each in its own tongue. There was bleating and barking and roaring and squeaking and mewing and yelping and the sonic *teek-teek-teek* of the bats whirling overhead.

"What is it?" whispered Billy. "What are they saying?"

" 'Father,' " said Rob. "I'm pretty sure they're saying 'father.' "

Sid bowed his head modestly before the multitude, a long string of drool dangling from his lower jaw. The six humans watched and listened.

"Children," he said again, "I have to go now. These two young human friends and I have a mission to accomplish." Sid tilted his head toward Phoebe and Rob. "They're taking a great risk to help us all."

Phoebe and Rob looked out at a sea of shining mammalian eyes, glittering in the darkness.

"I'll miss you," Sid continued. "I'll tell my spouse about each one of you, if she's still living and I can find her. She was worried that none of you would come into being. I'm worried, now that I've seen your world and sniffed your air, that none of you will last. You mustn't let your world die like mine."

At that moment a police siren blasted below them and headlights pounded up the hillside. Sid squinted, and a frightened murmur went up from the animals. Down the mountain slope two squad cars came to a stop. A small group of adults got out and started to walk up toward them: Sheriff Pete and Deputy Keith, Jane Traylor and Lucy Gates, and Nick and Janet Bright. Keith held a bullhorn in one hand and a long flashlight in the other.

"*Okay, you kids!*" Keith's voice barked over the bullhorn. "*Fun's over! Let's go! Come on down!*"

It was just dark enough that the adults at first didn't realize that the mountainside was covered with a multitude of mammals. Their first clue came from the bats: a vast cloud of them flew squeaking down the slope, darting this way and that, just above their heads. People ducked, and Lucy Gates, who was afraid of bats, let out a little scream. Keith switched on his light and shone it up at the bats, which filled the sky, circling and swooping. Then Keith lowered the beam of light, and finally the adults saw thousands of lit-up eyes staring down at them. And six middle school kids in the midst of them.

"Oh, my God," said Lucy Gates.

"What the hell . . . ?" said the sheriff. Keith played the beam around the hill, and everywhere the light touched, the scene became more impossibly bizarre. Goats, sheep, dogs, coyotes, deer, beaver, elk, racoons, horses . . . A bear? Four bears! Mountain lions!

Jane Traylor started bravely up the hill. "Phoebe," she called, frightened and angry, "you said you'd go *home* with it. You said you'd take it straight home!"

"You *let* them go?" said Lucy, turning on Jane. "You *allowed* them?"

"Ladies, stay right where you are!" snapped Pete. "Give me that thing!" He grabbed the bullhorn from Keith and put it to his lips.

"I don't know what's goin' on here, but you children are in serious trouble, you hear me?" Sheriff Pete headed up the mountain, drawing his revolver.

"Pete, for God's sake," cried Jane, "put that gun away!"

"You caused enough trouble, lady," said the sheriff. "I don't want to hear another word outta you! Back me up, Keith."

That's when the bears started down toward the adults, taking their time, and there were six of them by now, not four. The three mountain lions walked with unhurried pace in a line down the slope, along with the lynx, the bighorn sheep, the pronghorns, a single bison from who knows where, and a dozen or so coyotes. Sally May and Junior had somehow gotten out of the Mitchelsons' stables on the other side of the mountain; they whinnied loudly as they approached. The smaller beasts followed, until it seemed that an armada of mammals was moving slowly on the downcrest of a great wave. All the animals finally stopped, a vast wall of life facing the grownups. There was silence, except for a lot of panting and snorting and the squeak and teek of the bats, swooping above. Then one of the bears bellowed with amazing volume, and Pete retreated, almost stumbling over his feet in his haste.

Lucy shouted up the hillside, trying not to cry. "Rob, are you okay?"

There was no answer. "Rob?"

"Phoebe?" Jane shouted. "Guys? Is everybody all right up there?" It was impossible to see through the wall of animals. "Kids? *Please answer!*"

But the kids couldn't answer, because they weren't there anymore.

23
THE ROARING NAUGHTS

The Gang's first glimpse of Faith in 1904 was from the mountain meadow where they'd been surrounded by the vast horde of mammals a moment earlier. Suddenly alone, they saw below them the yellow glow of gas lamps, and heard, even from there, the raucous noise of a mining town that knew little of the law, and even less of order.

"Oh, this is just too much!" said Sid, exasperated, looking at the six breathless, wide-eyed kids and one yellow lab. "You others weren't supposed to come, just Phoebe and Rob!"

"Didn't do it on purpose," Aran said, a bit put out.

"I know, I know," muttered the diictodon. "It's not your fault. It's always the same—grown-up humans blunder in and ruin everything."

The six kids nodded, knowing this to be true from experience.

The ancient creature looked at the kids and the panting yellow dog and shook his head in dismay.

"My mate did not dream a whole gaggle of you. I believe it's Phoebe and Rob whose influence will allow me to take the Gorgon and go back—all the way back to our old home. But how am I going to get the rest of you back to yours?"

It was a question on all their minds, but Donna put a brave face on it. "I don't think it would be right to leave you guys," she said stoutly, "even if we could."

"Yeah, why should they have all the fun?" Aran said, and the others sort of collectively rolled their eyes.

"Aran," said Rob, "you're an actual idiot."

"Never mind, never mind," said the synapsid. "We'll cross that bridge when we come to it. Right now we've got work to do down there, and time is running out."

With Sid in the lead, and YL racing ahead and circling back, they headed down into Faith.

The darkness helped to hide them as they made their way along Main Street, but even so, they were noticed. There were not a lot of children in Faith in that era, and the kids' clothes and brightly colored backpacks were outlandish to local eyes. Suspicious faces appeared at windows and disappeared behind hastily drawn curtains. Rough-looking miners on the street changed course and crossed to the other side, eyeing them narrowly. The Gang walked in a tight knot, keeping Sid out of sight for the most part, but no one challenged them. This was a town where people tended to let others *be*, mainly because it could be dangerous not to.

Faith had exploded since 1890, when it was called Willow Creek. Now the silver boom was on, and the tiny prospectors' settlement had grown into a prosperous, chaotic, over-populated free-for-all. Wood-frame buildings stood jammed shoulder to shoulder with each other, and shacks with tin chimneys spread out from Main Street in no particular order. There were businesses cramming both sides of Main, with boardwalks lining the muddy, rutted road. There was a saloon every few feet, and no shortage of customers, judging from the number of horses tied up to hitching posts along the street. There was a majestic brick opera house that the kids recognized as Faith Rep's future home. The street was filled with music, shrill voices, and laughter. The kids' eyes and ears were filled with it all.

So much so that at first they didn't notice the woman who was bearing down on them, walking with a cane and calling their names.

"Phoebe Traylor! Robert Gates! Welcome!" cried Philippa Larson. "Aran, you made it! Donna, Angela, Billy—I'm so happy to see you!"

This was the sort of tone of voice that triggered YL's joy gene, and he jumped and capered all around the librarian, beside himself with happiness, although it's uncertain he'd ever met her before.

"It's Ms. Larson," said Phoebe, dumbstruck. One by one the kids realized it was so.

"But . . . but . . . how did . . . ?"

"How are you feeling, Philippa?" said Sid. "How's the pain?"

"Who cares? I'm living a dream! Just think, I was able to get my old rooms in the hotel!" she said. "Or rather, my new rooms—I guess they were old the first time I moved into them, but now they're brand-new. It's all a little confusing. Anyway, we mustn't stand out here talking—follow me. It's the twenty-seventh of May, Sidney—as you know, we don't have much time."

She turned and led them through a passage up to the back entrance of the Holy Moses saloon.

"Have you encountered our friends?" said Sid as they walked.

"Indeed. The malodorous one is in his favorite hidey-hole in the opera house, and yes, Sidney, there *is* a sort of tunnel from the theater down into one of the mines. You were right."

"And the other one?"

"He's in the saloon, about to do a great mischief according to everything I've read, so we really must hurry."

★ ★ ★

Serenity Parsons sensed trouble in the smoky air. It was a familiar sensation in the Holy Moses saloon, where men with too much to drink and too little (or too much) money in their pockets tended to over-react to life's little frustrations. There was always somebody accusing somebody else of cheating him, at cards or in the mines or with a woman, and half the time they'd be right. You wanted to step out for fresh air *before* they went for their guns.

But this was different. *He* had returned, as suddenly as he'd disappeared fourteen years earlier, and with as little explanation. The romantic stranger who had promised to give her a better life, far from the mines, had captured her seventeen-year-old heart. And then he'd gone, without a word, and stayed gone. Serenity's broken heart had eventually hardened. When Jeb Larson asked her to marry him, she'd said yes, but within a year Jeb was dead in a cave-in deep in the Argento mine. Childless, Serenity Parsons took care of her father, Lemuel, her uncle, Willis, and her younger brother, Jesse. Willis finally died of the black lung and disappointment, but Lemuel lived on, an invalid suffering from the same ailments. The one joy in Serenity's life was her brother. But Jesse was a man now, with a family of his own and little time for her since going into the mines himself.

Serenity at thirty-one was an old lonely widow, working as a saloon waitress. She should have spurned the man who called himself Patrick Mulcahy FitzHugh when he came back; she should have told him how much she hated him for deserting her. Instead, she'd clung to him, the way a person might cling to one last chance.

At the same time, she was afraid of him. She watched him from behind the bar as she washed glasses. He'd spent the day at the bank, checking into his accounts, he said, but now he was at a table against the wall, smoking and drinking whiskey and playing a hand of poker with one of the miners. Patrick Mulcahy FitzHugh had the look of a man who held all the winning cards, but there was something in his eyes that was infinitely cold.

Serenity had already been warned about him. The newcomer to town, the lady who said she was related to Serenity's late husband, Jeb, had urged her to be careful. Philippa Larson had showed up almost a week before FitzHugh reappeared, and taken rooms in the hotel and a job with Serenity behind the bar. She walked painfully, using a cane, and there were fading bruises on her face. She explained that she had hurt herself in a bad fall. She bore her injuries well, though. Once she'd purchased a second-hand pair of spectacles, Philippa Larson moved through town beaming as though it were her birthday, loving everything she saw.

Except for Patrick Mulcahy FitzHugh. Whenever he came into the saloon, Philippa would make herself scarce, ducking into the pantry or the kitchen. "Don't trust him, dear," Philippa said to Serenity when the two of them were alone together. "His real name is Jenkins, and he means no one well." Serenity knew somehow that the woman was right. But when the man invited her to his room, she'd gone anyway.

The saloon was packed, as usual. The gaslights flickered through the hazy air, thick with tobacco smoke. Jimmy Broadway was playing the piano, and a couple of the Sweet brothers, Tom and Al, were singing along. There were three or four other games of poker in progress. A table of traveling salesmen were eating beefsteak and potatoes, and at least a dozen miners were drinking up their most recent paycheck.

Then a young miner named Russell Gates came in, a clutch of papers in his right hand and a crazed look on his face.

"Which one of you is FitzHugh?" he cried hoarsely.

Jimmy Broadway kept on playing and the Sweet brothers went on singing, but when Russell Gates pulled a pistol from his holster everything went quiet. Gates shouted again, "FitzHugh! I want a word with you!"

The barroom was silent now, and Serenity edged toward the back pantry door.

"My name is FitzHugh," said Jenkins quietly. "What can I do for you?"

"You can tell me how you did it, damn you! You can tell me how you managed to know where every single lode would be! *Fourteen years ago!*"

Gates waved the papers madly in the faces of the other miners. "We don't own nothin'! It's all his!"

Tom Sweet took a step toward the younger man. "Come on, Gates, calm down now. You drunk or somethin', son?"

"Go over to the bank, Tom, they'll tell you! You thought the company checks were small, didn't you? You thought they'd get bigger by and by? Well, you can forget it, all of you! I was gonna cash out, get married, and get outta this dump! Here's what the banker fella give me." Gates threw a handful of coins on the barroom floor. "Twelve dollars! All that work, all that risk, twelve bucks!"

The miners slowly turned to look at Jenkins.

"How'd you do it, FitzHugh?" Gates demanded. "You didn't buy one acre where there weren't no silver—not one! No, you only snatched up the good stuff. How does a man do that *more than a decade before one ounce a' silver was found?*"

Jenkins smiled a thin smile. He spread his cards out on the table and said to the old miner opposite him, "Full house." To young Russell Gates he said, "Just luck, I guess."

Russell raised the pistol shakily, pointing it directly in Jenkins' face.

★ ★ ★

Serenity ducked out through the swinging door into the pantry and was about to step out the back door that overlooked Willow Creek when she hesitated. The pantry was dark. Was it breathing she heard? She turned and saw eyes looking at her, the eyes of children. The little room was filled with children. And a dog. And . . . oh, dear Lord, what *was* that thing?

"Don't be frightened, Serenity." The voice came from behind her, and Serenity whirled around. "These are some of my students," said Philippa Larson. "And a couple of their friends. They've just arrived in Faith. They're here to help us."

The kids themselves looked frightened, but Serenity Parsons was scared out of her mind. This had all happened before. She'd seen these very children before, years earlier. She'd seen this bizarre tusked creature before, looking up at her, just like now, a long string of drool hanging from his lower jaw.

Phoebe was crouched beside Sid, and Rob beside the labrador, scratching its ears. The only one totally at ease was the dog, who realized from the smell of things that he was back where he'd come from.

"Serenity, dear," said the librarian, "you need to get your father and take him to your brother's house up on Shotgun Hill. You need to stay there with Jesse and the rest of your family for the next twenty-four hours—don't let anyone leave. You'll be safe enough up there, but down here, very little of Faith will survive the fire."

"Fire?" whispered Serenity.

"Trust me," said Ms. Larson with the firmness of a schoolteacher. "It's in the history books."

Serenity nodded uncertainly and then edged toward the door, staring all the while at Sid.

"You don't know it yet, of course," said the diictodon, speaking up suddenly, "but you're going to have a child." Serenity's eyes windened in terror to hear the creature speak. "It will be a boy, and you'll likely call him Patrick." He turned to the kids.

"Children, meet Wynola and Adelaide's grandmother!" he said brightly.

Serenity turned and ran.

Philippa Larson coughed gently and shook her head a little.

"Did I say something wrong?" said the synapsid.

"The beast is in the theater now, Sidney," said Philippa. "We need to move."

"All right—let's go, everyone," said Sid. Rob was standing at the swinging doors to the saloon, holding one door open a crack and staring in. "Rob?"

Phoebe joined him at the door, opening it a bit wider to peer into the barroom.

The man they knew as Jenkins glanced suddenly at the pantry door and saw Phoebe and Rob there, staring at him. He laughed and said, "Well, that's just perfect," and turned back to the young miner with the gun. Jenkins slowly pushed back

271

from his table and stood. He picked up the whiskey bottle. The pistol in Russell Gates' left hand shook.

"Mr. Gates, I know kin of yours, as it turns out," said Jenkins. "I do believe he's a lefty, too."

Russell cocked the pistol, and Jenkins smiled his let-me-sell-you-something smile, shaking his head. Before anyone realized what he was doing, Jenkins had smashed the bottle on the table, slashed a bright ribbon of red across Russell Gates' shirt-front, and flicked a lit match onto the puddle of spilled whiskey on the tabletop.

The fire moved with unbelievable speed. As the saloon customers overcame their initial shock and rushed forward to smother the flames, a tongue of fire ran up the wallpaper. When it hit the gaslight above, the explosion tore a four-foot hole in the wall and spread the inferno to the adjoining dry goods store, thereby sealing the town's fate. Jenkins was long gone. He had run out the back swinging doors where Rob's and Phoebe's faces had been moments before. But they weren't there now.

Sid and the kids were running along the creek to the rear entrance of the opera house, the librarian hobbling along on her cane with surprising speed. They ducked into the loading dock doors a moment before Jenkins emerged from the rear of the saloon.

A small orchestra was sawing through a French music hall medley as Sid and the kids ran through the backstage regions. From the wings they caught a glimpse of a row of dancing girls onstage, wearing feathers and spangles. The sight of the high-kicking, beautiful women slowed the three boys down a bit, in spite of the terrible danger at their heels, and Phoebe hissed through clenched teeth, "Move, you idiots!"

They found the gorgonopsid on the little gallery overlooking the stage, exactly where Lucy Gates had encountered him a century later. He didn't even take his eyes from the stage when they pushed through the iron door at one end of the gallery. He seemed to be expecting them.

"Oh," murmured the Gorgon, staring down at the row of dancing women, "the humanity!"

Yellow Lab growled low and the fur along his spine bristled.

"Quickly now, old friend," said the Last Synapsid. "It's time. It's long *past* time, actually, and you know it."

"Friend?" said the Gorgon, still watching the chorus line. His yellow eyes flickered from the stage back to Sid and the rest of them.

"We have not a moment to lose," said Sid. "The town is burning."

"Who's the old broad?" said the Gorgon, and Philippa blinked as though she'd been slapped, but then she squared her shoulders at him.

"I'm not afraid of your sort," she said. "I'm a middle school librarian. I've dealt with worse than you!"

"Enchanté, madam," he said to Philippa. He leaned toward Sid, winked, and said in a stage whisper, "I *like* her. Got *spunk.*"

"Stop wasting time," said Sid urgently.

The Gorgon surveyed the kids and sighed.

"Oh, Rob Gates, Boy Wonder, yawn, yawn. And priss miss Phoebe Traylor, Earth Mother in Waiting." The beast half-lidded his eyes and glanced at the others. "Why do you all wrinkle your noses like that? Is it me? Would you tell me if it were?"

"Stop playing!" said Sid. "We need to go!"

"Where's the man?" asked the Gorgon, and all the kids glanced back over their shoulders nervously, expecting Jenkins to burst in on them at any moment.

"He's on his way, I imagine," said Sid. "He's just set a fire that will consume the town."

"Well," said the Gorgon, "that's him all over. I'm weary of him. I find him insulting."

"Then be quit of him, and come with me," said Sid.

"To die?"

"To reproduce!"

"You make me blush," said the Gorgon. "But I think you really want me to go back to die."

"To die when your time comes, yes. To live until then, and have offspring and as much life as you're allotted, and be grateful for it."

"Let us pray," said the monster.

"Don't you understand?" Sid shouted in the Gorgon's grinning face. "You're already dying! You're sick, you're dying, *you've run out of time!*"

"So have you, old fool!" the Gorgon hissed. "I can hear it in your breathing, I can see it in your eyes!"

"Yes! The two of us share the fate of our dying world! From the first breath we drew, our lungs were poisoned. But while we still do draw breath, we owe it to our world to live in it! To make what we can of the life we have left, so that other, later, better worlds might come to be!"

Below them, on the stage of the opera house, one of the dancers stopped, pointed toward the back of the audience house, and said something to the girl next to her, who looked back there and screamed.

"Fire!"

It's a terrible word to hear in a crowded theater.

"This should be good," said the Gorgon nastily.

"No!" Sid's nostrils flared in anger. "No, I'm telling you! No more malice! No more rejoicing at the misfortunes of others!"

The performers were fleeing into the wings, and the audience members were pushing their way chaotically toward the stage in a surging, shouting mass.

"As soon as I send these children to their home," shouted Sid in the Gorgon's face, *"you're going to return with me to ours!"*

The Gorgon said nothing. The diictodon turned quickly to the librarian. "Philippa, I know you wanted to stay here . . ."

"I had hoped to stay, yes," said Ms. Larson.

"I'm very sorry, but you need to make sure these kids get back home to their own time," said Sid firmly.

"I understand."

"You're a traveler now, Philippa," said the synapsid. "You've become a snag."

"As I say, I've been called worse."

Ms. Larson was holding one of Angela Cruz's hands and Billy was holding the other. Angela was trying to stifle terrified sobs as she watched the growing mayhem below. Donna covered her mouth and nose with her hands, and Aran held YL back by his collar. Rob and Phoebe looked lost.

"So are you all," said Sid, "each one of you, a traveler. Now, just think very hard about where you're going, and remember that a good part of you never left." Cries and screams rose from below, people crawling up onto the stage and others falling beneath the struggling mob and disappearing from sight.

"Hold hands, everyone," ordered Sid. One by one, the kids joined hands, making a semicircle with the librarian.

"Bye, Sid," said Phoebe faintly. "Good luck." She took Aran's hand with her right and Rob's with her left.

Rob was too stunned to say anything. His eyes stung. It was all happening too fast.

"Goodbye, dear Sidney," said the librarian, her eyes glistening. At that moment, Yellow Lab darted forward and licked Sid's face with all the love in his big dog's heart, yanking Aran forward with him. The screams of the opera house audience gave way to a great rushing wind and the light of thousands of shooting stars. When they all came to rest, they were back on the mountain with the vast gathering of mammals and the faint sound of a police radio squawking in the distance.

They were back in the present: Philippa Larson, Angela and Billy, Donna and Aran, and the yellow lab. And Sid. To his shock and dismay, Sid was there with them.

"Oh, for the sweet love of mercy!" said Sid.

Rob and Phoebe were alone with the beast in the burning town.

24
ANGELS AND DEMONS

The Great Fire of 1904 destroyed the boomtown of Faith in less than four hours. The flames ran along the wooden boardwalks, climbed the wooden walls, and leapt from storefront to rooftop to warehouse. There was no fire department, no fire engine, and no plan. Men hauled out hand-operated pumps, lowered them into the creek, and worked them feverishly, but they might as well have spit on the flames for all the good their little hoses did them. A few of the brick buildings endured, but of the wooden structures, only those few houses situated on the western ridge above town, near the cemetery, survived. It was from there that Serenity Parsons and her family members watched Faith burn.

For Phoebe and Rob back in the theater, it took a moment to realize what had happened. Their friends were gone. *All* their friends, Sid included. Where they had been standing, holding hands an instant before, there was nothing but smoke. YL had licked Sid's face, and they'd vanished.

"Looks like it's just us, kids," said the gorgonopsid.

He swung his massive head toward them, his fangs practically hanging in their faces. The creature's yellow eyes danced and his breath reeked.

"Just you, me, and a *whole* lotta crazy!"

The theater was filled with the screams of those who were still trying to flee toward the stage, and the screams of those who had fallen in the crush. It was the worst of nightmares.

"See how humans treat each other?" said the Gorgon with a nasty sneer.

"Shut up, you!" Phoebe barked.

"You want me to go back to my own era so that *these* miserable creatures may come to be? Give me one good reason and I'd do it! But no. These wretches started stepping on each other's heads the moment they learned how to stand upright. The earth will be much better off without them."

Phoebe brushed past the beast and gripped the iron rail at the edge of the gallery, ignoring the monster at her side entirely.

"Stop!" It was Phoebe's voice, louder than Rob had ever heard it. Even the Gorgon looked shocked.

"Stop!" she shouted again. *"The theater will survive the fire!"*

People on the stage below began to look up at Phoebe. Her face was fierce and her knuckles were white as she gripped the railing. *"The theater will survive the fire! Almost nothing else will! So stop panicking and stay where you are!"*

Rob joined Phoebe at the railing. More and more faces were turned up to them, and the din was subsiding a bit. People began to realize that the flames they had seen at the back of the audience house were actually on the boardwalk outside and across the street, consuming the buildings there. The wrought-iron and glass doors of the opera house and the sturdy brick walls had kept out the fire, although the vast structure was very smoky and the temperature was rising steadily.

"Tend the wounded!" Phoebe shouted. *"Find them, take care of them! They're your neighbors!"*

People looked up at Phoebe with awe on their faces. And then, amazingly, they began to do exactly what she'd told them to do. Rob in his whole life had never been so proud of his friend. The Gorgon looked at her thoughtfully.

(In the years that followed the terrible fire, the legend grew and spread through Faith: the miraculous story of the two angels who appeared in the theater and saved the lives of so many—one of them golden-haired with a thrilling voice, and the other one dark and silent. Eventually, as the story continued to be passed down from generation to generation, people left out the part about the grotesque demon who hovered behind them, over the angels' shoulders.)

As the work began below, Phoebe turned to the Gorgon, her eyes blazing. "All right, that's them. Now we've got *you* to save!"

"Oh, God, do we have to?" said Rob, and Phoebe was on him in a flash.

"What do you think?"

"Without Sid?" said Rob.

"Sid isn't here, Robert, in case you hadn't noticed, so yeah, without Sid!"

"But . . . but . . ."

"He spent two hundred and fifty million years looking for us, Rob. He said we might be needed. Well, as it turns out, we *are.*"

"But we don't know how to do it! How are we going to get all the way back there without Sid?"

"He's going to take us!" Phoebe said, jerking her thumb at the

beast. "And no funny business, Mr. Gorgon—I am *not* in the mood!"

There was still crying coming from below, the moans and sobs of those who had fallen in the crush and were being cared for on the stage floor. From outside the theater they could hear shouts and cries and bells ringing and the incomprehensible roaring sound of a town going up in flames. It was hot in the theater and becoming harder to breathe. Rob started to wriggle out of the backpack that he was still wearing, but Phoebe told him to put it back on because he was going to need it. Unhurried, the Gorgon looked steadily and thoughtfully at Phoebe and Rob.

"I must say, you surprise me," he said finally, in a low voice. "The species is more complex than one might suppose."

"Will you take us? Will you go?"

The creature's great head sagged for a moment, and the yellow eyes seemed to look far off—into his own unimaginable past, perhaps.

"I mean . . ." Phoebe hesitated. "Aren't you just a little bit . . . *tired*?"

The eyes, yellow and bloodshot, flickered back to the kids. The Gorgon moved to the iron rail and glanced down at the crowd below. "They're looking after the weak and the wounded," he finally murmured. "Remarkable."

"Will you do it?" said Rob. " 'Cause I guess we need to go."

"You understand," said the Gorgon, "I, too, am a synapsid."

The kids didn't know what to answer to this, so they didn't say anything.

"If I thought you would be my inheritors . . . ," said the Gorgon. "I mean, you two in particular . . ."

Rob and Phoebe didn't much relish the sound of that, but they said nothing.

"Follow me," said the Gorgon. He turned and disappeared into the dark door at the end of the gallery. He was fast as a lizard, and Rob and Phoebe had to run to keep up with him.

The old opera house was a bizarre maze, and the Gorgon seemed to know it by heart. Corridor gave way to corridor, the thick black tail always flashing out of sight ahead of them or disappearing down one iron spiral staircase after another. *Who built this place?* Phoebe wondered. It made no sense. The sound of the fire and the cries of the citizens of Faith faded from their ears as they continued to descend.

Now they were running down a long sloping ramp and the temperature was dropping. The gorgonopsid was no longer in sight ahead of them. The light was dim and growing dimmer. The wooden walls gave way to cement and then stone, and then the light failed entirely and they stumbled to a halt in pitch blackness.

"Hey!" shouted Rob into damp, earthy air that seemed to swallow his words. "Hey, where are you? Come back here!" Rob's voice seemed to come out of nowhere, the darkness was so complete.

"We're under the earth, Rob," said Phoebe. "Remember what Ms. Larson said about there being a passage from the theater into the mountain? We're in one of the mines."

"I can't see you," said Rob. They groped blindly until they found each other by touch. "Okay, let's go," Rob said.

"Forward?"

"It's like you said. If we don't go on with this, it's all over, isn't it? Or it never begins? Humanity and all?"

"I guess," said Phoebe. "Do you think Sid's going to come and rescue us at some point?"

"Maybe we rescue everybody else, and nobody rescues us."

"Maybe," said Phoebe. "It's an honor, I suppose. In a way."

"Yeah, right," said Rob.

They touched elbows and, keeping contact with each other that way, groped slowly forward in the blackness, their hands stretched in front of them, each moment expecting to step into nothingness. There were sudden drafts and squelching noises, sometimes distant, sometimes near, which, in their blind state, filled the kids' heads with images of nasty subterranean creatures slithering all around them in a pitch black world.

A warm draft sucked at them suddenly from the right.

"Look, Rob," whispered Phoebe.

The glow at the end of an earthen corridor on their right dazzled their light-deprived eyes. As their eyes adjusted, they saw two figures silhouetted before a flickering light. One was unmistakably the Permian-era carnivore they knew as the Gorgon. The other was beckoning them.

"What took you so long?" Jenkins' thick Texas twang was muffled by the earth. "Come on down! We're havin' a fire sale! Absolutely ever-thing must go!"

★ ★ ★

Night had fallen on the mountainside. Some of the mammals had laid themselves down to sleep—housecats mainly, and dogs and some of the sheep and goats—while others paced the hillside, snorting quietly or just breathing, their eyes glittering in the light of the half-moon. The bats kept swooping and *teek-teek-teek*ing and snatching mosquitoes as they swooped.

The grown-ups below were at a loss; the hordes of creatures on the hill still formed an impenetrable wall. The two moms had gone on calling for the kids, but whenever they or anyone else tried to approach, the larger animals (bears, mountain lions, pronghorns, and horses) would move gently but firmly to block their way.

The police radios in the two squad cars were squawking, and Sheriff Pete was speaking angrily into his microphone. His call for reinforcements from the Valley had been met with laughter. No one believed his story of what was happening on the mountain; they thought the old sheriff was trying to play some kind of prank.

Lucy Gates finally slumped to her knees and began to sob helplessly. Jane Traylor knelt beside her and held her shoulders.

"He's all I've got," said Lucy.

"I know," Jane whispered. "I know. They're all any of us have got."

When there was a sudden commotion from the beasts, excited yelping and growling and barking and baaing and snorting, the humans looked up at the mammal hordes in fear and wonder, unable to act, not knowing that the big to-do signaled the return of the Last Synapsid and the others.

The animals on the slope were overjoyed to have Sid back with them, but Sid was utterly distraught.

Drool roping down from his lower jaw, he turned to Yellow Lab. "This is all your fault!"

Yellow Lab said, "Bark!"

Angela, Billy, Donna, and Aran were all showing signs of shock—they were glassy-eyed and overwhelmed.

"Take care of the children, Philippa," said Sid, and she nodded, looking a little dazed herself. Sid looked out at the mountainside of mammals, each one of them watching him intently, their eyes shining, the joy genes in them almost bubbling over.

"Phoebe and Rob have your fate in their hands," he shouted, and the animals bleated and baaed and snorted and roared.

"They're just children, and they've got so much on their shoulders. I have to go back and help them."

The mammals were all in favor of it, whatever it was. Baa, snort, whinny, neigh, teek-teek-teek, bark, yelp, meow, purr!

"Goodbye, all!" Sid shouted. "Again!"

As the Gang of Six (minus two) watched, Sid seemed to look far off, and then he leapt—into the air, into the ever-moving current of time—and was gone.

A moment later (and a century earlier) the diictodon was racing from the mountainside slope where he landed down into the burning town, through the burning streets filled with fleeing people, and into the theater via the loading dock. The horde of humans inside, seeking refuge from the fire, drew back at the sight of him. He darted across the stage and raced up the staircase in the left wing until he stood on the gallery where he had left Phoebe and Rob moments before. He saw the crowd onstage, handkerchiefs over their mouths, looking up at him fearfully, and coughing and moaning in the smoke and heat. He heard the sounds of the conflagration outside in the town.

He was too late. Rob and Phoebe were gone, and so was the Gorgon. Where were they? Sid's tusked head drooped despairingly, saliva dripping from his jaws. Where had they gone?

Sid lifted his head abruptly and cocked it, listening. It was very faint, what he heard, and very, very far away.

"I hear you, Robert," he murmured. "I'm coming!"

★ ★ ★

They stood before a chamber of stone, deep within the mountain. Jenkins and the Gorgon stood silhouetted in the entrance, lit by a strange flickering light. "Come on in, guys," said the man. "This here's a sort of transit center for the ages. This

284

room is time's suck-hole, it seems, or one of time's suck-holes. It's how these critters first found Faith!"

At first Rob and Phoebe had stood paralyzed by the sight of Jenkins, who looked upbeat despite being splattered with blood and covered in soot. Not knowing what else to do, they entered the chamber. On its opposite wall was a large opening in the stone, and a black void beyond that.

Rob moved forward with a boldness he didn't really feel. "Listen, you don't scare us!" lied Rob. "We've got business with this creature here, this gorgonopsid. We've got some traveling to do, and you're not going to stop us!"

"Hey, little man," said Jenkins, grinning "dial it down, why don't you? You don't look so good, buster. And missy, frankly, neither do you, hon!"

Rob and Phoebe glanced at each other. Phoebe was shocked to see how the smoke and soot from the fire had blackened Rob's face and arms, and Rob saw in Phoebe's face, beneath the grime, deep lines of exhaustion and fear. He turned back to Jenkins.

"You should see how *you* look, you creepy little con man," said the boy.

Jenkins smiled again. "Sticks and stones may break my bones, but words can never . . . Oh, what's the point?" He glanced back at the Gorgon. "Come on, Halitosis, let's get us back to the action, leave these little muffins in the oven."

The gorgonopsid looked at Jenkins with hooded yellow eyes. "I beg your pardon?" he said. "What did you call me this time?"

"I'm thinkin' let's buy us up some New York City real estate— say, just after the stock market crash of 1929. Or, heck, Central Park in the eighteen hundreds, when it ain't Central Park yet. I mean, just for starters."

The man turned to Phoebe and Rob.

"So long, Shake 'n Bake!" he said with a grin.

That's when the Gorgon started quoting Shakespeare's *Tempest.*

"No more dams I'll make for fish," he said quietly.

"What the hey?" said Jenkins.

"Nor scrape trencher, nor wash dish," a little louder.

"Beg pardon? Talk English, why don't you? You don't want to annoy me, Sunny Jim!"

The Gorgon stretched his massive head toward Jenkins, his curved fangs dripping.

"Hey now, fella," said the man, "just let's go easy here, okay?"

The creature swung his head around and grinned wetly at Rob and Phoebe. The air between them stank.

"Let's bring him with us, shall we?" said the Gorgon.

"What's that? Don't you be whisperin', it's rude. Hey, didn't I always treat you good? Didn't I feed you goat and dog and cat and such?"

The Gorgon watched Phoebe and Rob closely, his yellow eyes flickering. "The play was good, wasn't it?" he said. "It's my favorite."

The kids, confused, exhausted, and almost at the end of their respective ropes, nodded numbly.

" 'Ban, 'Ban, Ca-caliban," the beast quoted in a suddenly huge, theatrical voice, *"has a new master . . ."*

His head swung back into Jenkins's face. *"Get a new man!"*

The beast, its forelegs outstretched, reared up on its hind legs and roared, and the four of them were swept off their feet on a wave of hot wind, flying into the emptiness of the cave's dark opening.

25
THE RIVER

Phoebe and Rob had traveled before, but this was different. For one thing, it wasn't over in a moment—it seemed to go on forever, and the current that was shooting them backward felt somehow like the very torment of the continents, tumbling them head over heel. Visions swept past them, an impossible cascade of sights as they flew through time. Momentary glimpses, split-second pictures of vivid color and ever-changing shape: empires and armies rising from the grass and disappearing into ash heaps; deserts flooding, and floodplains turning into deserts; forests burning and mountains exploding out of the seas in flame and smoke. And ice. Blinding white vastnesses of ice, whole worlds of ice. They felt in their bones the agony of the earth as it gave birth to itself, again and again, the land masses breaking apart and migrating and re-forming in cataclysmic upheavals, and they knew every instant that they would be crushed to powder, to dust, to atoms. It was terrifying, it was thrilling, it was almost more than any creature of earth could bear. They knew that they were seeing things no one else had ever seen and no one else ever would see. They knew it was a great gift, but also they grieved, because they doubted they would ever survive it.

The impact, when they finally landed, was shocking because it was so gentle after all that—so ordinary, in a sense. They tumbled out of an opening in a low hill and rolled down onto the moist sand of a beach. When they stood, their feet sank in just a little. They felt fine-grained sand between their toes and realized that they were barefooted. Their shoes and socks had been torn off. Their clothes were in tatters. Phoebe's braid was undone and her thick sand-colored hair fanned over her shoulders and down her back. Rob's backpack was hanging by one strap over his right shoulder, and his T-shirt was shredded. Jenkins lay sprawled on the sand before them, unmoving. Was it a riverbank they stood on? Was that a hill in the distance? The Gorgon stood between the two kids and—yes, it *was* a river. There seemed to be falling water somewhere near. In the distance there was the rumbling roar of a volcanic eruption. The air was tinted with a dull nicotine-yellow haze.

For a moment they tried to catch their breath. There was a stinging at the back of their throats.

Then the Gorgon swung his head left and right, comically. "Honey?" he called. "I'm home!"

Phoebe had a sudden shudder of realization, and she laughed out loud. The moment she laughed, a whole world which had never before heard such a sound seemed to listen. Jenkins raised his head blearily, and both Rob and the Gorgon looked at Phoebe.

"Sorry," she said, and hiccupped. At the sound of her voice, creatures they hadn't realized were there skittered over the ground and froze, staring, or came waddling up out of the swampy riverbed and out of holes in the ground—some big, some small, dozens of alien eyes watching the newcomers.

"I just realized—that picture we found?" Phoebe went on giddily. "The fossilized footprints that we thought were ours and Sid's? They were ours, all right, but they weren't Sid's pawprints, they were the gorgonopsid's! What a letdown. To be here at the end of everything, or the beginning, rather, stuck with the Gorgon and *this* guy. I mean . . . no offense, but . . . Sorry, never mind. I'm a little dizzy. I'll stop talking now. . . ." She trailed off into silence.

"Of course you're dizzy, Miss Lizzy," said the Gorgon, looking about. "The air's gone bad, you see. Just as it's going bad in *your* world."

"I wish Sid was here," said Rob in a tight, angry voice, and a tiny ripple of what he said launched itself on the river of time, speeding through the ages, toward the old diictodon's heart.

"I wish Sid *were* here," corrected Phoebe automatically. The two kids fell silent again, staring numbly at the world when it was young.

The creatures that stared back were unlike any they had ever seen. They had some knowledge of dinosaurs, of course, but the beasts they were looking at had lived their lives thirty million years before the first dinosaur appeared. They were so completely alien, it was difficult to take them in. Phoebe said later that if you had never seen a giraffe, or an aardvark, or heard of such an animal, it might take a while for it to sink in if you ever ran into one. That's what this was like.

Jenkins got to his feet, staring wildly. "Okay, fun's over, Stinky," he said. "You get me out of here and quick!"

"Let me introduce you children," said the beast, ignoring the man. "Genus Homo, meet . . . let me see now. The vegetarians keep well away from the meat-eaters at this party. Meet

estemmenosuchus. Have you ever seen anything so comical? I mean, apart from your friend Aran's ears."

"Here's another intelligent-looking fellow," continued the gorgonopsid sarcastically, nodding to a very large but timid-looking creature peeking out from a bank of ferns.

"Rocket science is never going to be his specialty," said the Gorgon, "but filet of moschops is rather good, and I'm also fond of the ribs."

"Eryops"
by Rbt. Gates Jr.

There was a splash near the shore. "Look out for that one. Eryops, an amphibian."

"He's a killer—and fast? He's so quick, you'd probably never even know he'd eaten you." The gorgonopsid looked about him and sighed. "Oh! I wish I could say it was good to be back."

"You just get me outta here!" hissed Jenkins. "Get me back to the twenty-first century! You hear me?"

"I have a feeling my traveling days are over," said the Gorgon. "Think I may settle down, do the whole raise-a-family thing." The beast looked sharply at Rob and Phoebe. "Make my contribution to the gene pool."

"The hell with that!" Jenkins was looking truly panicky now. "Please!" he pleaded hoarsely. "You can't leave me here! You can't!" The gorgonopsid ignored him.

"You know, boys and girls," said the Gorgon, "you think of that pompous old fool you call Sid as a father figure, but really there's as much *me* in you as *him.*" Phoebe thought she actually saw a kind of yearning in the Gorgon's yellow eyes, maybe even a kind of pride, but Rob was revolted.

"I'm not descended from you!" he said. "You're nothing like my father, or my father's father, or any of us! You're mean and cruel and you kill for fun and you disgust me, okay?"

"Rob, don't!" whispered Phoebe.

The beast was silent for a moment, his yellow eyes hooded and suddenly dangerous. Then he turned and slunk to the water's edge, where he lowered his head and drank. The other animals gave him a wide berth.

"Hey, listen up!" screamed Jenkins, pushing Rob aside and yanking Phoebe's head back by her hair. With a flick of the wrist, the folding knife was at Phoebe's throat. "Get me out of here *now*!"

"Let her go!" Rob shouted.

The Gorgon looked back over his shoulder for a moment. "You're threatening me with a *human*?" said the Gorgon. "You must have mistaken me for someone who cared." The beast dropped its head again and continued drinking.

Rob saw Jenkins hesitate for a moment, looking between the Gorgon and the blade at Phoebe's jugular. Then, suddenly remembering being blindsided once by Chad Scudder, Rob kicked Jenkins fiercely just behind his right knee and the man went down, pulling Phoebe down with him.

The tangle on the ground was fast and savage, Phoebe shrieking and a bright red stain spreading across her blouse and Rob frantically grabbing for her, trying to pull her out of reach of Jenkins' knife. Jenkins was on his back, trying to right himself, thrashing with the blade and kicking wildly. Rob got Phoebe under her arms in a lifeguard hold and thrust backward just as Jenkins brought the blade down, stabbing the sand between Rob's legs.

Above it all they heard the Gorgon's mirthless laughter. "Look who's here to pay his respects!" he exulted.

They looked up and froze. Jenkins said a four-letter word and the blood drained from his face. A large sail-backed creature stood at the edge of a coniferous grove, less than a dozen yards off. The ribbed orange-colored membrane that stood up from its spine was quivering and iridescent. The beast gave a birdlike squawk, scooted forward abruptly with the jerky speed of a salamander and stopped. It scooted forward again and stopped, then scooted again, until it was less than five feet from the Texan and the kids. Its speed was re-

"Dimetrodon" by Rbt. Gates Jr.

markable, given its size. It looked from Jenkins to the kids and back again.

"Dimetrodon," said the Gorgon, helpfully. "Meat-eater, in case you were wondering."

The creature's needle-like teeth glinted and its eyes glittered, whether with the anticipation of its next meal or just cu-

riosity, the kids couldn't tell. Jenkins was slowly getting to his knees, holding his knife toward the dimetrodon, his eyes darting about desperately. Rob and Phoebe still lay on the ground. Jenkins made a feint with his knife and the dimetrodon's ribbed sail flattened just a bit, the way a cat's ears flatten when it's about to

293

attack. Phoebe covered her eyes, and Rob, too, looked away, both of them bracing themselves. . . .

That was when Rob had his first vision. He saw Sid sitting on a little ledge of earth above the riverbank, looking down on him and Phoebe. Rob wished with all his heart that it really *were* Sid, he wished that he and Phoebe were back with their old friend, back in Rob's bedroom with Sid and a soggy tennis ball. And then, with a jolt, Rob realized what was wrong with the vision on the little hill: Sid had no tusks.

Sid's voice came back to him from ages ago—weeks ago, months ago, hundreds of millions of years earlier, or rather, later. "No, no, no—tusks are for show, tusks are for impressing the ladies!" Only the male diictodons have tusks. Not the females. . . .

There was an animal scream and a splash, and Rob turned back to see Jenkins running through river water up to his waist, while the dimetrodon shrieked and blood poured from a gash across its snout. The creature blundered down to the water's edge. It plunged in and swam rapidly in pursuit of Jenkins, but by now he was already emerging on the opposite bank, clambering up, streaming water and turning in terrified circles, brandishing his knife desperately. He turned and started to climb the rocky slope on one side of a narrow waterfall. He slipped and fell, scrambled frantically to his feet, and went on climbing. In the river, the wounded dimetrodon was joined by another of its kind, and then another, the three dimetrodons now swiftly climbing up out of the water to the opposite slope. The foliage was dense, and in moments Jenkins and his pursuers were lost to view. Rob and Phoebe heard the sounds of creatures running through undergrowth, and snorts and cries, and then those, too, faded to nothing.

The kids stood there numbly on the shore of the ancient river. "You're bleeding, Phoeb, are you okay?" said Rob finally.

"Is there a pulse behind the blood?" she asked, and rubbed the dirt and blood at her neck so Rob could see.

"I don't think so."

"Then I'm okay," she said lifelessly. "I want to go home."

Rob nodded silently, not thinking much of their odds.

"Haven't we done what we came for? Didn't we get the gorgonopsid back where he belonged, back where he can mate and reproduce his horrid kind so that someday we can inherit those awful genes? I mean, does somebody somewhere want something more from us? 'Cause I'm just about out of good deeds." Tears began to run down her face.

"We did more than that, Phoebe. If what Sid told us is true, we helped save a lot of good stuff. A lot of good things are going to happen because we brought the Gorgon back. Synapsids will evolve and survive the Great Dying and there'll be good things because of it. Things like paintings and music and horses and, I don't know, whatever's good. Baseball. Lasagna. Your mom and my mom, and Aran and Billy and Donna and Angela. Hey, remember all those mammals on the mountain? Remember Yellow Lab?"

Phoebe sniffed and nodded.

"All those good things are going to happen, and a lot more good stuff that we'll never know about. We did good, Phoeb. Anyway, we did our best."

Phoebe nodded again and reached automatically for a hanky in her pocket, but her pockets had been torn off on the journey. So she just drew her fist across her runny nose. "Rob," she said, "where *is* the Gorgon?"

Rob glanced down at the riverbank. The Gorgon was gone. Rob looked upriver along the shore and caught his breath. Phoebe followed his gaze and gasped.

Walking toward them beside the water was an impossibility. Phoebe put her hands to her mouth and fresh tears filled her eyes.

"It may not be real, Phoeb," warned Rob gently. "The Gorgon can make you see things, remember?"

But Phoebe walked toward the figure on the shore, and the figure walked majestically toward her. Johnny B. Goode, the magnificent black stallion and Phoebe's best four-legged friend on earth, raised his head and whinnied jubilantly. The girl ran to him and reached up and cautiously touched the horse's glistening flanks. Johnny B. Goode snorted, and his breath was hot and horsey. Phoebe put her hand to his mouth and the horse nibbled it with his thick, blunt teeth, wetly, warmly, affectionately. This just couldn't be an illusion.

"He's real," she said in wonder. "He's real, Rob. He's real, he's real, he's real!" Johnny B. lowered his great head for Phoebe to nuzzle him, and he nuzzled her, and Rob approached and put his hands tentatively on the creature's flanks. Yes, it was impossible, and it was true.

"That night in the stables," said Rob, "maybe the Gorgon, when he got close, maybe he accidentally sent Johnny B. back here, and he's been here ever since."

"And according to Sid," said Phoebe, "it's been only one day."

The horse, suddenly very agitated, neighed and reared up and whinnied again. A gust of warm wind passed over the kids with a wonderful smell of swamp and barn, and their skin tingled. A dear, familiar, gravelly voice pierced their hearts.

"It's true, Phoebe," said the Last Synapsid. "For your horse, it's been only a single day."

Rob and Phoebe wheeled about. Sid stood above them on the ridge with the second diictodon, identical to the kids' eyes except that Sid had tusks and the other did not.

"Here's *my* good news," said Sid. "*She's* still living, my most beloved mate—she waited for us."

The female diictodon smiled down at them with a kind of Sid-smile, which involved ropes and ladders of saliva.

"How do you do?" said Phoebe, and Sid's spouse gave a little bark. "Rob, say hi."

But Rob didn't respond. He was staring at another bizarre improbability, a little farther down the river's shore.

There he was. Robert "Jake" Gates, Rob's long-lost dad, walking toward him. No—this, surely was not possible. All the elaborate stories that Rob had invented to explain his father's absence flooded his brain at this moment. As wild as some of them were, none was as crazy as this.

"Rob?" said Jake Gates.

"Dad?" said Rob. Distantly, Rob heard voices—Sid's voice and Phoebe's—shouting at him, but from very, very far away.

"Where am I?" Jake said, looking dazedly at the insane landscape that surrounded them. "I've been here such a long time, but I don't know where 'here' is!"

"I don't know how you got here, Dad," said the boy, "but we'll get you back."

"Promise?" Jake whimpered.

"Dad! I promise!"

"Take my hand, son," said Jake.

Why were Phoebe and Sid shouting "No! No! No!"? Why was Sid leaping down off the ridge? Why was Phoebe shaking her head and waving her arms and running toward him? Nothing seemed real except the figure before him.

"Sure, Dad, of course." Rob extended his right hand to his father.

"No, son—I want that gifted left hand of yours. You may not remember, but I'm a lefty myself!"

297

Rob didn't remember, or he remembered differently. Hadn't his father been right-handed? Rob's forehead creased with a moment's doubt, but then he said, "Okay, Dad!" Rob stretched his left hand out to his father, and his father gripped it like iron.

"Dad! Hey, Dad, that hurts! Stop! Dad, stop!"

"So I disgust you, do I?"

Suddenly the vision changed. The shape that had seemed to be his long-missing father blurred, and thickened, and shortened, and began to stink, and suddenly Rob realized that it was the Gorgon that had his left hand gripped within its mouth.

Rob pushed his bare right foot against the creature's snout and with all his might yanked his left hand free. Rage and adrenaline surged through the boy. He hurled himself onto the gorgonopsid, circling its neck with his right arm and gripping its jaws with his bloody left hand. Rob wrenched the hideous head right, then left, and the Gorgon cried out in pain.

"I'll kill you!" cried Rob.

The Gorgon managed to speak with a choked voice. "Yes . . . you will. That's . . . what I give you, your inheritance: you become a killer like me."

Rob struggled to hold on to the writhing head for another moment, but then shoved it away in fury and disgust.

"I'm not like you! I'm not!"

"Rob," said Phoebe, and he realized that Phoebe was standing beside him on one side and Sid on the other. Phoebe was staring at his left hand.

Just then the sand bank beneath the Gorgon gave way, cascading half a dozen feet down into the river, the Gorgon falling along with it, his front paws beating the air. Immediately an eryops launched itself across the surface of the murky waters, intent on its kill. And then another. And another. A greenish blur leapt onto the gorgonopsid's back. The Gorgon bellowed in sudden pain and fear, his yellow eyes rolling back in his head.

"Oh my God," said Phoebe.

"We've got to save him!" cried Rob frantically. "All we've been through will be for nothing!"

Phoebe leapt up onto Johnny B. Goode's bare back, and horse and rider went into the waters with great wrath. The black stallion reared up, taller than any other creature in the entire predinosaurian world, and Phoebe clung to his neck. His whinny was like a trumpet blast. He crashed down and rose up again, sending up jets of river water. His hooves came slashing down amid the struggling beasts and the river seemed to boil. Phoebe held on fiercely as one hoof caught the eryops on the Gorgon's back squarely. It went flying. The other eryops all fled from the horse in terror.

The Gorgon bobbed limply to the surface, bleeding from several wounds. Sid leapt into the water and butted the gorgonopsid toward the shore with his head. Rob scrambled down onto the beach and, with his right hand tugging at a forepaw, helped the creature stagger ashore.

The Gorgon tottered and half fell on the sand, breathing heavily. Phoebe wheeled Johnny B. Goode around and the horse stepped up, streaming, out of the river. Phoebe dismounted and the horse snorted.

"My hand," said Rob, seeming to see the injury for the first time. He cupped his bleeding left hand to his chest and his face went paper-white. Then he collapsed in a dead faint.

Phoebe crouched and gathered up his head into her lap, tears springing to her eyes.

"We need water from your world," said Sid, his dark eyes on Rob's bleeding hand. Sid's mate silently joined him, staring at the unconscious boy.

Phoebe reached around and unzipped Rob's backpack. She pulled out a bag of smashed grapes, a soggy pack of trail mix, and a plastic water bottle. She poured the water slowly over Rob's injured hand. His eyes opened wide in pain and alarm, and then seemed to focus.

"Hi, Sid," said Rob in a whisper. "Hi, Mrs. Sid." The elderly synapsid tilted her head and nodded, her deep dark eyes riveted on the boy.

The Gorgon righted himself. He sat, winded and weak, on the sand. He coughed, and looked at Phoebe and Rob. "You saved my life. You and the boy." He coughed again. "I did my best to hurt him, and in return you saved my life."

"Don't remind me!" said Phoebe, bitterly.

As Phoebe watched, another gorgonopsid approached cautiously on the shore of the river. It was almost a mirror image of the other, except that the newcomer was smaller and more brown than black. The smaller gorgonopsid crept to the Gorgon's side. Its long rough tongue lapped at the other's wound. The Gorgon shuddered and his heavy eyelids closed. Finally, the Gorgon roused himself. He stood and looked long and wonderingly at Phoebe. He looked at the boy, and the two di-ictodons who hovered over him, staring back.

"If I could undo what I've done . . ."

Phoebe said nothing.

The Gorgon was barely audible when he murmured the words of Shakespeare's *Tempest* in Pangea.

"O brave new world, that has such people in it!"

The Gorgon turned and limped off. The other followed, and they were gone.

There was a sudden chorus of alien animals, yapping and squeaking, mewing and hissing and clicking and shrieking and bleating. Phoebe saw that a crowd of Permian-era beings had gathered on the riverbank above, including a little pack of wiener-shaped diictodons, all of them watching the humans. They had had an audience, evidently, and it was as though the creatures were now offering their applause. She turned back to Rob.

He managed a faint smile for Phoebe. He glanced up at Sid. "I thought you said you were the *last* synapsid," he murmured.

"But I *would* have been the last," said Sid, "these and my neighbors, had it not been for you and Phoebe. Because of your courage, *you* are our inheritors, you and the children you'll have someday, and their children. The synapsid line will endure as long as your kind survive."

Rob shook his head, looking at his injured left hand. "My hand," he said.

Sid's spouse finally spoke. Her voice was reedy, like an old woman's, and somewhat barky, like a dog's, but loving and comforting nonetheless.

Sid translated. "She says you have to believe this isn't the end of your story, Rob. It's the beginning."

Rob looked away.

His spouse spoke again, in the strange, gravelly barking language of her kind.

"She says humans will be the only creatures capable of the miracle of forgiveness," said Sid, "and the only creatures in need of it. She's so happy to have glimpsed her children again, and so very proud of them."

Rob turned his eyes on them. "You can't come back with us, I suppose?"

Sid shook his head. "You'll hear our voices again, one way or another. We'll be a part of you now, forever." Sid gently brushed a paw across Rob's forehead, glancing up at Phoebe. "You have done a great thing, you two. For the whole world."

Phoebe sighed a great shuddering sigh.

"Take him home," said the old synapsid. "You have the ability—you and Rob are travelers now."

Phoebe nodded.

Sid whispered in the stallion's ear, and Johnny B. Goode snorted and lowered himself to the ground the way Phoebe had seen trick horses do at the circus. Phoebe climbed onto Johnny B.'s back first, and then, with her pulling Rob's good hand and the diictodons gently lifting, they got the boy onto the horse, behind the girl. The stallion stood upright and whinnied.

Sid and his spouse reached the delicate digits of their forepaws up, touching the kids' knees.

"Oh, dear," said Sid. "I am going to miss you more than I can say."

The great horse began to quiver, his nostrils flaring and his eyes rolling excitedly. Phoebe wrapped her right hand around the stallion's neck, and Rob took one last look at his old friend, Sid.

"Me too, you," he whispered. And horse and riders were gone.

26
THE RETURN

As Philippa Larson described it, there came a moment on the mountain that night, as she and the kids kept vigil, waiting and hoping and praying for Rob and Phoebe's return, when the creatures of earth seemed for a moment to fade a bit, to become dreamlike and ethereal. As if none of them really existed. Everyone felt it; she and the kids and the thousands of gathered mammals all looked at each other, wondering, listening, watching, waiting with held breath. Billy said he could see starlight through Angela's hair, and Donna said she glanced at her watch and there was no face, no dial, no big or little hand. And then it passed, and all the animals on the mountain rejoiced, with a din of thousands of jubilant animal voices.

Soon a towering black stallion fell among them, landing gracefully and proud, with two children clinging to his back. As Yellow Lab raced joyously among them, shouting, "Bark! Bark!

Bark!," all the creatures of the mountain scattered, from the greatest to the least, from the lion to the mole. Bears went lumbering into the woods, and sheep and foxes and coyotes and squirrels and lynxes and hedgehogs and deer, and flights and flights of bats rose up into the night sky and disappeared.

The adults from below came running now, and Lucy Gates and Jane Traylor were ahead of all the rest. They stopped dead when they saw Phoebe sitting atop the long-missing stallion, and Rob slumped against her back, his bloody left hand curled against his chest. The two kids looked like they'd been through a war.

For just a moment, no one moved or spoke—they were too stunned.

"Look, Rob," said Phoebe, and his eyelids blinked open. "We're home."

★ ★ ★

Adelaide and Wynola Parsons had planned to use Richard Jenkins' (aka Patrick Mulcahy FitzHugh's) vast bank accounts to rejuvenate Faith—building a new library and improving playgrounds and schools and fixing anything that needed to be fixed, and giving every child in town the funds for a college education. The results came back from the lab in Albuquerque, and yes, they showed that the hair sample they'd clipped from Jenkins' head did indeed match their own DNA perfectly. Adelaide and Wynola thought, as the man's granddaughters, they should inherit the fortune that their grandfather had virtually stolen from the town. But no.

For one thing, according to the authorities, there was no evidence that Jenkins wasn't still living. Certainly no one at the bank had seen him run into the Permian wilderness, pursued by dimetrodons, two hundred and fifty million years earlier. For another thing, two octogenarians claiming to be the grand-daughters of a man the whole town knew couldn't have been more than forty or forty-five years old—well, the Parsons sisters had always resided on the far side of eccentric.

Their plans thwarted, Adelaide and Wynola decided to throw a party for the town instead, down at the gazebo near town hall, on the twenty-fourth of July, which was the twins' birthday. They baked red velvet cakes and peach and rhubarb pies and stirred up vats of fresh lemonade. Others brought fried chicken and ham and rolls and corn on the cob, although everyone agreed it was a little early in the season for corn.

Faith is a town that *loves* parties. Donna rode Johnny B. Goode down Main Street, with Angela at her side on Sally May. Billy and Aran ran alongside the girls' horses like a couple of idiots and paid no attention to Chad Scudder's halfhearted catcalls. Billy didn't sick up the red velvet cake, miraculously, but even ate a little more cake when Angela handed a piece down to him. When it got dark, Deputy Keith Springer set off fireworks from the slopes of Stair-Master, and the whole town had a great time.

Four of the Gang of Six were closer than ever, but neither Phoebe nor Rob attended the Parsons sisters' party. Rob still wasn't going out much.

He came out of the hospital with a lot of recuperating to do. His spirits, especially, needed looking after. In the Arenoso clinic, the night Rob and Phoebe returned, the doctors were deeply worried by Rob's left hand. Most alarming to the doctors was the infection that was already raging by the time they'd brought the boy in. They brought up the possibility of amputation.

"Never!" shrieked Phoebe, who was still smeared with silty Permian-era mud.

"No way!" said Lucy Gates.

Rob himself was unaware of the debate—he'd lost consciousness again on the ride to Arenoso.

Jane Traylor got on the phone to her ex-husband, who was good at pulling strings and getting things done. Within the hour, a medical helicopter was dispatched, and in the middle of the night Rob and his mom and Phoebe and her mom were flown to the biggest and best-equipped hospital in Denver. Doctors spent the morning doing what they could to quell the infection. Surgery began in the afternoon and went on into the night.

Around three A.M. two surgeons found Lucy Gates and Jane and Phoebe Traylor in the family waiting room. They all stood up with fear on their faces, but the woman surgeon beamed.

"We saved your boy's hand," she said, and Lucy started to cry.

The male surgeon said, "He's going to need a lot of physical therapy, but we think the prognosis is pretty good."

The first few weeks after the hospital were the worst. Lucy Gates barely slept for days on end, and she looked it. It was Rob's sadness that kept her awake. It was a sadness so deep, so silent and solitary, it seemed that no one and nothing could touch it. Lucy took him every day to physical therapy down in the Valley, and his left hand seemed to be making slow but steady progress. His spirits were another matter. When he wasn't in therapy he stayed in his room, day in, day out, alone except for the yellow lab.

It was Phoebe who came up with the idea of moving them all out of town for a while, to recuperate. Her mom reserved four cabins for them at the Elks, a beautiful old lodge on the banks of the Rio Grande, a couple of miles south of Faith. Each one had a little cabin above the sparkling river: Rob, Phoebe, Lucy, and Jane. The two moms did a lot of cooking together and they all did a lot of eating. Lucy quit smoking. Phoebe filled up

306

countless pages in her diary. But Rob stayed in his cabin with YL for the most part, except for meals, and even then he was mostly silent.

One morning, when the four of them were finishing a late breakfast on the deck, the other members of the Gang of Six showed up unannounced on their bikes. YL was so deliriously happy to see them, he actually fell off the deck and then pretended it had been on purpose. Even Rob couldn't help laughing. But then Donna brought out a copy of the latest *Faith Sentinel* with an article in it about the night the animals had massed on the mountain.

Rob's face darkened.

"They're saying it might have been caused by seismic activity!" said Donna.

"Yeah," said Aran, "and Sheriff Pete's telling everyone Rob was attacked by a bear that night and just doesn't remember it."

Rob stood up from the table and went to his cabin without a word.

★ ★ ★

It was a beautiful summer, and Rob and Phoebe and their moms often sat up late on the deck outside their cabins. They'd watch the night sky above the cliffs and listen to the sounds of the rushing river. The dog slept at Rob's feet and chased things in his dreams, twitching and snorting.

Sometimes they wouldn't say a word. Other times, the kids would tell their mothers a little bit about Sid and the travels they'd had with him. So, very gradually, the whole story came out. Given Rob's condition, the moms weren't about to tell him or Phoebe they were crazy, so they simply listened in the dark. Did the moms come to believe their story? Maybe on some level they did. There certainly was a lot of detail in what they said; detail that would be difficult to invent. Once, Jane asked Rob how old Yellow Lab was, and he said without a moment's hesitation, "I guess he must be about a hundred fifteen by now." He scratched behind YL's ears and said, "Ain'tcha, boy? Ain'tcha?"

Many nights Rob wouldn't come out, though—he'd go to his cabin right after supper and stay there. Phoebe told the moms that he was trying to learn to draw with his right hand. It was hard enough to button his shirts with one hand, or tie his shoes. Drawing with his wrong hand was a very tall order.

One night, out on the deck, Phoebe said to Jane, "Mom, what's wrong with Rob? His hand is getting better. The physical therapist says he's making progress every week. That's not it, somehow. I don't know what it is. I don't know how to help him."

Jane nodded in the dark. "I don't know either, honey," she said. "He's been through a lot. So have you, don't forget. Most of the time you *can't* save the world, Phoebe, or even your best friend. You can just do your best to take good care of yourself, and be there for him, if and when your friend ever lets you in."

"You sound like Sven," said Phoebe, and her mom laughed. "How is he?"

"He's good, honey, he says hi."

"August first is Rob's birthday, Mom, he's turning thirteen, we'll be the same age, finally. I'd sure like that to be more fun than a funeral, if you know what I mean."

"Lucy's planning a party," said Jane. "We'll just have to hope for the best."

Lucy came out onto the deck at that point with a big trash bag.

"I thought you should know about this," she said. "It looks like he's torn up all his drawings and paintings."

Phoebe turned pale. She opened the trash bag and rummaged

308

through the shredded sheets of paper. Dozens and dozens of sketches and portraits and landscapes—Sid and the marmots and Yellow Lab and Pinkie and the mastodons and still more drawings of Sid. She grabbed a large armful of the stiff paper and stomped off to Rob's cabin.

"Knock first!" he said testily, when Phoebe flung open his door. Rob was lying on his bed, playing Game Boy, and YL was sleeping soundly at the foot of the bed. Phoebe dumped the torn-up drawings on the bed.

"These were my memories, too!" she shouted. "You have no right! No right to destroy what we've been through together! *Jerk!*"

"You can keep your memories! They were *my* drawings, and I can throw them out if I want to!"

"Why? So you can feel even sorrier for yourself? What is the point?"

Rob didn't say anything, he just lay there.

"You are going to draw these all over again, you're going to paint the paintings and sketch the sketches from start to finish! I demand it!"

"Open that top drawer," said Rob, pointing with his injured hand.

Phoebe was breathing hard and not inclined to do anything that Rob told her to do at that moment, but finally she turned and slid open a wide drawer at the top of a dresser near the bed. It was filled with crude drawings.

Rob watched her face as she looked through them. He said, "They look like a baby drew them. Don't they. *Don't they.*"

Phoebe looked back at Rob. "So draw like a baby," she said finally. "Until you can draw better. I mean, Rob—what else can you do?"

Rob put his good hand over his eyes. After a moment he said,

"Where is he? He said he'd talk to us, he said we'd hear his voice. I don't hear anything, do you?"

Phoebe looked away and shook her head.

"I miss him. I miss Sid so much, Phoebe."

At the word "Sid," Yellow Lab woke up and looked left and right eagerly.

"Where's Sid, boy?" said Rob. "Where's Sid?"

The dog leapt down off the bed, his nails clattering on the wooden floor. He ran from the bed to the door to the window, as if expecting to see the old diictodon any moment.

"That's how I feel, Phoebe," said Rob. "That's how I feel every minute of my life. It's like, first I lost my dad. Or he lost me. Then Sid happened. I want Sid back, and he's not coming back."

Phoebe sat on the bed.

"Maybe not," she said in a small sad voice. "I guess that's why I wish we had some, you know, pictures to remember him by."

She sniffed, and her shoulders drooped, and she looked to Rob so lost and alone at that moment that something in him finally melted. He wasn't the only one who felt these feelings. So did Phoebe, and so did YL and probably so did the other guys in the Gang of Six. His mom, too—what was she feeling?

There was a long silence between them. Yellow Lab subsided and lay down on the floor with an indignant "humpf."

"Phoebe," said Rob at last.

"Yeah?"

"Get off my bed." Phoebe looked at him anxiously, and then felt a surge of relief when she saw a mocking gleam in his eyes, and the suppressed flicker of a smile for the first time in a long time. "Please. You've got your own cabin. Go there."

Phoebe felt laughter rising from a great depth.

"Go there," said Rob with dignity. "I've got stuff to do."

Phoebe stood up, and Rob reached into a drawer of his night

table with his right hand and took out a roll of Scotch tape. He arranged two halves of a torn drawing on the quilt before him, ignoring Phoebe.

"Shoo," he said, waving her away with his injured hand. "Shoo."

Phoebe smiled and nodded and left, shutting the cabin door quietly. Much later that night, she came down the long wooden deck from her cabin to Rob's. She saw the light still burning under his door. She went back to bed then, and she slept and slept.

ABOUT THE AUTHOR

Timothy Mason is a playwright. He has won a Kennedy Center Fund for New American Plays Award, the W. Alton Jones Foundation Award, the Berilla Kerr Award, a National Endowment for the Arts Award, and the National Society of Arts and Letters Award. Among many other titles, he wrote the book and lyrics for the Broadway musical *Dr. Seuss' How the Grinch Stole Christmas!* He lives in New York City.

ABOUT THE ILLUSTRATOR

Like Robbie Gates, Jr., fourteen-year-old **Paul Cronan** has been sketching for as long as he can remember. *The Last Synapsid* is his first illustrated book.

Paul lives with his parents and sister in Baltimore, Maryland, where he attends the Baltimore School for the Arts, a public high school for the performing and visual arts. Apart from drawing, Paul loves reading, cycling, music, and finding a great tree to climb.